# WILD RIDE

EVERYTHING EQUINE MYSTERIES

**BOOK TWO**

LENORE MITCHELL

Wild Ride
Published by Equisetum Books

Trade Paperback: 979-8-9868471-4-6
E-book: 979-8-9868471-3-9

Cover and Interior design: Damonza (New Zealand)

This is a work of fiction. Names, characters, businesses, places, events and incidents are either the products of the author's imagination or used in a fictitious manner. Any resemblance to actual persons, living or dead, or actual events is purely coincidental.

# PRAISE FOR DYING TO RIDE
## *Everything Equine Mystery Series Book One*

...this engrossing read hooked me from the intriguing opening to the end! Elizabeth T.

...interesting and surprising story with strong women characters! Couldn't put it down! Sandy S.

...The characters loved and hated and everything in between. I could smell the barn and the horses. Clues and red herrings strung us along until the very end. Loved the wrap-up! Don S.

...as a horse trainer and riding instructor, I loved this book! Fabulous job with mystery aspects and even better covering the horses! Vivid imagery that captures the senses. Tanya B.

...combines the thrill of a good mystery with a deep love and appreciation for horses. Peguin

...the mystery keeps you on the edge of your seat while you learn about the world of horses and riding. The author's passion for these animals is evident on every page. Charlie T.

...intriguing mystery that keeps you guessing all the way to the end! Patricia

...the author teases you with various suspects, each one with more motive than the next! Horses and landscapes come alive with the author's eye for detail. I couldn't put it down! Colleen G.

...enjoyable read with well painted images and great descriptions of horses and riding. Nancy H.

...wonderful escape to nature with twists and turns that engage the reader. Zippy

...the unique horse culture opened the door to the world of riding. An excellent read! Gnan P.

...An impressive mystery! Interesting and complicated characters make the book exciting and suspenseful. Plot is seamless, and the author's love of horses shows! Jan T.

For Bini Abbott & Kris Nixon,
horse lovers extraordinaire
and their years of hard work running
Rocky Mountain Horse Rescue
https://www.rockymountainhorserescue.org
Arvada, Colorado


And For


Every horse who has shared their life with me
for a day or for decades
especially Babe
and because they're cute & sweet:
mini Buffy & pal Petunia

# IMAGINE

### *a black mustang stallion running free under wide blue Colorado skies.*

Deep inside this stallion's bones, in his DNA, he carries the stamp of ancestors, the evolution of what came before, what passes on. Ancestral *Equus* evolved in what is now North America as small four-toed *Eohippus* beginning some fifty million years ago in the *Cenozoic* era. Fossil remains found in Wyoming's Big Horn Basin verifies this, and one *Eocene* bed lies but a few miles from the present Pryor Mountains that stretch from Montana into Wyoming. Mustangs still roam there and south into Colorado.

### *While the stallion stands watch over his herd, humans debate his right to exist.*

Although fossil evidence proves that the modern horse, *Equus caballus*, evolved into present-day form in North America, they became extinct here ten thousand years ago in the *Pleistocene* era. One theory connects this extinction to the arrival of early humans who entered North America by way of the Bering Strait and hunted horses to local extinction.

### *While the stallion feels the sun's warmth on his back, humans debate his right to exist.*

Fortunately for the stallion and all equines before and yet to come, another lineage of *Equus caballus* migrated from the Americas to Eurasia prior to continental drift, and evolved there into the Przewalski, the Draft horse, the Arabian, and eventually every modern breed. Wild horses are especially adapted for survival in wide-open terrain with sparse vegetation, surviving in ecosystems where other large grazing animals such as European cattle cannot easily survive.

*While the stallion lowers his head to graze,*
*humans debate his right to exist.*

Four centuries ago, a mere blink in geological time, ancestors of the stallion arrived in what was then called the New World. Spanish Conquistadors led by Columbus sailed the Atlantic to the Americas. With them came domesticated horses which carried the explorers and went on to transform the Native American way of life and then to facilitate settling land from Atlantic shores to the Pacific. These animals made life more bearable even for those who persecuted them. Some escaped or were released to become mustangs, or wild horses. The Conquistador's mounts represented a return of horses to their origin, the American continent.

*While the stallion quenches thirst with cool*
*water, humans debate his right to exist.*

Embedded in the stallion and his kind is an instinctive fear of predators, an inbred wariness of wolves, of lions. And of the humans who hunted equine ancestors for food, who domesticated them at times with kindness to harness their power but all too often with whips and spurs to force them into submissiveness. Thus, the horrid term 'breaking' a horse. Instinctive fear stands guard over horses, sustaining them on the uphill quest of all creatures, the quest for freedom, for life.

*While the stallion gathers mares to procreate,*
*humans with helicopters keep debating.*

# CHAPTER ONE

BEFORE MUSTANGS STARTED disappearing without a trace, I tried telling myself it was enough to catch occasional glimpses of them running free and wild. I loved horses, made my living giving riding lessons, training stout Quarter horses, leggy warmbloods, cute ponies. Margo Richards, Everything Equine, was not only imprinted on my business cards but on my soul. But mustangs were unlike any animal I worked with, often tougher, smarter, surprisingly adaptable. They deserved lush meadows under a warm sun. Reality spawned drilling rigs instead of grasses, threw fences around water holes. Reality came down to dollars, left out the sense.

The last straw was when the Bureau of Land Management on Colorado's western slope issued a bulletin declaring that despite decreasing numbers of horses at Soda Creek Cliffs, half of the remaining animals would be removed before the fourth of July, a mere six weeks away. Drought, grazing rights, and energy exploration were cited as reasons, but the gist was clear. Mustangs made the sky too blue, the moon too bright. They sinned by having no financial reason to exist.

The wild horse refuge I'd long dreamt about finally seemed like a possibility as well as a legacy to several special human beings. After last year's death of my beloved foster mother, Elizabeth 'Bow' Bowan, her entire thousand acre property was hopefully going to become a mustang refuge. A generous donation from Sam Connolly, an old-time rancher, offered seed money. My plan to provide a forever home for mustangs progressed from maybe never to maybe now. But stubborn obstacles remained.

Which was why my truck was parked outside the BLM office in Pinedale Springs on a blue-sky spring day, and I was inside confronting obstacle numero uno. Joe Gannon was a big guy, not so much tall as paunchy. A middle-aged, middle management sort with an over-sized plaque in the center of his desk proclaiming his importance: Joseph Herbert Gannon, Field Supervisor, Bureau of Land Management. Ever since his arrival less than a year ago, he'd taken advantage of every opportunity to whine that this little western Colorado town was nothing but an outpost on the edge of civilization. It didn't matter to him that area ranchers like me considered this edge a fine place to live.

Gannon leaned forward in his impressive leather chair, placed elbows on his impressive desk, and scowled. "Like I said last time, Miz Richards, there's nothing more I can do."

Everyone calls me Margo. Miz sounded weird, like I'd suddenly aged from thirty-five to sixty-five. Whatever. "C'mon, Joe," I said, attempting a smile without much success. "Nothing more you can do or nothing more you *will* do! The BLM has a mandate to protect mustangs, including those at Soda Creek Cliffs."

His scowl deepened. "BLM land has many uses, and oversight of wild horses is just one aspect, a minor one at that."

I clinched my fists. "So this next enormous roundup will proceed despite the already low numbers of mustangs, and despite the danger to foals made to run in summer heat. And what about the disappearances?"

"The next gathering is already scheduled. And you keep insisting horses are disappearing. But animals do die. You've ranched here all your life. Surely, you realize that horses don't live forever. Death is just nature taking its course."

My turn to scowl.

I may be female, I may be on the short side, and I may be so lacking in style that I hadn't bothered to change out of my breeches and muddy paddock boots for this meeting. But surprise, surprise, I've got a brain. I've got a temper, too, but managed to take a deep breath and aim a tight smile that didn't reach my eyes in his direction before responding. "Surely, you realize that nature leaves carcasses, bones. Disappearances leave nothing but questions."

He sighed, putting some effort into it. "Do you even know how many are missing?"

"Yes, of course."

"Well, then, give me a number."

"It's your *job* to know that," I said. There were at least six disappearances that I knew about.

"Now see here, Miz Richards, getting all huffy is not necessary."

I was tempted to provide a demo of huffy, but he wasn't worth the effort. I just shook my head. "You hate the mustangs, so why won't you authorize moving some of them to my private refuge?"

"Because those animals are on BLM land and under my jurisdiction."

I was on the verge of letting loose with a mouth-full of unlady-like, but managed to hold back. Mostly.

"The BLM wastes hellacious amounts of money on round-ups and then maintaining mustangs in those damn holding pens. I'm offering to save the Feds money. Taking some horses off government hands is a favor to taxpayers."

"I hear not everyone around here agrees with your plans to turn the Bowan property into a refuge."

"That doesn't bother me," I said even though it did. A lot. Not only did I have to convince the BLM, I had to manage the downright hostility some locals aimed my way. When it came to mustangs, tempers flared. Always had, always would. To some, wild horses symbolized the west, freedom. Others called them feral nags, considered them nothing but nuisances taking up space, depleting grasses needed for cattle, land suited for drilling.

Gannon stroked one of his double chins. "Best listen to those who oppose you. At any rate, you are wasting your time and mine. It is not going to happen."

"Shit," I muttered, pushing back my chair and storming out.

Patience never made it onto my skill-set, except when it came to horses. Neither did sweet talking bureaucrats. Not everyone in the BLM hated mustangs. In fact, the last district manager promoted darting mares with birth-control, but Gannon was the local head honcho now. I needed another plan. I needed allies, both inside and outside of the BLM. And soon. I had to establish the refuge before more mustangs disappeared and before Gannon got his way. Some BLM doodle-brains conjured up the sugar-coated term 'gatherings' instead of round-ups, downplayed the use of low-flying helicopters, but there was no way to sugar-coat the inevitable injuries and deaths.

I had no idea why mustangs were disappearing without a trace. Besides that, two foals died in the last round-up, trampled to death in the chaos as a helicopter stampeded thundering hooves toward catch pens. A mare and a yearling colt fell too, shattering legs. The BLM shot each of the injured on sight, leading to arguably more merciful ends than those destined to wallow in over-crowded holding pens the rest of their lives or end up in the Mexico slaughter pipeline.

Outside the BLM office, I took a deep breath to attempt lowering my blood pressure and hoisted myself inside the truck. Zap and Fetch delivered the usual tail-wagging greeting. My one-ton dually broadcast my sour mood as we rumbled loudly down Main Street. I considered Stopping for a double-dip butter brickle at the corner of 3rd and Main, but not today.

Too riled.

Always the happy dog, Fetch stuck his head out the passenger-side window, mouth open, tongue lolling while Zap cuddled beside me, dark eyes registering concern. Both Border Collies were perceptive, but Zap soothed while Fetch entertained. Despite the dog's efforts, I fumed all through town, on past Morton's Auto Dealership, the lumberyard, and Smith's Hay & Grain to ten miles of dirt road and home.

The ranch where I grew up served as my hub for the collision of life's highs and lows. Even though it'd been a year now since Bow's death, the sight of her barn and land next to mine remained an open wound pulling me back to times past, to others gone, tears shed. Establishing a refuge on her land would be an homage to her, a reminder of who she was and all she taught me about horses, about life.

Anyone who's ever loved horses relates to that mystical feeling of being transported into their realm. As always, I slowed down while driving past the dozen or so horses in my front pasture. Most ignored me, but Phantom and Babe knew the sound of my truck, lifted their heads from lush May grass and trotted toward the fence, inviting me to come stroke their velvet muzzles. Offering a snack was welcomed too, which was why I kept a bag of crunchy horse treats in the back. I pulled over, ducked inside the fence and spent a few minutes with Phantom, the sleek black mustang mare, talented and reliable beyond expectations. And always Babe, the fabulous Half-Arab chestnut who tolerated me as a kid and even now with greying muzzle, she still tutored me about the link between horses and humans.

A few minutes with these two mares rendered me mellow enough to face the rest of the day. Who needs Prozac with horses around. It would've been better if Roy was home, but he was in Salt Lake City on business, due back in a day or so. We were now husband and wife, and the delight of our six-month union hadn't yet worn off, hopefully never would. I still caught myself staring at the gold band on my ring finger with shock and amazement.

I was a married woman!

Keeping my last name seemed simpler for business reasons, and speaking of business, as much as I wanted to concentrate on establishing the refuge, that wouldn't pay the bills. There were horses to train, lessons to give, stalls to clean. I grabbed an apple and a handful of walnuts for lunch, put on a baseball hat and headed to the barn.

I barely got inside before my cell rang.

"Stop messing with those mustangs or you'll be real sorry," a man's voice began. He didn't bother identifying himself, just threatened to ruin my business unless I dropped my plans to save the mustangs. The voice sounded different from another anonymous foul-mouth who'd called two days ago and unleashed a string of expletives ending with something anatomically impossible about the horse I rode in on. I didn't say a word to either one, although I considered telling them to have a jolly good day and drop in soon for a cookie and a cup of simmering strychnine.

I plopped my cell on a shelf and proceeded to groom a skittish young mustang I'd be mounting for the first time. This buckskin gelding, appropriately named Hotshot, was brought to me by one of the locals who favored these animals for stock work, once the wild was gentled out of them. The rancher was too smart and too rich to risk his own skin when he could wave a wad of cash under my nose and let me be the first human to get cozy with half a ton of unpredictable horseflesh. It paid to be cautious. I've trained enough horses to know that working with any youngster isn't for those intimidated by mangled muscles or broken pride.

The phone made noise again.

I was more intent on gathering my equipment and my courage than on continued interruptions, and one threat per day seemed sufficient. Still, who knew, this might be a buyer for one of my horses or a client scheduling riding lessons.

"Margo Richards here," I said while continuing to groom Hotshot.

"Hi Margo," Jessica Parker said as if we'd spoken yesterday.

My fingers opened, and a brush full of horsehair plunked onto the concrete floor. Zap and Fetch sprang up from curled slumber and rushed to my side, ears up, eyes alert.

The last thing on my mind was yesterdays or former friends.

"It's been a long time, Jessica," I finally said, reaching down to pat the dogs.

"Yes, far too long. I've missed you so much. But we're always on the move. And things are... complicated."

Things always were, with Jessica. I lifted my baseball cap, swiped the back of one hand across my forehead, stuffed long blonde hair behind my ears. And waited, silent.

"I need to..." she cleared her throat. "This is...awkward."

Hearing her voice again twisted the present into the past, a swirl of moments remembered. I shook my head against a breathless inability to stop memories from sliding back to the bond between us that seemed unbreakable until it shattered from neglect.

"Well then," she said into the silence, "I can't blame you for being mad."

"It's… I'm not mad," I said.

"You have every right, though. Life just, like… happens. Too busy, you know?"

I opened my mouth, wanted to say something profound. Busy, I understood, but still. From grade school on through college, we'd been besties, a duo. After college, she headed to Nashville and a recording contract while I returned to Pinedale and the ranch. We stayed in touch, for a while, first through calls, then Facebook, Instagram. Then even those connections fell away amidst changing contact info, impermanent addresses. I'd tried telling myself it wasn't a big deal, but it felt like one more loss in a life too full of them.

Hotshot raised his head, snorted. Nothing like a spray of horse boogers to convey impatience. "I've got an antsy gelding here," I said, rechecking his crossties and murmuring "Easy now, easy."

Roy says I whisper those words in my sleep.

"I won't keep you," Jessica said. "I just…" She made a sound between a laugh and a groan.

I was tempted to groan myself. Time had suspended the ease between us, maybe erased it altogether. But something in her tone jolted me. "Is something wrong? Are you sick?"

"No, no. Nothing physical."

I exhaled, banishing half-formed visions of bandages, nurses with needles. Zap licked my hand and Fetch sat, fluffy tails working. I patted first one hairy head, then the other. Assured that no crisis existed, the dogs yawned and laid back down. "It's good to hear your voice. I just… I'm just surprised. Hold on for a minute, let me put this gelding in a stall."

"I'm sorry. Why don't I call back later."

"It's okay, just give me a minute." Hotshot wasn't yet used to standing tied very long, so I led him to a nearby stall. He was the type prone to sudden panic and the risk of having him pull back and get all excited would mean no mounting session today.

"I'm here again. So what's up?"

"Well, for starters, I'm coming to Pinedale Springs for a concert."

"Oh, that's a surprise. But great! When?"

"Like soon, about two weeks. I, well…"

"What? Tell me."

She sighed, loudly. "It's, like, complicated. To begin with, my career has, like, taken a nose-dive. And then, well, there's some guy… a crazy fan. He calls, sends letters, like, weird stuff. Didn't bother me at first."

"This guy is stalking you?"

"Kind of, yeah, but it's, like, under control, at least I think so. I'll tell you about it when we get there."

I imagined seeing her again, wasn't sure how that might unfold. "Where are you now?"

"Heading for San Antonio, our next gig. We've been on the road for weeks."

"Sounds exciting."

"Used to be, back when it seemed like I'd make it big. The bloom is off, though. Now it's just a whole lot of work. I'm looking forward to seeing you, spending a few days in Colorado. I wrote a song about mustangs called 'Running Wild, Running Free'. It needs to debut there. And… I need your help."

"Mustangs can use positive publicity, especially around here, but you know that."

"We need wild ones on stage. Yours, of course."

"On stage? Mustangs? You can't be serious!"

"This is important, Margo. Might be the last song I'll ever write. I need one final triumph."

"What do you mean? Your songs are still on the radio, you're still on tour."

"Yeah, but like I said, it's complicated. My career isn't, well, it needs a boost." She paused. "Besides, I'm homesick, thought we could pick up where we left off."

I wasn't sure where we left off, what fragments of friendship remained.

"So provide a few horses," she continued, "do this for me. You're still dreaming about a wild horse refuge, right?"

"Yes. It's more than a dream now. But I'm trying to save mustangs, not jeopardize them."

"Now c'mon, Margo. Yours are, like, trained and all, right?"

"Some. Others haven't been handled yet, some may never be. Besides, I have mostly Quarter horses. But even the mellowest of any breed wouldn't tolerate being on a stage in front of berserk crowds."

She sniffed. "I thought you'd help."

"What you're asking isn't reasonable. Why not show videos instead?"

"We're planning the big screen thing. We need real mustangs too, not some nags who wouldn't prick their ears if the stage burst into flames."

"I hate the word nags." She knew that.

"Sorry. But the audience, especially there, will know if the horses aren't genuine. And so will the press."

"The press?"

"Definitely. Publicity is crucial."

I imagined cameras, chaos. "You know enough about horses to realize what you're asking is, just, crazy."

She produced a dramatic sigh. "Are we friends or what?"

"I…now's not the time for this. I'm sorry, Jessica."

"They'll only be on stage five minutes, that's all, and in a secure corral. They'll be fine. My new song is soft, mellow."

"Some people around here hate the mustangs now, want them gone."

"Hate them? But why?"

"Money. Drilling, cattle grazing and big game hunting are profitable, mustangs aren't."

"All the more reason to show your horses off, make people aware," she insisted. "Having them on stage will remind everyone how beautiful they are, how majestic."

"Being on stage in front of a crowd would scare the hell out of most horses."

"But don't you still train horses for, like, movie producers?"

"Occasionally," I said, "but none of my mustangs have been around bright lights, sudden noises."

"If anyone could train, like, a few for this, it's you, Margo."

My turn to sigh. "Maybe," I muttered. As soon as I'd said that one word, I regretted it. I'd just turned absolutely not into something Jessica would run with.

"Make it three, no wait, like five. And I'll donate a chunk of the proceeds from my concert toward this refuge of yours. Everyone wins."

"It's not that easy," I said. "The herds out there are in real trouble. Some of them are disappearing."

"What do you mean?"

"As in gone without a trace. No carcasses, no bones, nothing except hoof prints."

"That's terrible. Who's behind it?"

"Certain ranchers, possibly. Certain BLM people, maybe. Or, could be the drillers. Anyone driven by greed. And time is running out. I need to get out there again, check the herds."

"Take me with you. I'd love to come."

"It's a long ride, might be dangerous."

"Don't give me that. One of the reasons I'm coming home is to ride with you. Besides, I've ridden at Soda Creek Cliffs before."

"That was years ago. Things are different now."

"The right publicity would, like, help them, raise some of the money you need. I want to go, see the wild ones, Margo."

She asked about Bow, and although it was still painful to talk about how my foster mother died, Jessica had loved Elizabeth Bow Bowan. "I wish I'd known," Jessica said when I finished an abbreviated version of last year's awful events. "I'm truly sorry I didn't keep in touch."

"I tried to contact you, but nothing worked, not Facebook, nada."

"I had to change my social media contacts, like, several times. It's been crazy."

I told her to call back in a few days, let me think about the mustang proposal. She had a point about the need for publicity. She also had the same old way of manipulating me. Even so, her ideas had some merits. The world was full of horse-lovers, and the more of them who knew about the mustangs' plight, the better. Then again, what the hell was I thinking. No way should I jeopardize mustangs no matter how much publicity resulted. I'd let myself fall right into Jessica's trap. Her singing career might be wavering, but her talent for dramatic flair and for playing old friends remained unchanged. I couldn't help but look forward to seeing her again, even though I hoped her visit would be low-drama, for once.

Fat chance.

I saddled Hotshot, led the gelding to the round pen, put one foot and a bit of weight into a stirrup. He allowed it. I stroked his neck, murmuring low, and eased myself onto his back. Born wild, some mustangs adjusted surprisingly well to domestication. But Hotshot was the type who smoldered with resentment at the loss of freedom, this association with puny two-legged creatures. My job was to change his mind. A few circles around the perimeter would complete the chestnut's first mounted lesson.

Someone had other plans.

Half-way around, a yellow ball landed in the middle of the pen, scattering dust, bouncing high. Any horse would've been startled, but the gelding got downright pissed. He snorted, sidestepped, then thrust his neck down despite my efforts to stop what I knew came next. First two bucks weren't bad, but then the little turd got serious.

I landed face down, the ball inches from my dirt-encrusted eyes. The thing was the size of a basketball, but smooth and shiny. Someone had gone to the effort of writing a message on it to clarify that this wasn't some random bouncing. Good to know.

The scrawl suggested I should "eat shit and DIE." That final word was enlarged and done in red.

The penmanship was atrocious.

# CHAPTER TWO

THERE'S NOTHING LIKE the sound of loud noise followed by a cascade of breaking glass to wake a person out of a sound sleep at 2am. My feet hit the floor before my brain fully activated. I shuffled into slippers, half-running, half-stumbling in the dark toward the living room, shadowed by a pair of barking dogs.

Zap and Fetch earn their keep by herding stray horses every now and then, but mostly by just keeping Roy and me company. They're fun, they're friendly, but fierce they're not. Intruders might get heavily licked or assaulted with dog breath. I shushed them, gave the sit and stay command. No sense risking cut paws.

I picked my way through glass shards to the window. Nothing to see, only shadows and stars. No strange vehicles, no movement. Maybe this was accidental, a rifle fired by some idiot hunter with bad eyesight or poor aim. Except this wasn't hunting season, to begin with.

I squinted into the darkness. Stars above, moonlight shadows below. The house was a good five hundred feet from the road. I turned on a lamp, scanned the room. Most of the front window had relocated onto the couch, glass fragments spilling over the rug, a glittering unworkable puzzle. My housekeeping was casual at best, but glass shards added nothing to the decor.

I didn't see the rock at first, because the thing had rolled into a corner. I reached down, picked it up, half expecting to see a message scribbled on it. But no, the thing careened through my window without comment. Better than a bullet, I supposed. The rock was small enough to carry a ways, large enough to demolish glass. I fished the handgun case from the bottom of my underwear drawer, unlocked it, shoved a single bullet in, pulled on jeans and raced down to the barn with Zap and Fetch in tow. Nothing out of place, nor did the dogs sniff out anyone to bark at or slobber on. Back at the house, I cleaned up the worst of the glass, taped a sheet of plastic over the window and crawled back in bed. Didn't sleep, maybe because of the gun, now within reach on my nightstand. I hated the cold power of it, the idea that something so small could inflict damage so permanent. I fired the thing rarely and only at paper targets because Roy insisted I keep in practice.

Commotions always happened when my husband was away, but traveling was inherent in his business as a Natural Resources consultant. If I believed in the fairy-tale concept of soul mates, although no, I mostly didn't, Roy Holden would be it for me. First and foremost, he loved riding, held his own in cutting horse competitions on a talented gelding he named Mutt. Roy was kind, supportive, extremely easy on the eyes. The last time he proposed, I shocked myself by accepting. So commitment, yes. Marriage, sure. I missed him when he was gone, but even if he'd been here, the window would've still shattered, whoever hurled the rock would still have been out there. I had a suspicion that the perpetrator might be the same one who'd caused the yellow ball ruckus.

I spent the rest of the night stewing over escalating enemies and wondering how to present my case at the morning's Saturday town meeting. If only I was better at speaking in front of a group. Not that I got nervous, but schmoozing wasn't my style. By morning, I was bleary-eyed from lack of sleep. I arrived early, still sipping from an oversized coffee mug to pump me up before facing my fellow citizens.

Millie Dickson came early too, stomped up to me, spit at my chest because she was too short to reach my face. I clinched a fist to deck her, but that wouldn't have been neighborly. She'd arrived agitated to begin with, mostly because that was her normal state but also because on my way into town, I dropped by her place to inquire about her possible part in the yellow-ball nastygram that precipitated a bucking bronco session with Hotshot, followed by last night's rearranging of my window glass.

She turned twenty shades of indignant. As expected.

I understood why she and others felt the way they did about mustangs. Didn't agree, but I understood. My parents supplemented their income by raising cattle on the eighty acres of meadows interspersed with hilly Ponderosa forests where Roy and I now lived. They considered animals commodities, means of supplementing their living. Nature was a force to conquer, an obstacle between them and survival. I grew up surrounded by the struggle to make it from snowdrifts in calving season to dried up water holes on summer grazing allotments. After sacrificing a pet calf I named Betty to the profit gods at Denver's National Western Stock Show when I was all of a pig-tailed nine, I developed a permanent aversion to red meat, a distaste for rodeo generally and calf roping specifically.

Still, I understood the need for livestock, admired real cowboys, the ones who put caring for their animals above their own comfort. I was totally awed by cutting horses and their talented riders. And I understood firsthand the challenges of ranching life.

Drilling rigs were a different matter. I had no desire to see those, although they sprouted around here like poison mushrooms. Only so much land, too many uses. Only so much money, too many struggles. Which was why Millie and her Dickson clan weren't the only ranchers who might stop at nothing to get rid of wild horses.

I managed to remain upright for my little speech about mustangs. When I finished, the applause was underwhelming, but the usual small group of supportive ranchers and town people gathered, and their presence felt like a warm hug.

Sheriff Blackmon approached too, waving me aside. "I hear you had a commotion last night."

I nodded. "Someone felt I had too many windows."

At first glance, Ben Plackmon looked like a stereotypical small town sheriff, mediocre in appearance, but there was more to him than the battered Stetson that covered his receding hairline. He was all business when it counted and plenty sharp.

"I assume you didn't see anyone," he said.

"Nope."

"Also heard you dropped by the Dickson place this morning."

"Yes."

"I warned the Dicksons to leave you alone. Be careful, Margo, and keep me informed," he said, turning to leave.

I was about to leave too when a tall stranger in an expensive-looking suit approached.

"Your love of horses is quite apparent," he began, smiling to show perfect white teeth.

"You must be from one of the drilling companies," I said, smelling expensive cologne and noticing the Rolex on his wrist.

"I am Juan Gomez, and you are correct. I represent Unified Energy Federation."

"So it's safe to say that you hate mustangs as much if not more than some others around here."

"Not at all, Ms. Richards, not at all. As a matter of fact, I own horses myself."

"Let me guess. Racing Thoroughbreds?"

He chuckled. "Why yes. How did you know?"

I shrugged. "For one thing, you said you own horses. Didn't say you ride. But enough chit-chat. I assume you have something to say."

His smile disappeared. "I do not wish to be confrontational, not in the least. As you know, the land at Soda Creek Cliffs contains vast stores of not only shale oil but also natural gas. I hope to convince you to stop considering energy companies the bad guys."

"And I hope to convince your companies to stop harassing the mustangs."

"We have nothing but respect for those hardy animals, and we are impressed by your efforts to save them."

"Sure," I said. "But why approach me? I'm not in charge of those horses. The land they occupy is controlled by the BLM."

"We're quite aware of that. We're also aware that your internet site and your other activities portray energy companies in a bad light. Negative publicity hurts our image."

I tightened my arms against my chest. "Since when do companies such as yours care about image? I thought accumulating wealth was the goal."

"You are mistaken, my dear. Public opinion is important."

"I am not your dear, Mr. Gomez. But you are right in regard to public opinion."

"Despite your adversarial posture, Ms. Richards, the Unified Energy Federation is prepared to purchase a tract of land for you to manage as a wild horse refuge."

"And where might this land be?"

"It's an expansive parcel in southern Nevada."

I laughed. "How could I possibly manage land that far away? And let's not forget it is the BLM that controls animals there too. Besides, Nevada has more mustangs than any other state. You want to ship the Colorado horses to some remote desert because it's closer to slaughterhouses in Mexico?"

"That is absurd. And it would be in your best interest to cooperate with us," he added, his voice smooth as silk but his eyes hardening.

"Is that a threat?"

"Of course not. That is not the way business is conducted." He reached into a suit pocket, withdrew a card, held it out.

I took it, but not because I planned to play in his sandbox.

"Survival of the mustangs goes beyond business, and I'll continue doing everything in my power to keep those animals safe. In Colorado."

"Do you have a business card?" he asked.

"Yes, but only for clients," I replied, turning to leave.

It was heartening to know that my message was ruffling some feathers. Energy companies wanted to drill every inch of the Soda Creek Cliffs area. They'd begun operations on the more remote edges of the cliffs and were seeking BLM permits to expand. But after what Juan Gomez had just said about relocating the horses to Nevada, I had to wonder why they were so anxious to get rid of the horses. I wondered if they also had their sights on drilling Bow's land, the very location I needed to rezone for the refuge.

"Hey wait, Margo, you okay?"

I turned, smiled. "Hi Beth, thanks for coming."

"So who's the guy you were talking to?"

I shrugged, shook my head. "Big shot fossil fuel guy."

"Thought so. C'mon, let's grab a bite."

Hunger was the last thing on my mind, but spending time with a friend sounded good about now. Beth Jensen and I were nothing alike, but our friendship began while cheering for Beth's talented young daughter. Eleven-year-old Nicole was one of those horse-crazy kids who rode with natural grace and accumulated well-deserved blue ribbons.

I tried being reasonable when talking about wild horses, but passion reared up, ran off with logic. As always, Beth listened patiently while we sipped iced tea and ate grilled cheese. She sent me off with a much-needed hug and a mellower outlook.

It didn't last long.

The morning after the town meeting and the run-ins with Millie Dickson and Juan Gomez, I awoke to find one of my front pastures empty, a bunch of my young horses meandering down the road. It was the time of year when spring grasses were nutritious and enticing. Although horses sometimes leaned over fences to snatch mouthfuls of grass, none had escaped from one of my pastures.

Until someone cut the fence.

Two names came to mind. But maybe it wasn't Millie Dickson or one of her clan. Maybe it wasn't Juan Gomez or one of his minions.

Maybe my name wasn't Margo Richards.

The dirt road was sparsely traveled, but the recipe for disaster called for only one vehicle. I sprinted out toward the wanderers, the dogs at my heels. Zap and Fetch demonstrated their herding abilities while I got a dose of aerobics. The first group we rounded up were Quarter horse yearlings and two-year-olds, and close inspection showed no cuts, no ill effects. The young mustangs were more skittish and cantered off a ways, which was no surprise. When I finally got closer, I saw red blotches along one side of each animals' rump. I gasped, fearing it was blood. But no. My horses had been spray-painted.

Anger and relief ran a race right then and there.

Anger won.

# CHAPTER THREE

**THE APPLAUSE WAS** deafening.

Jessica Parker looked at home on the outdoor stage, all fancied in sequins, microphone to red lips, mouth open wide. She swayed to the beat, mahogany curls dancing over slim shoulders in the warm May evening. I barely heard her, even sitting in the first row, because the audience was not only clapping, but singing along at the top of their lungs. I might've joined in but dogs yelp as though injured when I sing, and besides, I was too nervous. Couldn't believe I'd let Jessica talk me into came next. But even I couldn't help humming a little.

That's the way it is with a song like "Sweet Honey." Jessica wrote it to honor her manager and her 'one and only'. He must've dropped a barn-load of coin for the gigantic diamond decorating her ring finger. Fairy-tale wedding followed about a year ago. I wasn't there, in fact I wasn't aware that she'd gotten married. But knowing Jessica, it was easy to imagine her smothered in white lace, gussied-up little girls with baskets of rose petals skipping down the aisle to signal her grand entrance.

Frank stood in the wings now, a look of devotion on his handsome face. Anyhow, the tune propelled her to the top of the charts a few years back. It may have been her only major hit, but everybody still knew the words, they'd sung along with car radios, tapped their feet to the beat, belted it out in the shower. Even Roy liked the melody, and his tastes run more to jazz than country. By the time guitar players strummed the last chords, the blanket of dusk deepened and stars punctuated the sky like stage props.

Roy sat next to me, his arm around my shoulders. Beth and Steve Jensen were on my other side, everyone singing along and clapping with such force that I feared their palms would bruise. The Jensen's daughter, Nicole, was just as enthused.

I loved hearing Jessica sing, loved seeing her on stage, but as I looked at her this evening, I was also gazing into the past, wondering why friendships that seem so strong fizzle. We hadn't spent much time together, just the two of us, since she arrived. She came with a large entourage, for one thing. Time, or lack of it, was a major impediment. She and her people had a show to plan, to prepare for. I had horses to train, riding lessons to give. My life was just as governed by To-Do lists as hers. Schedules, obligations, and expectations took precedence over the desire to sit and chat for an afternoon or even one single hour.

All of which saddened me, although I knew better than to expect Jessica and I to somehow take up where we left off. She'd mentioned doing just that during one of her calls. Sounded good, but I knew better. Time doesn't slow down to allow for wishes and dreams. Regrets linger, but remain stuffed away in the back of emotional closets while lives race onward. My eyes moistened, regrets and sadness leaked out, clamoring for acknowledgement. I'm usually adept at keeping emotions in check. But I'd let Jessica's silky voice take me back to when things between us were simpler, to years ago when my parents were still alive, Bow still next door, back to when life seemed predictable, easy.

I listened to Jessica on Spotify, of course, but hearing her in person was different, wonderful despite the tinge of sadness.

She began blowing people away with amazing vocals back in junior high. Her talent paid her way through college, then whisked her out of small-town Pinedale Springs. Years before all that, though, beginning in first-grade, we held hands at recess, demanded identical pigtail ribbons, and stuck our tongues out at the same boys. As the years passed, we pledged to remain BFFs, to share secrets, to support each other through whatever came our way. But life itself came, and interrupted. Gradually, the friendship that'd begun so early and continued through college frayed first a little, then more as our lives unfolded and separated. I couldn't imagine what it was like to be Jessica now, to be famous, to feel at home in front of crowds, to open her mouth and have beautiful sounds come out, to watch people clapping, to feel so beloved.

As the next song began, Beth leaned over, whispered "She's so good!"

I nodded, glanced at Roy. "You like her?"

"Sure. Beth is right, she's really good."

"Strange," I whispered, grinning. "You look like a country fan, a cowboy, Stetson and all, but you're unpredictable."

He drew me closer, kissed me. "That's the plan." He gave me a look, let me know he'd seen my eyes, understood how I felt.

Knowing that gave me a surge of happy, that feeling you get when surrounded by friendship and love. Beth always had a calming influence, and Roy, well, we planned to spend the rest of our lives together. Yes, I felt sad that Jessica and I were no longer as close, that we'd gone our own ways, but she had Frank and other friends. I had Roy and my life too.

I'd met the two backup singers earlier, was struck by how much Evelyn Brooks resembled Jessica from certain angles, their hair the same color and length. But there was something about Evelyn's eyes, they lacked softness when she smiled. Bianca Romero, on the other hand, exuded happy, with her perpetual smile and mass of dark curls framing puppy-dog eyes.

Jessica's make-up and stage glitz made her appear too glamorous to be the friend I remembered, the one I'd hugged the day she arrived. That's when she revealed more about the erotic letters, the anonymous phone calls from some guy who idolized her, knew too much about her.

Last week she'd found all of her lingerie cut into shreds.

Fan turned fanatic.

At least her messages came from a fan. And she ended up with a perfect excuse to buy all new undies. After my own incidents, I was bracing myself for what came next. So far, no one had bothered my underwear drawer. Nothing in there qualified as lingerie anyhow, except for the red filmy thing Roy gave me one Valentine's. He peeled it off soon after I put it on. Waste of time, in my opinion. My detractors were more concerned with shutting me up than defiling my clothing. That might've been preferable to the bucking bronco thing, the shattered window, the spray-painted horses. I had the window repaired, relocated animals away from the front pasture and had ongoing chats with the Sheriff. I got used to extra vigilance, but when Roy wanted to cancel all his business trips to protect me, I told him no way. I welcomed his help, but this was my battle, not his.

And then Jessica Parker arrived with baggage of her own.

A glance at the ranchers and townspeople overflowing into a standing room only crowd revealed one unsmiling trio among the sea of Stetsons and baseball caps. Millie Dickson, her silver-belted husband and their muscular son stood scowling. I flashed them a grin, waved a bit. Annoying them was mildly entertaining. They topped my list of foes, had for so long it seemed ordinary, but I was more bothered by those as yet undeclared. Pinedale Springs was a small town, but recent increases in drilling activity meant new faces to the area, most of them muscled workers in Carharts and steel-toed boots, but also executives like Juan Gomez.

Odd that even though Jessica and I lost our tight connection, each of us had enemies, even though so far hers seemed fairly benign. Then again, these things tend to escalate. The silver-haired guy in front of us didn't fit my idea of a fanatic fan, but maybe he got off on writing raunchy letters. Or maybe that woman with the thick black braid several seats over kept spray paint in her purse and hated mustangs. Paranoia was overtaking common sense in my addled brain.

Beefy guys patrolled the base of the stage. I'd watched people arriving, scanned faces for weird expressions, random oddities. Jessica wanted to be a regular person again, ordinary, safe. I put my bones and my butt on the line with horses, but entertaining a bunch of strangers was something I couldn't imagine. She assured me most fans were great and no one could bother her on stage. I hoped she was right, tried to enjoy the show, but dread for what came next kept building.

After the last notes of other tunes, a curtain of colored fog billowed up, obscuring Jessica and the band, and then the stage lights faded to black. Murmurs arose from the audience, and Roy and I hustled from our seats to the holding pen behind the stage. This was the part I dreaded, the part I'd let her talk me into even though I knew better.

Shocking how desperate I was to make more people love mustangs, to make them care.

I demanded metal corral sections on stage, those portable kind that grace stables everywhere, but was told they'd look crude. Roy suggested stout wooden rails with hidden metal reinforcements, and that seemed workable. Stagehands hustled things in place and Roy and I led the horses up a ramp and into the enclosure.

I brought five mustangs, the calmest of the dozen or so I currently had. In an effort to acclimate them, I followed the same procedures I used to train Quarter Horses for several Hollywood films shot nearby. I took them into the round pen and gradually blasted CDs of live concerts, introduced bright lights, sudden noises. They adapted better than expected, but the wild in them simmered, and I felt guilty for subjecting them to things they had every right to fear.

The fog cleared and I stood off-stage beside Roy, chewing my lip as soft lights illuminated Jessica and the two backup singers. They'd changed into Levi's and fringed chaps, western shirts and black vests. No sparkles in sight. Jessica asked the crowd to remain quiet, calm, hold applause.

The fencing formed a long narrow rectangle so all five animals could be seen. First came Phantom, a solid black mare and in my biased view, a gem in conformation and also the calmest of the group. Next was Outlaw, a mellow gelding from Pryor Mountain, Montana, buckskin with distinctive dark highlights. Then the blue roan gelding, black and white hairs mingling, the effect more gray than blue. Close behind stood the pinto filly, splashed in brown and white. Last, a bay filly, dark coat glistening.

The crowd murmured, softly for such a large group. I kept watch on the horses' eyes. Those expressive brown ovals would register a warning if things headed south.

Guitar notes sounded, mellow and soothing, and then Jessica lifted the microphone. "Running Wild, Running Free" told the haunting tale of mustangs galloping under blue skies, and her voice mesmerized the audience. Even my mustangs stood quiet, necks up and eyes alert, unaware of their kin moving silent but bigger than life on the screen behind them. If anything could change a few minds about wild horses, maybe this was it.

I drew in a deep breath and lowered my shoulders a notch.

Then a noise blasted from somewhere, the corral fell as though made of toothpicks, and my mustangs burst across the stage in a blur of flying hooves.

# CHAPTER FOUR

THE MUSTANGS MOVED as one, a jumble of legs bolting across the large space, looking like they'd dive right off an edge, then whirling around at the last instant, necks high, eyes wide.

I moved onstage, fast but not running, my eyes on the frantic horses. What if they fell or jumped, breaking legs, crashing on top of people. Phantom was the leader, the others mirroring her movements. If I could catch her, settle her, the others would calm down too.

Jessica, the two backup singers and half a dozen band members ducked this way and that, scrambling to avoid the horses. "Gather together, leave the stage, slow," I said, keeping my voice calm, although my pulse revved to a gallop. The audience milled around, some shouting. "Jessica, ask the crowd to vacate the first rows, everyone else to stay still, quiet."

None of the mustangs wore halters, and in my rush, I'd neglected to pick up the ones I used to lead them onstage. I slipped off my belt and coiled it in my hands. If I could ease up close to Phantom and loop the belt around her neck, and if I managed that before she and the others plunged off the stage, everything might be all right.

Might be.

Roy stood to one side, ready to help but well aware that the horses would respond better to just one human to begin with. They huddled together in one farthest corner now, panting from nerves rather than exertion. They could run for miles, if their instincts dictated the need. Fear ricocheted from one to another, fueling them with urgent confusion. "Easy, now, easy," I murmured, stepping toward them.

Phantom looked at me, snorted and pawed the floor as if to take off again.

Didn't.

I lowered my chin toward my chest and repeated "Easy, Girl, whoa now." I watched her without staring right into her eyes. Predators stare, and horses react by escaping. I wanted Phantom to concentrate on me, to remember that I was her friend.

Her neck relaxed a bit, ears flickered. She wanted to be rescued, wanted this to end. The other horses squeezed together behind her, awaiting the slightest signal to run. They all knew my voice, had taken carrots from my outstretched hand, felt my touch on their muscled bodies. Two of them had allowed me to settle a saddle briefly on their backs, the other three were ridden regularly. But they weren't looking to me for leadership now, they were looking to one of their own kind, to Phantom.

Everything rested on the trust between the black mustang and me, the blonde-haired human. I'd worked with this mare for several years, using the same techniques for starting all youngsters. First came gentling, touching, then haltering, bridling, saddling. I'd gotten to the point of riding her long distances, enjoying and trusting her enough to make her one of my main mounts. Impossible to say how any horse regards their human rider. Most likely, Phantom wanted to ask why the hell I brought her and the others here. Everything we'd worked for hovered on this moment. Either we were enough of a team to end this together, or not.

There's a bridge of understanding for humans and horses to cross, hard to say who travels farthest to form the necessary partnership. Twenty feet and our different worlds separated Phantom and I at the moment. I took one step, then another.

She stood her ground, eyes softening.

But then came footsteps behind me, not running, but approaching all the same. "Stop, stand still," I said without turning around.

"Get back here," Roy's voice from the sidelines was soft but urgent.

Phantom remained where she was, but the pinto filly's neck rose and she side-stepped away.

The footsteps kept on coming.

"Stand still, damn it," I said, keeping my voice calmer than I felt.

"Got a coupla' halters," a loud male voice said.

"Stay there, stay the hell there until I have one of them."

"Whatever, Lady."

Phantom snorted again. I reached for her, but her instinct to run, to escape this madness, won out. With a toss of her head, she raced away with the others close behind, headed this time for the ramp leading offstage. Halfway across, though, the lead guitar player dashed out, arms waving. Tall but boyish-looking, Eric no doubt meant well, but he should've been off stage by now. Jessica had mentioned that he loved horses, especially wild ones. Matter of fact, he'd helped her write this song in their honor. But the mustangs had no intention of stopping, not now and certainly not for some human flapping like a goose at take-off. Phantom and the one I called Outlaw swerved to the right, the bay and the pinto swerved left, but the blue roan didn't swerve quite far enough either way and ran right into Eric, knocking him flat.

Gasps rippled through the audience. Someone screamed.

Eric sat up, groaning. Blood seeped through one leg of his jeans. Roy and Jessica rushed out to him.

The horses huddled together now on the opposite side of the stage, but they'd either missed the ramp or didn't trust it. I began moving toward them once again, pausing to pick up one of the halters and lead ropes that were deposited on the floor by the idiot who'd insisted on approaching, then finally left.

After minutes that passed like hours, I closed the gap between myself and the mustangs, slipped a lead rope around Phantom's neck and secured the halter, murmuring to her and the others all the while. The ramp leading offstage stood only yards away, so I coaxed the black mare downwards, the others following in a tight group. Roy came too, close behind the knot of horses. A corral, metal this time and on solid ground, stood far enough behind the stage to be relatively quiet.

Roy stayed outside the enclosure while I entered along with my horses and just stood there for a moment, watching them settle, allowing myself a deep breath. This wasn't the first time I'd let Jessica talk me into doing something crazy. I was steamed, but not as much at her as at myself. We weren't kids anymore. I knew better now, knew I should've found another way to find approval for my mustang refuge.

And I also knew that corral shouldn't have fallen apart. Everything happened too fast to replay events in my mind with certainty. Maybe the noise came first, before the corral collapsed. Hard to know. But something went wrong, and I had to figure out what. And why.

"I'm going to check out that fencing," Roy said as if reading my mind.

"Thanks."

I looked over each animal, checking for cuts or bumps, was trying to reassure them when I heard footsteps.

"Are they all right Margo?"

"They seem to be," I said, turning to see Jessica's husband. Frank Stanza was impossibly handsome, and knew it. He favored black turtlenecks and crisp tan slacks, his Italian leather loafers shone as though freshly polished. I'd met him earlier, and we'd chatted just enough for me to recognize that underneath his suave exterior, he was used to being in control, used to getting what he wanted from everyone in the Parker Company.

"And how about you, Margo?" he asked now. "I trust you are holding up as well?"

"I'm okay," I said, although at this point, that was a stretch.

"I am sorry this happened," he said. "I'll find out who is to blame. In the meantime, do let me know if there is anything I can do for you."

All I wanted him to do was leave me alone. After he walked away, I grabbed a few flakes of grass hay. Chewing would calm the horses, take their minds off this bizarre episode. They seemed fine physically, but I'd let them all down, especially Phantom. It'd take a while to regain their trust. I remained with them for a while longer, just standing quietly.

Finally, I returned to the stage area to check on Jessica and the others. Some horse trainer I was. To Roy's credit, he'd never said this seemed like a crazy plan, although we both knew it was. He rode cutting horses, among the Einsteins of horse intellect, but he understood how dangerous some horses can be, how many chances I took.

The reseated crowd buzzed with excitement. The ranchers and other horse people in the audience were no doubt astounded by what they'd just witnessed, no doubt blamed me for allowing my animals on stage. I might never live this down. Millie Dickson wouldn't have to bother spitting at me now. She'd busy herself using this to further discredit mustangs. And me.

Paramedics were loading Eric onto a stretcher, carting him offstage. He rose up on one elbow, waving to the audience, and a cheer arose.

I was about to return to the horses when Jessica reached down and grabbed my hand, pulling me onstage. I had no desire to be there again, but her grip was strong, her eyes pleading. If I struggled, I'd only create a scene, look stupid.

Standing on center stage and still gripping my hand, she introduced me as her best friend, assuring everyone that it'd been her idea alone to put my mustangs on display. "Thanks to Margo's way with horses," she went on, "no lasting harm done." The audience clapped politely, and I tried to smile, feeling like a fool. A real friend would've refused to let this disaster happen. Jessica clasped one arm around my shoulders and continued. "Despite this little mishap, folks, mustangs are wonderful creatures, magical. I wrote the song in their honor."

Someone booed, a few hissed, but disapproval was drowned out by applause. "Sing!" One guy began chanting, and then more joined in. "Sing! Sing it again!"

Jessica smiled at me and then at the crowd. She was their darling, their hometown girl. Celebrity status granted her dispensation from blame. I slipped back to my seat; she and the band started up again with one of the other guitar players stepping into Eric's spot. The song was good, and the clapping was enthusiastic.

I slipped backstage where Roy was still checking out the corral boards which were heaped into a pile. Several bolts were missing from one of the corner posts, he said, and a sweep of his flashlight spotted them on the ground, but they were noticeably shorter than the other bolts. Odd, possibly ominous. He and I approached each of the stagehands, but aside from comments like "those broncs were wired" and "totally wild" they turned palms up, shrugged. Saw nothing, knew nothing. Or so they claimed. One of the crew, a kid named Jake Campbell, came and helped us load corral posts and each bit of hardware into the back of Roy's pickup.

The whole thing could've been an accident, but if not, the suspects began with Millie Dickson and her family. Others around here rode with that bunch. No telling which one of them signed up for the job of harassing me yet again. On the other hand there was Jessica's fanatic fan, the guy whose dark shadow lurked around unknown corners, stretched along twisting paths. Out of reach, but ever lurking, lingerie scissors at the ready. Maybe he'd moved on to jimmying fences, but that seemed unlikely.

After rechecking the horses, Roy and I returned to the stage area and watched Jessica shaking hands, signing autographs, a smile pasted on her face. Goop highlighted her cheekbones, false eyelashes and glitter enhanced come-hither eyes. Soft curls framed her glamorous face. My own straw-colored top always looked windblown and sun-bleached from hours on horseback, but also because I never bothered with beauty salons or bottles of stuff that would only gather dust on the bathroom counter. Sometimes Roy said my hair looked nice, but I figured he was either kidding or horny.

After she signed the last autograph, Jessica let her fake smile fade and turned to me, her eyes sparkling. "That was exciting, don't you think? Those mustangs looked awesome, racing across the stage."

I frowned. "It was a disaster."

"Not at all. Crowds love something like that."

Roy's eyes widened, but he stayed silent.

"You've got to be kidding," I said. "It's also lucky that Eric wasn't hurt worse."

She flipped manicured fingers through her hair. "I thought he knew better than to wave at them like that, and he should've followed us off the stage. But he'll be okay. Broken leg, according to the paramedics."

"Bad enough," I said, "and my horses were traumatized."

"They'll be fine, Margo. They've got you to take care of them."

"I need to figure out what happened."

Jessica shrugged. "The corral came apart. Maybe someone forgot to tighten a bolt or one of your horses kicked it. Leave it to Frank. I'm sure he'll check things out. Anyhow, the media loves excitement."

"We have the corral in our truck, so Roy and I will figure out what happened. And I don't give a damn about the media right now."

"You don't mean that. The more publicity the mustangs get, the more people will care about them. And hopefully, another benefit of this concert will be selling more of my music, which will raise your percentage of profits." She turned to Roy. "Don't you agree that publicity will help your cause?"

Roy looked from me to Jessica, shrugged, said nothing.

"Making money isn't the main goal, not for me," I said.

"Making money isn't a bad thing, Margo, and you're the one who said you need approvals for zoning permits and also money for your refuge."

This was beginning to sound too much like an argument. I shook my head, got up to leave.

"No, wait, please wait," She said, closing her eyes. When she opened them, her expression had changed. "I didn't mean to upset you. I am sorry about tonight. I know how much you care about your animals."

The only time we'd talked in person was when she first arrived. It would be awkward if the years had extinguished the glow of our friendship, the connection we had. "You really sounded great," I said.

She took hold of my hand. "Thanks."

I thought about the old Jessica, the way we used to finish each other's sentences. With the exception of Beth, I had only casual friends now, the kind who exchange smiles, comment on the weather. "Come stay with us," I blurted before I could think better of it.

"But I couldn't impose. And Frank flies to Tulsa tomorrow, finalizing arrangements for my next concert."

I bit my lip, trying to decide if she didn't want to come, but exploring what was left of our friendship seemed suddenly urgent. "Bring him out to the ranch overnight," I said, "you stay on with me, ride, relax."

She smiled. "I'd love to see your place again, and, like, I really do want to ride. But Frank insists on, like, having guys around, watching out for me." She turned to Roy. "Is this, like, okay with you?"

He nodded. "Of course. We'd be happy to have you and Frank too. I'll have dinner ready by the time you arrive."

Jessica's jaw dropped. "You cook?"

Roy smiled. "Yes, I enjoy it, matter of fact."

I hugged Roy, and we kissed. "He's talented in many ways," I said, turning to Jessica. "So you have bodyguards?"

"They're stage hands, actually. But they look the part. Nothing bad has happened, not yet."

Before I could reply, the backup singers appeared. "Great publicity!" the taller one said. "I'm Evelyn, by the way, in case you don't remember me." She paused, inhaled a lung-full of smoke from the cigarette she held up in her right hand. "I handle the media, and their camera guy got pics of those stupid nags." She took another drag of smoke, exhaling it almost in my face.

I stepped back.

She frowned. "What?"

"C'mon, now, Evelyn," Jessica said. "You blew smoke right in Margo's face!"

"Oh, did I?"

The shorter backup singer inserted herself between us. "Hey, now," she said, looking up at first Evelyn then me. "We were all worried about the mustangs, and they're beautiful." She might've been the younger and the shorter of the two, but she assumed the peacekeeper role with ease. Bouncy black curls framed her wide smile.

Evelyn shrugged. "Whatever."

"This is Bianca Romero," Jessica said.

I nodded at the cute singer. "Hi, yes I remember you."

"Hi, yeah, I'm Bianca. And... well, it was kinda' exciting, seeing the horses acting all wild. Anyhow, I'm shacking up with Damian tonight."

"Which leaves me alone, as usual," Evelyn said.

Jessica looked at me. "Uh, she doesn't have anyone to stay with. Could she crash on your couch?"

Evelyn stared down her nose at me. "I can take care of myself."

I stared back. Sometimes there's clarity the moment you meet some-one. That's the way it was with Evelyn. No possibility of friendship. "Okay, sure," I said without much enthusiasm. My couch was as nonde-script as the rest of my furniture, but it could serve as a place to sleep. I wouldn't relish having this chick sit there and foul the house up with smoke, though. Bad enough it'd been assaulted by shattered glass two weeks ago. Now that window sported brand new glass.

"Great," Jessica said, looking relieved. "And there's Louie, a dog who considers himself human," Jessica added. "Craves attention. He's in our van."

"No problem."

"I'll call the hospital first," Jessica said, "check on Eric."

Evelyn didn't acknowledge my offer, just kept smoking.

"You'll have to smoke outside, Evelyn," Jessica said.

"Whatever."

"Anyhow, like… oh, there's Damian," Bianca said. "Catch ya later."

Jessica and I walked over to her tour bus, opened the door and Louie burst out, tail wagging. Inside, on the driver's seat, was a long white box with Jessica scrawled in block letters, red ink.

Maybe more defiled underwear. It could get expensive if this fan of hers kept cutting up clothing.

She opened it, gasped.

There was no note, not a word. No lingerie, not this time. But there was a knife, one with a monstrous blade.

"Don't touch it," I said.

Jessica nodded, sucked in her breath again, turned pale.

I peered into the distance, saw only darkness.

# CHAPTER FIVE

"Michael Turner, that's his name," Jessica said.

My jaw dropped. "This fanatic fan of yours?"

She nodded.

"You know him?"

"Just the name. Never met him, not that I know of. But he must come to my concerts. Knows specific details, tells me which outfits he prefers, how he likes my hair a certain way."

"Ever threatened you before?"

She winced. "Never. He's been, well sort of sweet on the phone, but his letters are steamy."

"He broke into your personal space, cut up your underwear last week, right?"

"True. But... I mean, that seemed, like, different, sort of erotic. This is..."

"Yeah, way worse." I took out my cell, dialed the Sheriff. Within minutes, a deputy showed up, asked questions, examined the package, the knife. I told him about the corral falling apart, said I thought it might be connected either to the stalker or to me. My incidents had escalated and so had Jessica's. Strange, for sure. Then again, who knew.

The deputy made notes, took photos and left with the knife package, promising to let us know if fingerprints were found.

Frank and his crew had gone into town searching for parts to repair one of the band's ancient amplifiers. Jessica called him, took a while to assure him things were under control. The plan was for him to meet us at my place soon as he could. Jessica and I found Evelyn still smoking and we all walked to Roy's truck. We loaded up the mustangs and headed to the ranch, tailed by a black SUV with the two bodyguard types. Ten miles to a world of difference from town, even the sparsely populated Pinedale Springs. The best thing, next to all the animals who shared our place, was the near-silence. Roy and I thrived on the quiet, the rhythms of the animals, the ever-changing sky, now glittering with distant stars. I got out of the truck and stood there, inhaling the cool night air, the scent of home.

But peace would have to take a back seat to suspicion, for now.

I grabbed a pillow and some blankets for Evelyn, and she laid on the couch, denied being hungry and closed her eyes.

Roy and I settled the horses in a paddock with a tank full of water and scattered grass hay for them. Roy headed up to the house while I checked out the barn. The other horses were out on pasture, so only Socrates rummaged inside one of the stalls, and he was who I'd come to see. My raccoon considers me the only human worth associating with, and I was about to pet him when he bristled, wrinkled his nose in disgust and executed a disappearing act just as one of Jessica's bodyguards appeared, gun raised.

"Shit!" I shouted. "Lower that gun!"

"That's a big-ass 'coon there. Dumb critters, mean too. Got to make sure ain't nobody hiding."

I scowled at him. "You leave that raccoon alone! Don't you dare shoot it, or anything else."

The guy shrugged. "Whatever, Lady."

All I needed to top this night was this over-muscled idiot calling Socrates stupid. This particular raccoon was the latest in a long line of ring-tails to reside in a corner of my barn. He was one of Ramona's babies and elected to take up residence with me, which I didn't mind one bit.

Anyone who's spent time around raccoons knows they can be affectionate, funny, and far from dumb. Can't say the same for some humans.

Back at the house, Roy was in the kitchen fixing sandwiches. He had a big grin on his face and told me the other bodyguard had roamed the house checking closets, under the beds, behind the shower curtain. "You never know where scary boogey-men might be hiding, waiting to pounce," he added, rolling his eyes.

"Might be a long night," I said.

Roy nodded. "Yes, and before we go to bed, I'll make sure the guns those big guys have aren't loaded. They're probably squirt guns, anyway."

I laughed, then joined Jessica on the porch. She was right about her dog, Louie. With over-sized ears, soulful eyes and a wiry coat that stuck up this way and that, he was thirty pounds of cute. My dogs performed their welcoming ritual, running circles around the newcomer in the patchy grass among tall Ponderosas in front of the house. After that they engaged in some serious butt sniffing and tail wagging. Canine socializing lacked complexity. Either they got along or they drew blood. My border collies were friendly except when they sensed danger. Nothing about Louie seemed the least bit threatening.

"So here we are," I said, yawning and snugging a sweater tighter against my chest. The night air was crisp, the stars brilliant. One of the big guys stood nearby, the one who'd appeared at the barn stationed himself in a parked SUV at the top of the driveway.

"What a night," Jessica said, shaking her head. "I just want all this to stop."

This time I couldn't call her a drama queen. I wanted this to end too. Unfortunately, I had a feeling things were just revving up for both of us.

Roy brought out a platter containing sandwiches, pickles, an assortment of fruit and cloth napkins. "Be right back," he said, and soon returned with a pitcher of lemon water and glasses.

Evelyn was fast asleep, so Roy turned off the living room lights.

"How about your bodyguards," he said. "I'm happy to give them sandwiches."

"That's ok. They bring their own food," Jessica said. She took a bite of sandwich and grinned at Roy. "Delicious! Avocado even. Do you always make gourmet food?"

"Of course. Margo insists," he said, winking at me.

"Everything he makes is fabulous," I said. "It's one of the reasons I keep him around."

He lifted one eyebrow and grinned. "Shall I provide details about my, ah, additional skills?"

"Let's stick to your cooking, for now," I said, grinning back.

He bowed. "As you wish, My Lady."

I reached over, socked him on the arm.

Jessica laughed. "Just when things could've gotten interesting. Ok then, so how do you manage when Roy isn't here to feed you?"

"I can answer that one," Roy said. "She grabs apples and walnuts, eats them on her way to the barn."

"No surprise," Jessica said. "When we were college roomies, Margo always had a bowl of apples and a bag of walnuts on her desk. Supplemented with double dip butter brickle cones now and then."

"I aim for consistency," I said.

After we finished eating, Roy gathered the leftovers and headed for the kitchen. "I'll wrap a few sandwiches and put them in the frig for Frank. Then I'm off to bed."

"Thanks for letting Evelyn come," Jessica said after Roy left.

"Sure," I said. "There're extra towels for everyone in the guest bathroom."

"Now that we've finally gotten back together," Jessica said when we were alone, "I'm so…" She stopped, looked to one side, gasped.

"What? What?"

The bodyguard moved closer.

Jessica's eyes widened and then she giggled. "Is that a… chicken over there?"

I sank back into the chair, drew in a big breath, forced it out through puffed cheeks. Henrietta perched on her ledge not far from us, beak tucked beneath one wing, waiting for a last hand-out from me before I put her in the coop. "She imprinted on me when she was just a fluff-ball," I said. "Follows me around, considers herself half human. She's actually one in a long line of Henrietta hens, beginning over at Bow's place next door."

"She's… cute. And no wonder you have chickens. I remember that Bow always had them, too."

I nodded. "So, tell me what you know about this fan of yours."

Jessica shrugged. "Like, nothing concrete. The name is likely a fake."

"Figured that."

"We checked online stuff, and Frank talked to a company that tracks stalkers. Most clients are famous entertainers, athletes. Ridiculously expensive, way out of our range. They advised us to keep a log of everything, letters, contacts. We were already doing that."

"Sounds good. What else?"

"The cops checked previous letters for fingerprints. Nothing. We talked with other performers who've dealt with this. There've been some tragedies, but most say that either the person reveals himself or the threats stop after a while, that even if the guy is right under your nose he's hard to identify. I need help, Margo… need you to check this out."

"Me? Get serious. Leave this to the pros."

"They can't do squat. Just like that deputy tonight, they ask questions, make reports, say they're working on it. And we can't afford real bodyguards, much less threat professionals. You don't know what this feels like."

"Maybe a little," I said. "A nastygram bounced into my life recently. And someone rearranged my living room window, then liberated my horses from the front pasture, spray-painted them."

"You're kidding."

"I seldom kid."

She rolled her eyes. "Yeah, so what'd you do with the real Margo?"

"Stuffed her full of hay and turned her into a scarecrow," I said. "Meantime, I have some real concerns. With the exception of your unfortunate undies, all these current incidents involve mustangs. Maybe even the knife in your truck somehow. You came here to sing about wild horses, had them on stage, and I've been hounding people around here about the need to establish a refuge before the next big roundup in early July. Not everyone is against it, but some sure are."

"I don't get it. Why hate mustangs?"

"Like I said when you called several weeks ago. Money... root of everything. Cattle and drilling rigs are profitable, wild horses are not. Throw in pure hatred of mustangs and stir. Millie Dickson is the one with the biggest spoon, but the drilling companies aren't exactly fond of me either. Neither is the local BLM guy."

"So what's the plan?"

"How should I know?"

Jessica laughed. "You're as sarcastic as ever."

I grinned. "I try to keep up. Anyhow, tonight we rely on those oversized guys of yours to stay awake and keep fans and knives behind the velvet rope. Tomorrow we'll powwow with the sheriff, sniff around the corral posts, bake some cookies for the Dicksons."

"You'd have to figure out where the oven is for that."

"I think I saw it once. Damn thing looks dangerous, which is why I let Roy handle food prep. Besides, there's something sexy about a cooking cowboy." I looked at my watch and yawned. "So if Roy doesn't feel like baking, we'll buy the cookies. Anyhow, in less than five hours, the horses will be expecting room service."

She yawned too. "Frank should be here soon."

"He's cute... how's he in the sack?"

"Probably not as good as your cooking cowboy," she said, raising one eyebrow and tossing her hair back.

"Sorry to hear. But Frank looks like the type who expects his squeeze to wear fabulous lingerie. Breeches and boots are more my style."

"Nobody ever accused you of having style."

"They'd better not." I yawned again. "Speaking of sacks, mine is calling to me. We can argue over Frank some more in the morning."

"Actually," she said, "you can have him if you want."

"Seriously?"

"More than you'd think," she said. "I mean, I do appreciate Frank, and he does take care of me. But he's so damn controlling. Thinks he always knows what's best for me, for everyone. He is a good manager, but let's face it, I've never been a really big star."

"You've got a lot of talent."

"Thanks, but that's not all there is to it. I'm tired of this rat-race, this constant pressure to perform. I used to love singing, loved it so much. But now all I think about is how many songs can I make into hits, how much money can the Parker Company bring in."

"Maybe you just need a vacation, a break from everything."

"What I need is a different life. Eric and I talk about moving somewhere together, maybe Montana. He's tired of performing too."

"So you and Eric are an, uh, an item?"

"Well, like, sort of. Ok, yes."

"Does Frank have any idea how you feel?"

Jessica shook her head. "Are you kidding? He's not about feelings. We should never have gotten married. When I leave, he'll just find some sexy young thing who can sing and mold her into a star. Meantime, I'm so glad to see you again. It's been way too long."

"I agree," I said, yawning.

Daylight came before I was ready to welcome it, but animals get cranky when the buffet is late. The worst one is Maynard. I love donkeys, and he's my favorite. But his braying carries for miles. Roy and I stepped out the back door, followed closely by Zap and Fetch, headed to the barn for chores. Maynard brayed, but softly just to encourage us. Early morning sunshine cast a warm glow on the horizon, softened the edges of our barn, backlit the pastures, the horses, each blade of grass. The routine began with the mare and foal enclosure, ladling out grains formulated to enhance lactation, allowing myself a few minutes to enjoy the sights and the antics of this year's Quarter horse fillies and colts, the last ones bred by Bow. After the death of my beloved foster mother last year, I moved all the horses, including brood mares, to my place. Watching the foals brought a mixture of joy and sorrow.

Roy handed out supplemental grain for pasture inhabitants. I loaded the wheelbarrow with half a bale of hay, a bucket of grain and headed to the round pen where my five mustangs had spent the night. One of the day's goals would be starting to undo any damage from last evening's fiasco.

Back at the house, Roy began breakfast while I tiptoed into the living room. The couch was empty. No Evelyn. Even the blanket I'd covered her with was gone. I hadn't heard anyone in the bathroom, but I went to check. Bathroom empty. Odd. The house had three bedrooms, but one was where Roy and I slept, one served as an office, the other was a guest room now occupied by Jessica and I assumed Frank, who'd arrived during the night. I checked the office. Nope.

I hadn't seen Evelyn outside, at least not in back or anywhere near the barn. I opened the front door to an empty porch. The black SUV was way down at the ranch entrance, and I assumed both bodyguards were inside. No other vehicles in front.

Jessica said one of the stage crew planned to bring Frank here last night. Maybe Evelyn had left with that person.

Dense shrubs and towering evergreens formed a windbreak in front of the house. I stepped off the porch, wandered into the greenery, and hadn't gone far when I saw a pair of legs poking out from beneath low hanging branches.

Evelyn was on her side, curled up on the ground as if asleep, the blanket I'd given her last night loose around her shoulders.

# CHAPTER SIX

I BENT DOWN, touched her. "Evelyn," I said. She smelled like cigarette smoke.

Nothing. No movement, no sound. Eyes closed.

Her cheeks were devoid of color, mouth open, jaw slack. A bit of drool seeped over her lower lip. I pushed two fingers into her neck, gently, feeling for a carotid pulse. Her skin felt cool even though she was fully clothed. Nights in May can be chilly, and no telling how long she'd lain here on the ground.

A swirl of possibilities flooded my mind. I repositioned my fingers on her neck, thought I detected a pulse, hoped I did.

I shook her again, harder. "Evelyn, wake up, wake up."

I held my breath.

And then she groaned.

"Open your eyes."

She groaned again, her eyelids fluttered. "Wha – ohhh," she mumbled, bringing a hand to her head. Long mahogany curls framed her face. That hair made it easy to see why people sometimes mistook her for Jessica.

First aide classes warned not to move someone with a possible head or neck injury, but she sat up before I could stop her, wobbling.

41

I put an arm around her shoulders to steady her. "What happened?"

"I, uh…" She paused, frowning. "I'm cold."

"Yeah, I know," I said, snugging the blanket around her shoulders. "But what are you doing out here?"

She looked around, blinked. "Woke up to pee, stepped out for a smoke."

At least she was awake, talking.

She pulled her legs under her, started to get up. "Cold," she said, "I'm cold."

"C'mon," I said, helping her, "let's get you inside."

She was stiff, and her knees began to buckle once, but I held her up, guided her in, settled her onto a chair.

I went to the kitchen, told Roy about Evelyn. He poured her a cup of tea with milk and honey, came to the living room.

Evelyn sipped, hands trembling.

"You went outside to smoke?" I asked.

"Um, yeah, I think so."

"Did you trip and fall?"

"I saw somebody," she said, frowning.

Roy and I exchanged glances.

"One of the bodyguards?" Roy asked.

She shrugged. "Hit me." She rubbed the back of her head. "Here."

"Maybe you bumped your head when you fell down," I said.

"Someone hit me."

"We'd better have a doctor look at you," I said.

Jessica swept into the living room, her red robe shimmering, making her look glamorous even with mussed hair. Louie padded at her side. "What's going on? I was in the bathroom, headed back to bed, but…"

"Someone hit me," Evelyn repeated.

Jessica's eyes widened. "What?"

I told her where I'd found Evelyn, what she'd said.

"So you saw someone?" Jessica asked, yawning.

Evelyn shrugged. "Not the face. Too dark. Heard something behind me, glanced around." She paused, sipped more tea. Her hands seemed steadier now. "And then I felt a big pain in my head, knew I'd fall."

"Oh my God," Jessica said, "you poor thing. You laid there on the ground until this morning?"

"Must have."

"What time did you go outside?"

Evelyn shrugged. "It was dark."

Jessica turned toward me. "What about the guys?"

"Haven't seen them yet. The SUV is still down at the ranch entrance." Jessica buzzed them on her cell and they rushed up to the house, searched awhile, found nothing.

"I should wake up Frank," Jessica said, "but he got in so late. Looked exhausted."

"Evelyn must've gone outside after his arrival," Roy said.

"Yeah," Jessica said. "How you feeling now, Sweetie?"

"Better," Evelyn replied. "Just a big headache."

"You may have a concussion," I said.

"No," Evelyn said, "I'm fine."

"Well I'm taking you to the emergency room, let them check you out," Jessica said.

"I can take her," I said. "You're still tired."

"No, that's okay," Jessica said. "I'm awake now, I need to go with her. But watch Louie for me, don't let him out of your sight."

Pinedale Springs had a ten-bed hospital and lacked a real emergency department, but doctors were always on call.

One bodyguard drove Jessica and Evelyn into town, the other soon appeared and resumed patrolling the ranch. For stagehands switched to bodyguard service they were probably better than nothing, but real professionals would have seen Evelyn go outside, known if someone had hit her. Frank dressed them in tight black shirts which outlined muscular torsos, so they at least looked the part.

I called the Sheriff's office and a dispatcher asked pertinent questions, informed me that Sheriff Plackmon himself wasn't due in for an hour. She offered to send out the night shift deputy, but I told her no, asked to have the Sheriff call when he came in.

After that, I left the dogs inside and went out for a look around. Pine needles and old leaves layered into thick mulch under the trees, and I surveyed here and there, looking for anything out of place. Maybe something shiny. Or Evelyn's cigarette butt. I usually didn't allow smoking anywhere on my property. Smoke gave me an instant headache, for one thing, but more important, the thought of smoldering ashes scared the hell out of me. Fire would be bad enough here around the house, but down by the barn, one carelessly tossed butt could ignite a haystack and reduce everything to cinders before a fire engine left the station.

The bodyguard hadn't found anything. On my first pass, I found Evelyn's cigarette butt which looked less than half used. If someone had been out here, it appeared that they'd left no sign. Maybe Evelyn had simply fallen on her own, imagined someone hitting her.

I was about to head back inside when I got a whiff of something, a faint odor, unpleasant and out of place, different than lingering cigarette smoke. I knew right away what it was, but bit exactly where the smell originated. There was a new-looking fluff of pine needles way beneath a tree, over near the house. Probably the work of a squirrel scratching around, hiding some treasure that'd begun to rot. Black Abert's squirrels with long tufted ears inhabit the ponderosa forests on our property, and although their main diet consists of pinecone seeds, they also raid our bird feeders for sunflower seeds. Like all squirrels, they forget where half of their caches are, so sunflowers sprout in odd places every summer.

I almost didn't bother approaching it because I only expected to find a few seeds and something disgusting like a smelly piece of food, but I walked over there anyhow.

This wasn't the work of a squirrel. The closer I got, the stronger the smell.

An inch or so of dirt had been pushed aside, making a small depression filled with wads of chewing tobacco. A piece of wrapper imprinted with one legible word: 'Skoal' stuck out. Someone had been here, someone with a bad habit. Close up, the stench made me gag. There was quite a lot of the stuff. Still moist. Took some time to chew that much.

The guy at the feed store on the outskirts of town kept a brown wad between his discolored teeth and lower lip. Sometimes when he spoke, a little dab of spittle oozed out the side of his mouth. Every now and then, he spit into a coffee can. His breath smelled like cow turds.

The beefier bodyguard had a noticeable B.O. problem, but neither one of them were chewers. I can smell that stuff across a room.

So Evelyn was right. Someone had been here not long ago. Must have been waiting for a while. But waiting for who, and why?

The guy who called himself Michael Turner was one obvious culprit. Maybe he was playing peeping Tom, just trying to get a glimpse of his supposed one true love. He could've gotten all frenzied when he thought it was Jessica coming outside, ran up to her, hit her over the head. No telling what his intentions were. Must've run off when he realized it wasn't Jessica. He couldn't have driven onto the ranch, not with that black SUV stationed right by the only entrance. He must have parked down the road somewhere, ducked under a fence and circled up through trees to the house.

Seemed odd that Zap and Fetch hadn't barked during the night. They seldom failed to alert me to visitors, although their barking signaled more excitement than threat. They seldom growled. Roy and I had a bedroom on the opposite side of the house, though, and they slept on the floor next to the bed. Maybe they were thrown off by the houseguests and the bodyguards. No warnings from Louie, either. So the intruder and his brown spittal had slipped in and out undetected by dogs or humans.

I thought about that big knife Jessica found last evening. Meant to shock, to warn. Ominous for sure. I needed to check the people on the Parker Company list. I looked at my watch. Nearing seven. Too early for the stage crew to be up and about. I could call the dispatcher back, have her send the deputy out, but this was no longer an immediate emergency. Better to wait and see what the doctors had to say about Evelyn anyway.

The smell of coffee and tea brewing filled the kitchen, and Roy gave me a hug while I told him about the chewing tobacco. "I don't like this. Things are escalating."

"I agree. Sheriff Plackmon will call when he gets in."

"Let's eat before he comes. Eggs and toast?"

I nodded. "Sounds great." While he cooked, we discussed Evelyn and the mystery intruder.

The sheriff called just as I was finishing the last bit of egg and said that no fingerprints were found on last evening's package or the knife inside it. He told us to be cautious. I assured him we'd let him know right away if anything else happened. There'd been so many incidents in such a short amount of time that it was tempting to believe everything was related somehow, but it was hard to link the same person or group to both Jessica and me. When I brought that up to the sheriff, all he said was "We'll consider it."

Jessica was right about the difficulty of getting official help. Yes, Sheriff Plackmon was appropriately concerned, but he had no more concrete information to go on than we did. No way of knowing who bounced that yellow ball to spook Hotshot and land me face down in dirt. No way of knowing who aimed the rock at my front window or cut my fence and spray painted my young mustangs. I suspected it was the Dicksons, but no proof. Same issue with incidents involving Jessica. Most likely this latest culprit was her stalker, but no proof.

After breakfast, Roy went to do another check on the corral panels that'd broken apart so readily at the concert. He concluded that those panels appeared to have been fastened in such a way that they'd fall apart extremely easily. On purpose, in other words.

"I suspected that was the case," I said.

"Yeah, that's not good. Means someone wanted to create chaos last night."

I frowned. "They succeeded. Now the question is why? Were they aiming to embarrass Jessica or go after me and the mustangs?"

"We need to find out."

Before I got bogged down in what promised to be another day packed with problems, I had to fit in some training sessions. Enough horses needed my attention, and working with even the most challenging animal would be a joy, a respite from this insanity.

I scribbled a note to Frank, told him to help himself to toast and coffee or grab one of the sandwiches Roy had put in the frig, said Jessica was in town, would explain things when she returned.

Roy thinks I'm too tied to this place, too bogged down with training schedules, riding students, wilderness pack trips, prospective buyers for my Quarter horses, advocating for the mustangs. But I love all of it.

Challenging and time consuming, yes, but I not only enjoy being around horses, I need to be with them so much that I hesitate to call it work except maybe on subzero February mornings when I'm shoveling ice out of a frozen water trough because one of the tank heaters quit. Wouldn't mind having regular help shoveling shit from stalls or throwing hay bales around. Ranching is hard work and Roy helps when he's here. He didn't plan to travel much this summer, so I hadn't hired anyone.

In some ways, I preferred to see all horses running free, not just the mustangs. There's something at once wonderful and yet sad about domesticating such elegant creatures, whether Quarter horses, warm-bloods or ponies. That was why it didn't bother me in the least to know that many of the mustangs I planned to rescue were too old or just too wild to ever be ridden. I felt a combo of pity and fury for people who called these animals useless. Fortunately, some people not only under-stood my plans but backed me up. A small chunk of the townspeople and possibly a third of the local ranchers were in favor of a mustang refuge. Others were at least neutral to the idea, so I shuffled them into the favor-able column. If it came down to a vote to make the BLM approve my plan, it'd be a close call.

My most important ally was Roy Holden, of course. Not only was he totally in favor of establishing the refuge, his love of all animals was one of the many reasons I fell in love with him, finally agreed to walk down the aisle, exchange rings. I hadn't worn a fluffy white dress and Roy hadn't worn a tux. But the vows we exchanged were solid, and we even took a honeymoon, traveling to Montana to spend time at the ranch Roy's family owned. Naturally, while we were there, we rode lots of horses, made tons happy memories.

Tall and slender, Roy looked like a stereotypical cowboy. Originally from small-town Montana, he now traveled throughout the West and occasionally internationally as a PhD Natural Resource consultant. Our relationship flourished because we loved one another enough to grant each other space. He loved me and he loved our ranch, but staying in one place day after day wasn't his thing.

I've always considered myself somewhat of a loner, although after Bow's death, the word lonesome was more accurate. Having Roy and a few select others as allies kept me sane, at least somewhat. Friends like Beth Jensen helped too. But the truth was that horses were more responsible for my sanity than anyone or anything.

It thrilled me when any of the wilder mustangs allowed me to approach. For a wild creature to accept my presence was the first step, leading eventually to touching them, then proceeding gradually from there. A sustainable mustang refuge could provide forever homes for some, introduce more people to the joy of either owning one of them or just spending time watching them.

I hadn't finalized the details yet, but the concept was a combo of training select mustangs to sell, training people to work with mustangs, initiating equine therapy for humans, and charging visitors to view mustangs from a distance. None of these ideas were new, but the hope was to perfect each aspect and bring in sufficient funding to build a sustainable and reproducible model for other refuges.

I squeezed my eyes shut, took a deep breath. I'd dreamt of establishing a mustang refuge ever since I went to live with Bow after my parents died in a plane crash when I was twelve. Those dreams stayed with me, helping me through the sadness back then. It all seemed closer to reality now.

Roy assured me that the challenges were worth it, that everything would work out.

I wanted to believe him. I wanted to be optimistic. I wanted to kick the BLM's butt.

Morning sun, still low to the east, cast a sideways glow, the one photographers seek. Sweet light, they call it. One Quarter horse mare and foal in the nursery pasture were backlit as if posing in the midst of a luminous halo. If I wasn't so rushed this morning, it'd be fun to capture this maternal scene with a camera. But the foal moved, the moment passed.

I proceeded to the barn, told myself to stop dreaming, get to work, keep alert. Nothing seemed out of place, no intruder lurked behind a corner or inside a stall. I went down the aisle to the tack room for a halter and lead rope. Someone was coming in a few days for a look at one of the Quarter horse yearlings, so I brought him in from pasture. Although this bay gelding wasn't yet old enough to ride, I'd worked him regularly on the basics; halter manners, leading, groundwork, the feel of a light saddle. Today all he needed was a quick review. In half an hour, he was done, rejoining his pasture buddies.

Next on the agenda were the three mustangs I was training for a local rancher. This was the first time to ride Hotshot outside the arena, into the forest. After the bucking session in the round pen a few weeks ago, he remained skittish, probably wondering when another yellow ball would bounce down from the sky. Now, I rode him beside the pasture fence, beyond the boundaries of the ranch, and into the forest. He was too inexperienced to carry anyone for long, but I wanted to see how he handled himself in rough terrain with a rider on his back, a feat which changes a horse's center of balance and hence their movements. Hotshot's muscular frame attested to the fact that he'd spent the first years of life running free with other rugged Piceance Basin mustangs. This area west of Meeker held another of Western Colorado's wild herds, but unlike Soda Creek Cliffs, adoptees had been taken from there recently and offered to the public. Gas drilling operations threatened to decimate that herd entirely.

Somehow, I had to prevent the roundup of the Cliffs' herd that was planned in only a few weeks or better yet, move all those rounded up to my new refuge. At the same time, I had to stop Jessica's stalker and figure out who besides the Dickson clan were intent on stopping my plans for the refuge.

If only I had Wonder Woman on my side.

# CHAPTER SEVEN

THE CHESTNUT DIDN'T mind going out alone, a good sign. He crow-hopped a few times, a mild version of a buck. His back legs came only a foot or so off the ground, just enough to test this load he'd rather not carry. I sat still, keeping my balance until he realized that acting up wasn't worth the effort. He didn't bother getting light in the front, so no rearing tendency now. As soon as he settled down, I gave him a looser rein, encouraging him to stretch out his neck and look where he was going. Once we reached rockier terrain, his steps grew tentative, and then he started jigging. I knew what came next. He whirled and tried to head back down the trail, then dropped his left shoulder. I collected the reins, sat deep in the saddle and chanted "Easy now, easy there" to coax the little guy to relax. These words served to calm both horse and rider. Hotshot tried to argue, which was neither unusual nor unexpected, so I guided him in a circle until he stopped jigging and finally stood still.

I rode him up the trail a ways more before turning him around toward home. He jigged some here and there, bucked for real once, but I stuck with him and we circled some more until he calmed down. Not bad for a quick first outing. Hotshot was smart, he'd make a fine mount, although he'd need hours under saddle to raise his reliability score. If the rancher who owned him hadn't named him Hotshot, I would've called him Wiley Coyote. He was the type who'd always take advantage of fearful or beginning riders. Fortunately, his owner fit neither category.

The rancher's other two mustangs came next. Lady, the little bay filly, was a dream to work with, smooth-gaited and trusting. The gelding, Trooper, didn't give me any trouble either, although his straighter shoulder made for choppier gaits. When I finished with them, I spent some time with my five mustangs who'd had too much excitement last night. I began by doling out carrots, then brushing each one, trying to reassure them. I saddled Phantom and my fabulous black mare and I enjoyed a quick but relaxing ride that let me know she held no grudges. I rubbed her down afterwards and led her and the others out to pasture. The message on my phone alerted me that Sheriff Plackmon had called, said he was on his way to my place.

At first glance, Sheriff Plackmon looked like the type who'd kick back a cold one while rooting for his favorite team on an oversized flat screen. But a more complex human being inhabited that middle-aged body. He was a man of few words who preferred wine to beer and shared an impressive collection of books with a wife young enough to be his daughter and smart enough to be the only psychologist in town. The friendship between us wasn't perfect, but it was honest and easy even if I did have a tendency to step out of bounds now and then. Whorls of dust announced the arrival of his silver truck.

"I hear you've had more excitement," he said.

"Sufficient," I replied. He'd gotten reports from his deputies, of course, but he'd come in person for details. I told him everything I'd seen, beginning with Evelyn and the stash of chewing tobacco. He walked around, gathered a sample of the stuff, made a few notes. He asked if the bodyguards chewed, and I told him no. I would've noticed that smell.

"You know as much or more about this stalker than I do," I began.

He nodded. "Ms. Parker's husband called before they came to town, told me about the letters, the calls, the lingerie business. I said we'd keep an eye on things, do what we could while she's in town. But we're not equipped for surveillance. I don't have enough deputies, to begin with."

My turn to nod. "Which is why Jessica asked me to help."

"And you love to go poking around."

"Poking around is a hobby of mine, I guess."

"Now look, Margo Richards, this is serious, dangerous."

I blinked at him. He usually called me just Margo. "She's a friend of mine. We grew up together. I need to look out for her."

"You need to look out for yourself first," he said. "You've had problems of your own lately."

"Everybody needs at least a handful of enemies, so I selected mine years ago while the pickings were good."

"None of this is funny. You could've been hurt. Even that spill you took could've been worse."

"As far as spills go, that was at least good, possibly excellent. I assume Ruth Dunn was the one who blabbed about it. She tends to exaggerate, you know." Ruth Dunn was seventy but ran the B&D Tack Store and her own ranch while serving as the local source for gossip. She spread news faster than the high school kids on TikTok, Discord, or whatever.

"Any idea who lobbed that ball at you?"

"Ideas, sure. Proof, no. I don't tend to see much when I'm face down in dirt."

"I'd tell you to be careful, but I know you too well," he said, shaking his head. "I assume you think it was also the Dickson clan who broke your front window and then cut your fence and spray-painted the mustangs."

"I can't help it if people keep doing nasty stuff, and yes, I suspect the Dicksons. Which brings us to the mustang fiasco at the concert."

Roy emerged from the house and joined us. "This corral was rigged to fall, sheriff. Let me show you."

The corral pieces were still behind my barn. The three of us walked over and had a look at the wood. Roy pointed out the shorter bolts.

"Does look suspicious," the sheriff agreed, rubbing the back of his neck. "Someone might have meant to disrupt the concert, another scare tactic. I don't want you or your friend getting hurt, Margo."

"My sentiments exactly," Roy said.

"Your mustangs all right?"

"Seem to be."

"Hard to prove it was more than an accident."

We reviewed all the incidents with Jessica's stalker, and the sheriff nodded grimly. "This guy is escalating."

Roy nodded. "We know."

"I'll do what I can to protect your friend while she's here. Don't you go trying to find this guy, Margo."

"I plan on jumping to answers."

"Be serious, Margo," Roy said. "The sheriff is right. No telling what this stalker could do."

Sheriff Plackmon sort of smiled, touched a finger to the brim of his Stetson. "Keep me informed, both of you," he said before climbing inside his truck. Whorls of dust came back to life as he drove off.

"I believe that he'll do what he can, Roy. But we both know it may not be enough."

"I want Jessica to be safe, but you're my main concern. I'm sticking around here as much as I can."

"I love you, Roy."

He pulled me in for a hug. "I love you too."

We walked back to the house hand in hand.

I called Jessica's cell to check on Evelyn.

"Her brain scan was fine," Jessica said. "And she wasn't molested, either. They're discharging her. A deputy came and spoke to us."

"I know," I said, "the Sheriff was just here." I told her about finding chewing tobacco.

"So there was someone outside last night."

"Yes."

"Evelyn feels fine and plans to stay in town with the others. The doctors told her to rest, but she claims she has stuff to do."

"What stuff?"

"Well, she coordinates publicity for us, and she's good at it."

"Okay. So it's time to get serious about this fan of yours. Tell me about the men in your life."

"All of them?"

I had to smile at that. Knowing Jessica, the list was probably endless. "Any guys you've… uh, spent time with, in the last year," I replied. "And I need to know if any of them chew."

"Oh," Jessica said, catching her breath. "Well, Ian does sometimes, but I haven't been with him for a couple weeks."

"Weeks? But you're married!"

"True."

"So Ian chews."

"Sometimes, yes."

"Uh huh, so you were with him, as in bed?"

She laughed. "C'mon. Bed is boring. He's got this private deck where we get naked, look up at the moon. Great sex."

"Sure, whatever. I assume Frank doesn't know."

"No way. He's the jealous type."

"What kind of guy is this studly Ian?"

"Not a stalker. He was my drummer for a while. Totally a good guy."

"Great, but I'd like to call him, ask a few questions." Jessica provided his name and address. "Anybody else you're messing around with?"

"Well, Eric Jakowski, he doesn't chew, but we get together."

It was safe to assume she was referring to something other than band rehearsals with Eric Jakowski. Even though he didn't chew and was still in the hospital with a broken leg, I added him to the list. "How about the other band guys, the stagehands?"

"None of them are my type."

"Any of them chew?"

"Nobody in the band, but several stagehands use the stuff. I get a whiff sometimes. Foul, but reminds me of Ian. Let's see… Ken uses it, and a couple others."

"How about the bodyguard guys?"

"No, I'm sure neither of them chew."

After scribbling down the names Jessica provided, I closed the call, took a shower. I pulled on clean jeans and the first knit top in the stack. It happened to be purple. I did an underarm check for holes, which is about as fancy as it gets toward making a fashion statement. Roy was in his office, and I kissed him, said I was planning a few calls, just snooping around. I was headed outside to sit on the porch when the guest room door opened.

Frank's dark hair looked a bit tousled, fine stubble outlined his chin, and I nearly broke out into a sweat just looking at him. Chiseled features, that's what magazines say about men like him, for starters. Impossible not to stare, he was that good-looking.

"Morning, Frank," I said, hoping my voice sounded natural.

He nodded and winked.

Heat rose in my cheeks and embarrassment spilled out of every pore. Maybe my hormones were out of whack. I wasn't the flirty type, and even though I saw nothing wrong with appreciating handsome males, this guy made me feel like a schoolgirl, vaguely inadequate, definitely uncomfortable. I flashed back to my first crush. The kid's name was Greg, and he never did acknowledge my existence despite the fact that I scribbled his name over and over at the back of my math notebook and awarded him a starring role in junior-high daydreams.

Frank moved closer, raised one eyebrow and asked, "What are you doing up early?"

I glanced at the clock above the kitchen stove. "It's almost noon."

"Oh, of course," he said, shaking his head, "Jessica told me you rise at dawn."

Roy joined us, and I glanced from one to the other. Two very handsome males, but I moved close to Roy, put my arms around him, glad he was my guy. There was something about Frank, something a bit off.

"Jessica isn't here," I said.

Frank nodded. "I know. She awoke me in what seemed like the middle of the night, told me about Evelyn. How is she?"

"Seems all right," I said. "The doctor did tests which came out fine."

"Good. I must make some calls, tighten security. I am quite concerned about Jessica. This is not the first episode. There was another fanatic fan three years ago, kept sending chocolates. Arrived by UPS every single day for an entire month. Always the same, two pound boxes of chocolate covered cherries. I did not allow her to open a single box. After someone made sure nothing had been tampered with, we distributed the boxes to nursing homes. We heard that the confections made a big hit."

Roy and I smiled, and I imagined white-haired people licking their fingers, reaching for more. "She didn't mention that to me," I said.

"It was quite different, amusing at first." He paused, shook his head. "But this time there is nothing humorous, not in the least."

"You spoke to threat management agencies, right?" Roy asked.

"Some provided advice, but they are all prohibitively expensive," Frank said, nodding. "I therefore devised another plan, one which shall bring an end to this maddening situation."

"Well," Roy said, "that might be good." He paused, waiting for Frank to provide details on his plan, but Frank said nothing. "Something to eat?"

"Perhaps a splash of coffee and a bit of toast," he replied.

I was out the door and seated on the porch with Zap and Fetch nearby when my cell phone rang.

"You hear about the mustang?" Ruth Dunn's voice sounded so high and agitated, that I almost didn't recognize her. She rode an old and grumpy appaloosa named Gus, but she'd always loved the mustangs.

"What happened?"

"One of those bays out at Soda Creek Cliffs," she said. "Someone shot it."

"Is the horse dead?"

"Yes," Ruth said, "hikers found the body. Been there awhile."

I grimaced, sucking air through my teeth.

"Hope it was quick, poor thing didn't suffer," she continued.

"Was it the stallion?"

"Haven't heard. The women who found it didn't know much about horses. Only said brown with a black mane and tail."

Which described a bay, one of the more common colors. Still, only one bay stallion ran in Soda Creek Cliffs, and he was the most striking animal of them all, a wondrous mix of raw power and intelligent eyes. Half a dozen or so bands had bay mares, but the other stallions included a buckskin, two pintos, several chestnuts.

"Anyone seen the bay and his harem?" I asked, holding my breath.

"BLM agents haven't been out there yet," Ruth said.

"Um, 'course not," I said. It wasn't just that they wouldn't care, with one exception. There were also too few agents with too many priorities. Like most government agencies, the Bureau of Land Management was perpetually under-staffed and over-budget. They'd send someone to investigate the shooting. Eventually. They'd be hard-pressed to devote enough manpower to finding the culprits.

My stomach knotted. Almost a month since I'd visited the Cliffs to survey the mustangs, check on them. Somewhere out there, a horse lay dead. I closed my eyes, imagined the stallion and his band. If that magnificent animal was targeted, his genes would no longer infuse offspring with greatness. "This isn't like the others."

"No," Ruth agreed. "This one didn't just disappear."

"Right, and what about that, the dwindling herds." A rhetorical question. At least six mustangs had disappeared from a total of slightly over one hundred animals within the past year. The official BLM report blamed winter die-off or an unidentified infection, neglected to mention why not even one carcass had been found. I'd searched more than once, failed to find a single bone. Someone must be capturing mustangs out there, stealing them while the BLM sat back and did nothing. But shooting one of them was different.

After ending the call with Ruth, I pressed my lips together and shook my head. All I could think about was who shot the mustang. One name came to mind. I punched in another number on my cell. "

"Who did it?"

Millie Dickson knew why I called, wasn't the type to play games. "How should I know. I'm not the only one who realizes how worthless those critters are. But if I planned to put bullets in them one by one, I'd a done it years ago."

I gritted my teeth. Millie was a bitch, and not only because she hated mustangs, not only because she was an outspoken enemy of Forever Free, the main mustang watch group I supported. Years of cattle ranching had weathered her skin and soured her attitude. Her husband and son towered over her in height and muscle, but she dominated with razor tongue.

"How did you find out about the mustang so soon?" I asked.

"I have sources, just like you. Too bad you grew up around the likes of Bow, got you all soft and sentimental."

Of course she didn't care much for Bow, my foster mother who'd taught me everything about horses, about life. Millie Dickson grew up around nature but seldom really saw it, considered it her enemy.

"I'll find out who did this." I ended the call before she could reply.

I imagined the mustang, running free, falling suddenly, a bullet lodged in its flesh.

# CHAPTER EIGHT

NEXT, I CALLED the Bureau of Land Management office, hoping to talk
with the one good friend I had there.

Luke Barnes grew up on a cattle ranch near Meeker, a part of western
Colorado so rugged that it made the Pinedale Springs area seem like Eden.
We met years ago when he bought one of my young Quarter horse colts.
Long-legged and lean, with that tight cowboy butt, tanned face and soulful eyes, he was one of the sexiest guys I knew, except for Roy, of course.
Luke competed in team roping all over Colorado and Wyoming when he
wasn't stuck in front of a BLM computer. I felt sorry for those little calves
he chased around even while admiring the skill it takes to accurately throw
a rope from the back of a galloping horse. I tried not to hold his choice of
recreation or his job in Big Government against him, although I kidded
him mercilessly. He came back at me about my preference for English
saddles and my choice of Roy, declaring my new husband "citified."

We dated off and on before Roy came into the picture, and our
friendship could've evolved into something more at one time. He loved
horses and open spaces. But he loved women, too, loved them one and
all. He never married, but seldom slept alone. He would've made a hor-
rible, cheating husband, but he was a loyal friend.

"Mr. Barnes is not in," the secretary said when I asked for him.

"This is Margo Richards. Do you know where he is?"

"Oh hello, Margo," she said in a somewhat less formal tone. Mary Lou was one of those efficient types with an ageless face and perfect hair. "He hasn't been here for two days," she added.

"He out in the field?"

"I don't believe so. Mr. Gannon hasn't assigned any trips."

"So is he home sick or something?"

"Sorry, I wouldn't know." A note of impatience crept into her voice, her subtle way of trying to end the conversation, get back to her files.

After that call, I entered Luke's number. No answer. Odd. He merely tolerated being tied behind a desk, but he seldom failed to show up for the Monday to Friday grind. There was one exception that I knew of. This past June, after his boss denied a request for vacation days, Luke called in sick in order to participate in one of the season's biggest team roping competitions. The reason I knew this was because he'd told me how much money he'd won, which was a lot more than he made in an hour or even an entire week at the BLM. He'd also told me what he thought his boss could do with the paperwork that'd been stamped 'time-off denied.' Sounded like something involving considerable discomfort.

Luke was one of the few local BLM guys who loved the mustangs his department was charged with caring for. He always volunteered for field assignments when it involved places where the wild horses roamed. He'd adopted several and gave them free range of his modest forty-acre spread north of town. In addition to the mustangs, he owned two Quarter horses. By his own account, he lacked ambition, at least in regard to monetary gain or a cubicle nearer the windows, so he remained subordinate to nearly everyone in the office. He drove an old truck, pulled an old horse trailer, but he never skimped on care for his animals. Maybe he'd gone to a roping event last week-end, gotten hurt somehow.

I called the BLM office again.

"Yes, Margo?" It wasn't a question. Mary Lou didn't try to delete the impatience from her tone.

"I'm concerned about Luke," I began. "I tried calling him at home."

"I already said I have no idea where he is," Mary Lou said. "I can tell you that Mr. Gannon is not pleased about his absence."

As far as I could tell, Joe Gannon was probably born with a scowl on his face and an oversized helping of badass attitude. The chief honcho of the local BLM office kept his uniform starched and his outlook sour.

"Can you connect me with him please?"

"He's a very busy man," she said. She sounded surprised that I'd dare to ask to speak with such an important person. Either that, or she didn't want to risk irritating him. According to Luke, Joe Gannon sprang to life minus any sense of humor whatsoever. Luke and another office prankster perpetrated jokes on their boss to elicit a laugh. The more he scowled, the more fun they had.

"I'll only take a moment of his time," I said.

"Let me see if he's available. One moment, please."

A click, and then that stuff they call elevator music. So-called easy listening, irritating mush. There was another click, then a clipped male voice. "Gannon here."

"Hello, Joe," I said. "This is Margo Richards."

"I know. What now?" He sounded less than thrilled. He associated me only with Forever Free, which had an adversarial relationship with the BLM in general and Joe Gannon in particular.

"I'm calling about Luke," I said. "I'm concerned."

"Concerned?"

"Mary Lou said he hasn't been in for two days."

"Yes, and if Barnes is playing hooky from work to ride his horse in some stupid contest again, I'll fire his skinny ass."

"He doesn't answer his phone," I said. "I'm wondering if he's okay."

"Well he won't be okay unless he has an appropriate excuse for missing work. And now if you don't mind… "

He was about to hang up on me. "Wait," I said. "What do you know about the dead mustang?"

"Not much, not much at all."

"I'm curious about where it was found."

"I haven't been able to send anyone out there yet." Impatience radiated from each word.

"I know, but can you tell me what the report said?"

"Citizens can come and view public portions of any report during business hours."

"I'm trying to be reasonable," I said, "so can you just drop the canned crap?"

"This office has jurisdiction on over thousands of acres of Federal land," he said in a don't-mess-with-me tone. "We'll investigate this dead animal in due time."

He was right, of course. So damn right that I was tempted to tell him where to stuff it. My attitude needed adjustment as much as his did.

"If you could just provide a bit of information, I'd appreciate it," I said, choking on my attempt at sweetness.

"Hikers found the thing several miles from the main entrance. That's all I can divulge."

"Several miles in which direction?"

"Report didn't say. Those hikers were from out of state, Pennsylvania, as I recall. Just stumbled on the carcass, barely knew where they were. Called the State Trooper's office, didn't even know enough to call us."

I thanked him in an almost polite tone and hung up, congratulating myself for holding back on calling him names no mother would approve of. I wanted to ask him more about the others, the horses who'd disappeared, but there was no point. I'd have to rely on Luke for that. And if I made even more of an enemy in the twisted halls of government bureaucracy, say with someone like Joe Gannon, I'd have to reply on Luke for help with that, too. He'd been increasingly frustrated with the BLM in general and his boss in particular. Maybe he'd just walked off the job, quit without giving notice.

Joe Gannon would never come right out and say he hated horses, but he sided with ranchers like the Dicksons who believed mustangs took up space better occupied by cattle or sheep. He seemed more relieved than concerned about the disappearances, and he wouldn't lose sleep over a mustang who'd been shot.

Someone was behind the dwindling herd at Soda Creek Cliffs. Maybe that same someone was behind the shooting. If Luke suspected something, he might've ridden out there without waiting for the BLM to send him. I had to get ahold of Luke, and soon.

Frank appeared with a suitcase, said he had a plane to catch for a quick trip to Oklahoma and called for the bodyguard to take him to Pinedale's small airport.

I went back inside, poured myself a cup of tea, carried it into our office and rummaged in my bottom desk drawer.

Roy turned to watch me. "What're you searching for?"

Today's prize, the topo map of Soda Creek Cliffs, was the last item to surface. I held it up.

"A topo? Why?" he asked.

"Are you up for a long ride?"

He shrugged. "Maybe. Where and why?"

I told him about the bay mustang, told him Luke Barnes was missing.

"Okay, when?"

"Tomorrow," I replied, "we have to find that horse. And Luke."

"Maybe Luke camped out there."

I shrugged. "Maybe. But we need answers."

He nodded. "Let's go."

GPS was readily available for road trips, but a large topo map still provided info for roadless areas. I unfolded it on the desk. Even though I didn't ride there as often as I rode in the Flat Tops Wilderness, I knew some trails by heart, could visualize curves leading from Coyote Canyon Trailhead into twisting canyons enclosed by rocky cliffs and pinyon-juniper dotted plateaus. Staring at the map renewed the place and the distances in my mind. Over thirty-six thousand rugged acres, a third of that designated an official Wild Horse Range, all of it under BLM jurisdiction.

It'd be difficult to find the culprit, but not impossible. The first step was locating that carcass. Horses are herd animals, seeking the company of their own kind for protection and comfort. It was unlikely that mustang had been alone, so the shooter either targeted it at random or singled it out for some reason. It'd take hours to ride the entire trail system, so narrowing the search was imperative.

Joe Gannon hadn't revealed much, but he did say that the hikers reported their find to State Troopers. One of my riding students, Kerry Jamison, had a dad who was a Trooper. When Jim Jamison wasn't busy patrolling the highways around Pinedale Springs, he often delivered his horse-loving daughter to her Thursday afternoon lesson. He was a nice guy, approachable. He didn't ride, but he brought carrots for the horses.

It took more than one phone call to reach him, but when I asked him to check specifics on the hikers who'd reported a dead horse, he said "No problem, Margo. I know who wrote it up. I'll contact the guy right now, call you back in a bit."

Connections help.

While I was waiting, there were things to accomplish before Roy and I could ride into the Cliffs area tomorrow. In order to keep things flowing, I kept a detailed schedule, the same as any businesswoman. Instead of stuffy offices, my clients came with manes and tails or breeches and boots. I kept notes with progress and problems on all my riding students and the horses they rode. I kept even more detailed notes on all the horses I had in training. When a horse was ready to return to its owner, I provided a copy of the file and kept the originals in alphabetical order according to the horse's name rather than the owner. If an animal returned for additional training, the record of previous encounters proved invaluable.

I had to clear tomorrow, reschedule lessons, rearrange training sessions. I arranged for one of my high school aged riding students to feed tomorrow evening if we weren't back, made notes and started other calls.

I couldn't forget about Jessica's stalker, and I also needed to figure out why a tobacco-chewing guy had been hanging around last night, what had happened to Evelyn. I was looking at the list of tobacco-chewing guys that Jessica had made for me, mulling it over, when the phone rang.

It was Jim, and my Trooper friend provided not only names but also the phone number of the motel where the Pennsylvania hikers were staying.

I called the place right away.

The hikers were available, talkative, and gave me their cell numbers. College students, two coeds on a first visit to Colorado. They'd read that the Cliffs area was one of only a handful of ranges in the United States set aside for wild horses. They'd gone backpacking there, hoping to see real live mustangs. All they'd found was the dead one. They'd ridden at rental stables a few times back in Pennsylvania, said they loved horses. "It was like, so awful, all the blood," the first girl, Kiera told me, sobbing, "like, so sad." She sniffled, sobbed some more. There was a pause until the other coed came on the line. "It was, like, brown," Heather said. "But the wild ones are all different colors, aren't they? I mean, like, some of the photos we saw show gray ones or black and white ones."

"Right," I said. This wasn't the time to explain that some grays were called blue roans, black and white were piebald pintos. Location was the concern, not color.

But neither Heather nor her friend Kiera could provide specifics about where they'd found the body. "It was steep," Heather said, "real rocky. There were, like, these drop-offs."

That described more than one place. I asked how many hours they hiked, named a few of the trails to jog her memory.

"I dunno," she said. "We didn't have, like, a map, just headed out there. We couldn't wait to see wild horses. Neither of us felt so good after like, a few hours. Guess it was like, the altitude. We thought we were in shape." She paused, laughed a little. "We camped out, and we were, like, freezing all night. It's such a big place, like wilder than we expected. All we could think about the second day was getting back to civilization. We kinda' like, freaked out, when we saw that poor horse."

"You said it was shot. Did you hear anything that sounded like a rifle at any time you were in the area?"

"Huh-uh, the State Trooper guy asked that too. He asked if we saw any other people. We didn't see a soul."

"How was the weather?"

"Hot, mostly, a little afternoon thunder, like, a ways off. No rain."

A rifle was loud, might've sounded like distant thunder.

"You had a good look at the horse?"

"I knew, like, right away that it'd been shot," Heather said. "My Dad's a hunter. I've seen, like, carcasses. Deer and stuff." She sucked in a big breath and finished off with a loud sigh.

"Go on," I said. "Any details might help."

"Uh, right. Well, Kiera backed off, screaming. I felt like screaming too. But I made myself walk closer. There was, like, a lot of blood."

"Fresh or old?"

"Like, dark red."

Meaning the horse might've been dead for a while. There was no delicate way to ask the next question. "Any, uh, big black birds?"

"Not right there. Some big ones were, like, flying in circles way high, though."

Vultures.

"Did the body smell bad?"

"I, uh, some, I guess. I was, like holding my nose, about to hurl. Shouldn't have looked," she said, her voice wavering. "It's bad enough with, like deer, but who'd shoot a horse?"

Who indeed.

They were headed back to Pennsylvania soon. I thanked them for speaking with me and hung up without learning much except that these coeds said 'like' all the time and that I'd have to check out every one of the steep trails for a body which had been there over a day now. Might take more than one trip. I hated to admit it, but in this instance Joe Gannon was correct. The hikers provided little useful information. Like, almost none. They'd started at the Coyote Canyon Trailhead, though, so it was safe to assume they hadn't hiked many miles from there. I took out my topo map again, circled an area that spread out from their starting point. With any luck, Roy and I could cover all those trails tomorrow.

Someone had gone out there, shot a mustang, left it to rot.

# CHAPTER NINE

I WAS ABOUT to call and reschedule tomorrow's riding lessons just as a car approached in a fog of dust, squealing to a stop in front of the house. Jessica jumped out, followed by Louie the dog, Evelyn, and one of the bodyguards.

"Look, look at this!" Jessica said, running towards me. In her hands was a box, a small one.

I hurried down the porch steps. "What's that?"

She caught her lower lip between her teeth. "I haven't opened it yet." She held it out. "See this?"

Scrawled on the outside of the box was a simple message. Simple but disturbing. "Mustang Mayhem." The box was cardboard, small but heavy. I shook it just a bit, and there was a slight rattle, like metal on metal. I slipped my pocketknife out.

"You shouldn't open that," the bodyguard type said. "Could explode or something."

"There's no ticking," I said, slicing through the tape.

The bodyguard took one step back and then another. I almost laughed. Looking tough doesn't always mean much. I peeled tape, ripped paper and even though I was fairly sure I knew what the box contained, I held my breath for the final reveal.

By themselves, the contents couldn't cause any harm. When loaded into a rifle by someone with ill intent, however, the box full of bullets would be deadly. Ammunition, enough to wipe out most of the mustangs at Soda Creek Cliffs.

I blinked, nodded.

Evelyn moved away and pulled out a cell phone.

Jessica crowded closer. "Oh my God. Do you really think…"

I shrugged. "I don't know what to think, not yet, but I do plan to ride out to Soda Creek Cliffs tomorrow, find out what's going on, do everything I can to protect those horses."

"Tomorrow? Perfect!" Jessica said. "That's the day we're shooting the video out there."

"Video? What video?"

"I… oh, it's been so crazy I forgot to tell you. It's a music video to promote "Running Wild, Running Free." Frank's good friend has a professional film crew, and they agreed to come to Soda Creek Cliffs, but they're only available tomorrow."

"You've got to be kidding."

"Isn't that cool? You can provide horses, right? It'll be Evelyn, Bianca and me. We'll cover expenses, of course. I am sorry it's such short notice."

Evelyn had finished her call, moved back toward us. "Great news!" she said, smiling. "Some guy from the Denver Post is in here in Pinedale Springs, and I told him about all these nasty threats. He's on his way over to do a story on us, Jessica."

"Publicity is a necessary evil, in my opinion," I said, "but it's all you ever seem to think about."

"That's not true," Jessica said. "Evelyn is in charge of our publicity, and she works hard to come up great ideas. And as for 'Running Wild, Running Free,' I wrote the song to help the horses, to make people care about them."

"You wrote the song mainly to make money," I said.

"You're wrong," Jessica said. "Wrong."

"All she's been talking about is coming here, saving those scruffy mustangs," Evelyn said. "It was her idea to come to this hick town in the first place, debut the song here. I wanted to do it in a bigger town, but

I have to admit that there are good possibilities for stories here since the mustang range is nearby. I told the reporter about the threats to you and your horses," Evelyn said. "He'll interview you too."

"Think of all the people you can reach through this reporter," Jessica said.

I just stared at her, shook my head.

"So please take us tomorrow, if not for me, then for the horses."

"I let you talk me into putting my animals on stage. Look how that turned out."

"This is different. Just a nice ride, that's all."

"With a film crew tagging along and possible danger lurking around every hill? Let me guess. You want some dramatic shots of wild horses running into the sunset, you and your backup singers riding in the foreground looking glamorous."

"The film crew will only be at the trailhead, that's all. Bianca is a good photographer and she'll video parts of the actual ride. The final thing will be edited later, blended into a soundtrack. So how about it?"

"For one thing," I said, "I'm serious when I say it could be dangerous out there. Someone already shot one mustang. This box of bullets is no joke."

"I know," Jessica said. "But you were planning to ride out there alone."

"Yeah," Evelyn said. "It'll be safer with a group."

"Depends on the group," I said, "and Roy is riding with me. Can you and Bianca even ride?"

Evelyn smiled. "I competed in Hunter-Jumper classes all during high school and part of college."

She looked so proud of herself that I didn't bother pointing out that riding in an arena was a whole different deal.

"Bianca grew up on a Texas ranch," Jessica said. "She's great with horses. So how about it?"

I shook my head. "You won't stop until you get your way."

"Can't help it. This is extremely important."

"Important enough to die for? This box of bullets you just received should scare you."

"If this new song fails, my career is over, my dream dies, and that's scarier than the bullets. And the band, the stagehands, everyone else loses too. We're on the brink of financial disaster, Margo. This is a matter of survival me, for our entire group."

"We'll make it, Jessica," Evelyn said, sneering at me. "If Margo won't help us, I'll find other horses and we'll ride there by ourselves. One way or another, we are filming tomorrow."

"Soda Creek Cliffs is rugged, to begin with," I said. "You can't go alone."

"Then take us with you," Jessica said. "Please. Do this for our friendship."

"I'm beginning to question this friendship."

Jessica bit her lip. "Oh Margo, none of this has worked out the way I envisioned it. I did want to reconnect with you, really." She paused, sniffled, began to cry. "We'll just cancel tomorrow."

"No way," Evelyn shouted. "This video will make lots of money, put the band back on its feet. We've got to do this. We'll help, Margo, do whatever you say. I can handle a gun, and the bodyguards can come along too."

I sighed. One way or another, Jessica always got her way, and Evelyn seemed even worse. "Call Bianca, have her come out here. We'll take a little trail ride, see how all of you handle a horse. As for the bodyguards, no way they're going."

"Whatever you say," Jessica said, wiping her eyes. "You don't know how much this means to me."

"I didn't say I'd take you yet," I said. "Meantime, let's get back to this box of bullets. Where'd you find it?"

"That's what's so weird," Jessica said. "Someone called on my cell when I was at the hospital with Evelyn, asked for you."

I frowned. "Me?"

"Yeah. Said there'd be a package on my car, that I should bring it to you."

"Did you recognize the caller?"

"No. Voice was muffled, hard to understand."

"Male or female?" I asked.

"Male, I think."

"But not your stalker."

"Not unless he was talking through a, I don't know… through a funnel or something."

"Did this person say anything else?"

"Told me to be careful, and then whispered something I could barely hear. Sounded like 'I love you,' but no way to tell."

"You're sure this wasn't your stalker?"

"He's never disguised his voice before."

"Okay, I'm calling Sheriff Plackmon, let him know."

The sheriff asked questions, told me to be careful and strongly advised against riding out to Soda Creek Cliffs.

I said Roy and I had to check on the mustangs and look for Luke, and that Jessica insisted on tagging along.

If the bullets were intended for the mustangs, it was unclear why they were given to Jessica rather than directly to me. Why involve her unless that caller was her stalker. But if that was the case, what did he have against horses? Maybe he was just being dramatic, or maybe he was a total loony. This didn't seem to be Millie Dickson's style, either. Her main beef centered on my plan for a refuge. She and her family were more than capable of harassing me, capable of doing a lot of nasty stuff, but they were ranchers, had horses of their own. Shooting one mustang out at the Cliffs, much less threatening to shoot them all seemed out of character, even for that family.

The only thing we knew for sure about Jessica's stalker was gender. A guy made the phone calls, and he knew her schedule. Michael Turner was surely a fake name. It'd be hard to figure out who he was, harder still to nab him before things escalated even more.

Roy and I had both done some checking on the internet, found that celebrities plagued by stalkers often contracted with an agency belonging to the Association of Threat Assessment Professionals, or ATAP. Jessica had said that Frank spoke to several agencies, but the cost was prohibitive. Some police departments have Threat Management Units, but only in large cities. A small Colorado ranching community like Pinedale Springs lacked the money and manpower for specialized units of any type. Sheriff Plackmon and his deputies handled whatever happened around here, from traffic stops to murders.

Which left me to protect Jessica and find out who her stalker was before things escalated to the point of no return.

# CHAPTER TEN

MY MIND WAS swirling with possibilities and, worse, with doubts.

Jessica sat beside me on the front porch. Evelyn drove into town to pick up Bianca.

"It'll all work out, Margo. No worries."

"But I am worried, I'm worried sick that I won't be able to find your stalker and stop him."

"Oh no, no. I shouldn't have asked you to help with that, Margo. I mean sooner or later, it'll all work out. Frank and the bodyguards will take care of things. You've got a lot of other things on your mind. I feel awful about the way things are going. This was supposed to be so much fun, getting together again."

I sighed. "We're not kids anymore, and life gets messy."

"That's for sure."

"I just don't want anything bad to happen. There's too much out of our control, especially for the ride tomorrow."

"We've already discussed that," she said.

"You don't understand how serious the danger is."

She looked away, then back at me. "And you don't understand how much I need one last success."

"There's no point in arguing."

"Right. So… are we still friends?"

I shrugged. "I thought so, but I don't know. Are we?"

"It's me, damn it, me! And I need you. We've just renewed our friendship, Margo. Let's not lose what we had."

"You always want something."

"Friends help each other. What's wrong about that?"

"Nothing, to a point."

"You're not the easiest person to talk to," she said.

I've been told that before. I tend to be blunt. Still, when Jessica first arrived, I thought she and I were reconnecting. Now I wasn't so sure. We'd both changed, maybe grown apart.

Communicating with horses was so much easier, challenging, sure, but less complicated. Non-verbal cues tended to the basic, the raw truth.

Jessica was watching me, eyebrows raised. "How does Roy cope?"

"He travels a lot."

"You're happy together?"

I nodded. "Very. And we give each other space. Makes the time we spend together more special."

"So you've been married just six months."

I grinned.

"That's great! I guess I did see a ring on Roy's left hand."

"Mine too," I said, holding up my hand. "He's a catch, for sure."

She laughed. "You two look so happy. But no diamond?"

I shook my head. "Not my style. So how about you and Eric? Are you really thinking of leaving Frank for him?"

"I don't know. Once I snag a guy, the fun's gone."

I shook my head and laughed too. "You're still a hustler."

She laughed again. "The word is slut, although no money exchanges hands." She paused, looked away. "I used to dream about settling down, having babies. You ever want kids?"

My eyebrows rose. "Me? I can't see myself being a mother. I like kids, though, especially once they're old enough to ride. Speaking of which, let's get going."

"I haven't been near a horse for a while, you know. I'm rusty. And there's something else," she said, swallowing hard. "Last time I rode… the horse ran away and I fell off."

"Everyone who rides much has fallen off, including me," I said, "You know that."

"It was different when I was a kid."

I led the way to the barn. "You'll do fine." I was glad she'd admitted the fear but wondered how it might affect her on tomorrow's long ride. A riding instructor's first goal is to instill confidence. Success begins in the mind. Then again, if she rode badly, I could use that as yet another reason to talk her out of going.

"I'm looking forward to seeing those mustangs," she said. "Do you go out there much?"

"Not as often as I should. Once I iron out the logistics, though, I hope to offer more rides into that area. Good way to let people see the horses, publicize their plight."

"What's your overall plan?"

"The ideal would be more areas set-aside for mustangs to run free, but pressures on the places already in use result in too many gathers, too many mustangs languishing in huge holding pens that are nothing but permanent prisons. So the next best thing is a system of sustainable refuges and better methods of training them so more can be placed in good homes. There are some prisons that allow inmates to train mustangs, and maybe that could be expanded."

"There are other private refuges, right?"

I nodded. "But not enough, because sustainability is the issue. Too many horse recues operate on razor-thin financial margins, and the ones who take in mustangs are even harder to fund. It has to be economically feasible to run those places, to begin with. The other issue is birth control to keep numbers in check."

"Your eyes sparkle when you talk about mustangs."

"Seeing wild horses running free makes me feel more alive."

"You're lucky, Margo."

"Yeah. In many ways, I'm extremely lucky. Anyone who admires horses is lucky. I make a living training horses and giving riding lessons.

Roy loves horses as much as I do. I get the feeling that Frank doesn't like horses very much."

"He tried riding once, back when we were dating. Didn't enjoy it, said horses have no place in modern life."

"I'm not surprised."

Jessica frowned. "Why?"

"To begin with, I can't imagine him with dirty hands, much less with horsehair soiling his tailored clothes, mud on his Italian loafers. Some people who dislike horses have a bad experience, fall off or something. Some are simply frightened by how big horses are."

"Everyone around here rides, right?"

I nodded. "A lot of people do. You remember that from when we were kids. But even around a ranching community, there are a few who don't even want to stand close to a horse." And as I said that, I was thinking of Beth Hanson. Although she wasn't exactly afraid of horses, Beth had never ridden. Her young daughter, Nicole, had somehow been bitten by the horse bug.

"So what happened to make Frank dislike horses?"

"Nothing specific. He didn't fall or anything, just couldn't wait to get off both times he rode with me." Jessica paused, swallowing hard. "We get along fine, I suppose, but it seems best not to analyze our relationship too much."

"Opposites attract," I said.

She shrugged. "I used to think my soul mate was out there, but that's just a dream."

My cell rang just as we entered the barn. It was Evelyn. She and Bianca would be out in an hour.

"This means you get a private lesson," I told Jessica. We went to the tack room for a halter and lead rope. "C'mon, they're all out on pasture."

"I remember how to ride. I don't need a lesson, Margo." She paused. "Well, if I'm being honest, I am a bit nervous. Like I said, last time I rode, I fell off."

"Did you get hurt?"

She winced. "Only my pride."

She wasn't the first person who'd loved riding until something scary happened. Horses inspire longings and daydreams, but in spite of their gentle and willing nature, they're large, powerful. Up close, a horse can easily melt a person's bravado.

Jessica raised a hand to shield her eyes from the afternoon sun as we neared the pasture gate. "Wow, your horses are gorgeous."

Some of the animals ignored us and kept grazing, but half a dozen came running.

"They're expecting hand-outs," I said.

"Oh," she said, looking uncertain. "I see three of those you brought to the concert. The black one is spectacular."

"That's Phantom," I reached over the gate to pat the mare's neck and gave her some apple. "She's amazing, and one of my favorites." I pointed out which ones were Quarter horses, told her a little about the mustangs in this enclosure. Sassy and Bucky lived up to their names, while Wind Song and Jet were less excitable, more willing to accept humans.

I unlatched the gate, we eased inside, and I waved away all the animals except Hawk. A brown and white pinto, chunky, he teetered in height between pony and horse, head on the large size. Not the best-looking animal on my place, until you got to his eyes; big brown ovals, soft and wise. In temperament, he was pure gold.

Jessica stayed behind me. "Meet your new friend." I said.

She peered at him, took a deep breath. "It was a pinto that, uh, I fell off of."

"But not this one." I patted her shoulder, handed her some apple chunks. "Go ahead, give him a treat."

Hawk stood still, sensing this new human's hesitancy, but he stretched out his neck. He was an expert beggar. Seeing him always reminded me of Dawn, who'd ridden him last year and was one of the many who'd grown to love him.

Jessica's laughter brought me back to the present.

"Oh, aren't you cute," she said, holding out a piece of apple. Hawk closed soft lips around the prize. He munched, then reached for more.

By the time the entire apple had disappeared down Hawk's throat, some of Jessica's nervousness had also disappeared. She slipped the halter on, led the little pinto up to the barn, and I coached her through brushing and saddling him because that gave her more time to get to know Hawk, to relax around the little guy. We talked while leading him to the arena, reviewing some basics, especially the proper way to halt.

Hawk was such a seasoned lesson horse that my presence was almost unnecessary. He knew what to do, standing like a statue until asked to move, then traveling only at the pace requested.

"I love him, I just love him," she said after riding a few circles around the arena. "He's a treasure."

As always, Hawk seemed to understand the praise. Either that, or he knew that looking cute earned him more hand-outs. If only I could clone him.

"You're doing fine, at a walk. Try trotting."

She and Hawk trotted around the arena a few times without incident.

"Great," I said. "So let's pick up the pace."

"You said we'd just be walking the horses tomorrow," she said. "Why do I have to ride faster today?"

"What if they spook, start running?"

"Hawk wouldn't. He's too sweet."

I gave her a look. Confidence was one thing, reality another. "Any horse's natural impulse is to escape from fear."

She swallowed hard. "Yes, of course, that's logical."

"Hawk carries lots of green riders and he's never run away with anyone," I said, "but preparation is the key to prevent misshaps, maintain control. Let's see what happens. Besides, you're not a green rider. You just need a confidence boost." I reviewed the proper cues for cantering; outside foot and leg back a couple inches, press that leg against horse, reins in contact but not too tight. Hawk understood better than his rider and struck out in a large circle, smooth and steady. But Jessica gripped the saddle horn as though strangling it, falling forward and then flopping side to side like a sack of oats.

"Sit back, Jess, sit tall," I said.

"I'm trying. He's running away!" And then she screamed.

Oh brother. "Whoa, Hawk, trot now, easy," I chanted.

The little guy slowed to a trot, halted.

"You're not ready for tomorrow."

She brushed the hair out of her face and sat up straighter in the saddle. For a minute, she said nothing. "I can't believe I'm such a wimp."

"No worries, just chill."

She took a deep breath. "I'll be okay if he doesn't run away."

"What if he does?"

"I won't let him."

I folded my arms and wiggled my shoulders back. "A horse is a powerful creature, even one as sweet as Hawk. You know how to ride, Jessica. You just forgot how to relax."

"I know, and I can do this. I have to."

"You've got to at least canter without freaking out, know how to stop him."

"I will, I need to. I used to ride with you all the time. And I am going tomorrow," she said, staring at me.

I stared back. At the moment, she reminded me of Melody, the twelve-year-old whose Wednesday riding lessons gave me headaches. Melody had a horse she couldn't handle and a mother with fistfuls of money and expectations of blue ribbons for her spoiled child.

"You need to be comfortable with the basics or I won't take you." It was the same thing I said to Melody before horse shows. Her mother didn't care much for me, kept beseeching me to be easier on her princess. They kept coming, though, and in time, Melody might turn into a decent equestrian with skills to match her expensive horse. Blue ribbons were another matter.

"Are you rude to all your students?" Jessica asked.

"If I need to be," I said, smiling.

She blinked, then smiled too. "I'll show you."

It was exactly what I wanted her to say.

The next attempt wasn't much better, even though Hawk remained smooth. Jessica lost both stirrups and listed so far to one side that she almost fell off. Always the gentleman, the pinto sensed her distress and slowed before I asked him to. I could've kissed him. Matter of fact, I'd done so, many times, right on his cute over-sized nose.

She didn't scream this time. On the next try, she managed one full circle in canter. Her grin was wide. "So?"

"Umm, better," I said.

"Oh c'mon, Margo, admit it. That was great. And now I'm ready for tomorrow, for anything." She stroked Hawk's neck.

I had my doubts. I proceeded to explain how to slow a runaway horse, which usually involved circling. Novices or scared riders tended to lean forward, which shifted the center of gravity and made it easier for the animal to gallop onward. It was a talk I gave to anyone who rode trails with me, novice and experienced riders alike. Review never hurt, and stopping under controlled circumstances in an arena differed from dealing with an out-of-control horse in wide open spaces. "You know all of this," I said, "but it's hidden beneath the memory of that one fall."

"Let's not talk about that right now."

"You're holding onto it. Which is why you had trouble cantering."

"So what do you suggest?"

"Put your fear into a box," I said.

"Huh?"

"You can only concentrate on one thing at a time, and that one thing shouldn't be fear, so lock up bad memories in a box, put them aside. Think about relaxing, enjoying."

"Interesting concept," she said.

"Sounds simplistic, but it works."

"I'll try, I really will. It's so peaceful here." She looked around, sighed. "I forgot how the breeze whispers through those tall ponderosas, how beautiful clouds are against this impossibly blue sky."

I nodded, but I doubted that the day ahead held only whispering breezes and beautiful clouds.

After Jessica transitioned Hawn from trot to canter several more times, we put Hawk out in pasture, went to the house for lemonade and were settling on the back porch when a car arrived.

"Joe Clark, Denver Post," the driver said. "And this is my photographer, Bill. Evelyn Brooks said this was a good time to interview you."

Nothing like just dropping in. Still, I had to remind myself that the more publicity the mustangs got, the better. Jessica excused herself, hurried into the house for makeup and a change of clothes. She reappeared looking glamorous about the time that Evelyn and Bianca arrived. The photographer filmed the singers and almost every horse on the place, even aimed his camera at Henrietta, who clucked in alarm and scurried inside the barn as fast as her chicken legs would go. If Socrates was around, my raccoon would've hidden so he couldn't be found. No self-respecting raccoon wants to be photographed, especially not by strangers.

When Jessica finished gushing about herself and how much she loved mustangs, I told the guy about the mustang that'd been shot and about wild horses endangered status. He asked a lot of good questions and said that the article would appear not only in the Post but also in other syndicated news markets.

"That was more interesting than I expected." I said after the newsmen left. "Now we need to go saddle some horses."

Bianca clapped her hands. "Great. I miss riding. I'd love to ride one of your mustangs."

"I won't have to ride one of your scruffy things, will I?" Evelyn asked.

Ever the charmer. "No," I said, scowling at her. I had no intention of letting her on one of my mustangs anyway. I put Jessica back on Hawk and selected Flash, a good-looking and unflappable bay Quarter horse for Evelyn. I put Bianca on Wind Song, a seasoned grey mustang and saddled Phantom for myself. After a few turns around the arena, we headed into the forest. Evelyn rode reasonably and Bianca looked at home on a horse. Even Jessica seemed relaxed. I still wasn't all that enthused about taking them tomorrow, but if they went out on their own as they'd threatened to do, I'd end up looking out for them anyway.

I had a feeling that Luke Barnes had played hooky from his BLM job to ride out there, maybe pitched a tent, stayed to watch the mustangs. I needed to find him, see what he knew about the one that was shot.

Conditions at Soda Creek Cliffs were different from the forest we were riding in. Rocky trails, steep ledges and little shade, to begin with. Unforgiving terrain, unpredictable dangers beginning with the dead mustang. I doubted Jessica's stalker would show up out there, but no telling. More likely that Millie or one of her group might cause a disruption of some sort, but despite the threats she'd already sent my way, I doubted that she or her followers would go so far as killing horses or people. Their target was removing mustangs, their goal was financial gain.

While Roy and I were doing evening chores, I mentioned that Jessica and her two friends were joining us on tomorrow's ride, made it sound casual.

"Can any of them ride?"

"I checked them out. They're not bad, and they insisted on going."

"Swell. Do you still want me along?"

"Only if you'll protect me from anything and everything, Cowboy."

"In sickness and in health, in danger and in foolish fun, my Sweet!"

"Oh, golly gosh! Why, I might just faint right here on this hay."

He smiled mischievously, scooped me up, laid me down on the hay, and then... well, this wasn't the first time we'd enjoyed a roll in the hay. I hoped this newlywed bliss would never end.

Afterwards, we sat together, hugging. "So back to business," he said after a bit.

"Right," I said. "but didn't we just..."

"Yup, sure did, but the other business, the dangerous stuff."

I sighed. "I don't know much yet, but we need to get out there, find the dead horse, for starters."

"Who knows what's going on."

"Right. Tried to talk Jessica out of going."

Roy shook his head. "She always gets her way, but this might be a lot harder than she thinks."

"For sure."

Frank was in Oklahoma preparing for their next gig, but he called Jessica, then spoke to me about sending the two pretend-bodyguards along, assured us they'd be armed. He wanted them to follow us on four-wheelers. Impossible, I told him. Some of the trails were too narrow, for one thing. The damn things would be way too noisy for another, spooking my animals, drowning out any chance of seeing wild horses. Motorized vehicles are prohibited on most of the trails anyhow.

I handed the phone to Roy, and he finally convinced Frank that the bodyguards wouldn't be able to keep up, for one thing, and more importantly, that they weren't needed. Frank wasn't the type to give in easily. He was too sophisticated, too controlled to raise his voice, but the steel in his tone was unmistakable.

After the call ended, we agreed that we not only disliked Frank, but we didn't trust him, either, although we couldn't say quite why.

"I need to check him out," Roy said.

I agreed, said I would check others as soon as possible, too, beginning with any of Jessica's crew who chewed tobacco.

Roy planned to secure his rifle to his saddle for tomorrow's ride, and at Roy's insistence, I agreed to pack his long-arm Colt 45 in my saddle bag.

We went to bed hoping neither of us would have occasion to pull a trigger.

This was the west, but it was no longer the wild west.

# CHAPTER ELEVEN

Gravel scrunched beneath the horses' feet. I closed my eyes for a second, relishing the rhythmic sway of Phantom's walk and the soft sound of hoof beats. Riding was like breathing to me. Under the equine spell, the world seemed enchanting and the view from between Phantom's ears transformed everything for the better. Even though today's ride had the goal of searching for the mustang who'd been shot, being in the saddle still felt relaxing.

The best outcome would be finding Luke Barnes, hearing how he'd spent the last few days watching over the remaining mustangs. Soda Creek Cliffs smelled like nature itself, from the scent of pine trees to the brisk breeze. Faint aromas of well-oiled leather and horse sweat added to the mix. No roads, no fumes, no buildings, just trees and sky and the sun rising to the east.

This Coyote Bluff Trail at Soda Creek Cliffs began on flat rocky ground, curving around sagebrush and tall junipers on its way into Rockwall Canyon. Tiny pink spring beauty flowers danced beneath mountain mahogany shrubs with their own emerging leaves. The promise of growth, of the coming summer, was everywhere.

Roy rode beside me this day, always a treat. His bay Quarter horse, Mutt, was not only a much better-looking animal than the name implied, this gelding was an accomplished cutting horse, muscled and agile. Although rodeo in general was not my favorite sport, cutting competitions were primo demonstrations of horse and rider teamwork and mutual intelligence.

I loved riding Phantom. This black mustang and I connected in a special way from the moment I adopted her as a wild filly several years ago. It's impossible to say why some people clicked, became friends. It's the same with a horse and rider who became allies rather than just two creatures traveling the same direction, merely tolerating each other.

I closed my eyes, inhaled a lungful of happy. But then I heard the others chatting, so I looked back to check on them.

The three women rode close behind. First came Jessica on Hawk, and the little pinto could be counted on to always mind his manners. Next came Evelyn on my bay Quarter horse gelding Flash; lastly Bianca and her small video camera on Wind Song, my dark grey mustang.

Jessica looked elegant in jeans and a red plaid shirt, mahogany hair cascading around a face full of make-up. The backup singers also wore jeans, but their shirts were brown. The make-up people had plastered their faces with goop too. They even approached me with their jars and brushes, but I shook my head at that nonsense. They informed me that faces looked pale under photographer's lights, but all I cared about was the fact that, if we were lucky, this film might help save the mustangs. Roy was even less enthused about cameras and made it a point to stay out of any filming, although he tolerated it when Bianca pointed her simpler video camera his way. All three women wore new-looking cowboy hats which contrasted with the much-used Stetson Roy and the wide-brimmed straw hat I wore.

Frank designated Evelyn as manager of the professional crew who filmed only at the trailhead before we rode off. That spot included a vista of tall peaks in the background, so after the scenic aspect was ensured, the crew captured the horses and riders, and then pulled in even more for closeups of the singers' faces.

After the film crew left, Roy and I took charge of keeping the riders safe while looking for Luke and also the dead horse and, if luck and the wind were blowing right, checking on one or two of the wild mustang bands. I lead the way while Roy brought the up rear, leaving the women sandwiched in the middle. The sun remained soft and low to the east as we headed down the main trailhead of Western Colorado's showcase wild horse range.

Jessica and her backup singers looked happy and carefree, and I hoped they hadn't forgotten everything I'd said about the potential for danger. There were many places where a bad dude could hide out here. And not even Roy or I could see through cliff walls or around twisting trails.

Bianca trotted Wind Song around the others and up beside Phantom.

"Wow, this place is incredible," she said, grinning.

An expanse of orange and reddish cliffs peppered with pinyon pines stretched to the far horizon above irregular canyons. In the distance, barely visible, the hoodoo spires rose in rocky layers like a castle fortress. Sagebrush and sparse grasses defined the edges of this first trail. Loose layers of shale rock were strewn about as if by a giant with attitude. Incredible, yes, an unpolished magnificence. Best of all, there were no drilling rigs in this part of the mustang's range, at least not yet. But Juan Gomez and his conglomerate of energy companies had already invaded areas north of here, and I had no doubt this was their next target. What I couldn't understand was why they considered the mustangs so detrimental. Many parts of the west played host to both drilling rigs and wild horses. True, their co-existence was always tenuous, but I'd never heard of mustangs interfering with drilling operations. The horses kept their distance from humans. Access to water was always an issue, and drilling operations always took precedence. The fact that mustangs were here first seemed unimportant.

"It's amazing that mustangs can live out here," Bianca said.

Indeed. The wild horses who survived in such inhospitable environments deserved respect. Sometimes they got it. "Mustangs, and horses in general, are built to survive on sparse grasses and land that isn't suited for ruminants like cattle," I said, "but you're from Texas, so you know all that."

"Sure, I guess. So when will we see them?"

"Hard to say," I answered. "May not see them at all."

"How many are there?"

"Used to be over a hundred," I replied, "but now their numbers keep declining."

"I love horses and Wind Song is great," she said, sounding breathless. "I'm so happy to be riding again." She paused, pushed unruly curls away from her face.

Some people feel uncomfortable with silence, maybe because they've grown accustomed to noisy cities. I hoped Bianca wouldn't babble the entire ride. Still, her enthusiasm made her impossible to dislike. The love of equines, the need for them, beats strongly in many peoples' hearts, sometimes beginning in childhood before a real horse was ever encountered. It's impossible to analyze exactly why this happens to some and not others.

Humans benefit greatly from forming connections with other animals, from horses to dogs, from cats to chickens.

Evelyn seemed content to let her friend do all the talking. It was surprising that she handled publicity with such enthusiasm. Whatever. Today, my concern was everyone's way with horses. I'd taken them for a short ride yesterday to assess their skill. Jessica's nervousness still concerned me a little, but the other two knew the basics. I checked out anyone before allowing them on any of my horses. Part of that was for the rider's sake, part for my own liability, but also for the horse's sake. A nice gallop is fine, when the horse is in shape, when circumstances call for speed, when the rider knows what they're doing. But anyone whose burning desire is to reenact their vision of a pony express ride by galloping a horse to death is not welcome to ride with me. Some people watch too many westerns.

Jessica improved during yesterday's lesson, and this morning she seemed more relaxed than expected. Hawk worked his magic, of course, reawakening her love of riding. She still looked a little stiff in the saddle, but when I smiled at her, she managed to grin back. If anything went array, having Roy along would help, and the ride also provided more opportunity for both of us to get to know the backup singers, assess them.

Bianca grew silent, so we rode on in blissful silence broken once by the distant roar of a jet, a jarring reminder of civilization. After the first few miles, the trail began curving upward, ever rockier and narrowing to the point that we had to travel single-file with me in front and Roy still bringing up the rear. Now and then, Bianca lifted her small video camera and aimed it here or there.

We rounded a bend and a startled jack rabbit raced across the trail ahead of us, propelled by comical outsized hind legs, long ears bouncing up and down.

"Oh, look at him go," Bianca said, laughing, videoing the rabbit's retreat.

I turned and Jessica waved at me. "I'm so glad we came. I adore Hawk!"

I nodded and smiled. Everyone who rode Hawk fell in love with him.

Pinyon pines and scattered juniper trees grew taller on north-facing slopes, but most vegetation was sparse in this high desert-like country. Desolate to some eyes, beautiful to others, a harsh and demanding place for all. Water, never plentiful, varied in quantity and quality according to time of year and amount of winter run-off from distant peaks. Now, in spring, the wild horses would remain closer to whichever creek held moisture. The women wanted the thrill of seeing horses in the wild. I wanted the opportunity of seeing them to count numbers, check if more had disappeared.

And of course there was the dead horse. Seeing it wasn't going to be pretty. I'd have to prepare the others. Last thing I wanted was for one of them to faint or scream. I'd have enough trouble keeping myself together. An hour passed, and then another, and we'd covered about six miles uphill and back down again.

"My butt hurts," Evelyn said. "And I'm thirsty."

"Me too," Jessica agreed.

"And here I thought you guys were tough," I said.

"Nah," Jessica said. "We're wimps and we admit it."

"Speak for yourselves," Evelyn said. "I'm tough."

"Yeah, right," Jessica teased. "You look like you're about to fall right off that saddle."

"There's a little spring up ahead," I said. "About a mile. We'll rest there."

Cougar Gulch Spring was one of the most reliable year-around water sources, the flow abundant now in spring. The gulch opened out at this point, affording the mustangs who frequented the place a good view and therefore relative safety from the spring's namesake predators. We dismounted, unbridled the horses and secured them at intervals on a tie-line. They weren't all that tired nor hot, but I still wanted them to rest a bit before I let them drink their fill from the spring.

"I'm just famished," Bianca said. "How about you, Evelyn?"

Evelyn blinked and shrugged. "I could eat."

I'd gotten reacquainted with Jessica by now, and it was obvious that Bianca was not only at home in the saddle but also a relaxed and friendly sort. Evelyn was harder to pin down.

Trail rides generated big appetites. Horses did most of the work, but human hunger exploded anyhow. Roy always brought extra food for everyone, seldom had much left over. We settled down on the ground and dug into sandwiches, polished off apples, drank our fill of water.

"This sandwich is delicious!" Bianca declared between bites. "What's in it?"

Roy grinned. "Banana, almond butter and honey."

"Wow, yummy," Jessica said. "Do you always make such good food?"

"I can answer that," I said, nodding. "Everyone needs a cooking cowboy."

"No kidding!" Bianca said. "Can I take him home?"

"No way!" I said. "I don't share my man."

Everyone laughed, even Evelyn.

A pair of red tailed hawks circled high overhead, wings outstretched, dipping to follow the thermals. Hunting for a lunch of their own, no doubt.

Jessica was looking up, watching the birds circling. "Beautiful," she said. "This place is amazing. I knew it was rugged, but it's been so long since I've ridden out here that I forgot how magical it is."

"It's fantastic," Bianca said. "And even if we don't see the mustangs, this ride has been great. And it's so good to be back on a horse!"

Jessica smiled and nodded at her enthusiastic backup singer. Even Evelyn smiled a bit.

"So about this dead horse," Jessica said.

"The trail ahead forks," I said, "Upper Deer Trail to the right, Lower Deer to the left. The Upper is where I think that horse may be. The coeds found it on a ledge trail with steep sections."

"Steep?" Jessica said, her eyes wide.

"Hawk will do fine," I said. "All the horses are surefooted. Besides, steep for a human is different than steep for a sure-footed horse."

"Right, but…" Jessica's teeth clamped down on her lower lip. "I don't care much for heights."

"Neither do I," I said. And I didn't. Drop-offs always made me nervous, but I forced myself to take deep breaths to avoid conveying anxiety to my horse. "It's high, but the horses don't mind."

Jessica frowned. "How high?"

"I dunno, exactly, but the trail is decent, although it could be muddy this time of year. Upper Deer isn't the steepest trail in the area, but it sounds closest to what little description the coeds provided. There is a ledge, a hefty drop off, but the trail is plenty wide enough for a horse."

"I bet the views will be just great," Bianca said, ever the optimist.

"Best get going," Roy said.

"I don't want… I mean, the thought of seeing that dead one," Bianca said, sounding as if she might cry.

I looked at her. "Did one of your favorite horses die?"

She nodded. "It was awful."

I nodded too. "There are some things you never forget."

"I second that," Roy said quietly.

"Good chance of seeing mustangs any time now," I told them, "So keep a look out."

"What if they're on the ledge trail?" Evelyn asked, gripping the saddle horn and sounding panicky, "what if they run right into us?"

"Never happen," I assured her. "They'd hear us coming, clear out way before we got close."

She frowned, but said nothing more. The look on her face made it clear that she didn't believe a word I'd said.

"It'll be all right, Evelyn," I said, smiling at her. "Trust me."

The corners of her mouth twitched as if she was trying to smile back, but she ended up grimacing instead.

Upper Deer Trail ascended slowly at first, looping through more pinyon pines and scraggly junipers, then sharp curves back and forth. I glanced around to assess my charges every few minutes, although if problems arose, I'd be sure to hear scrambling or worse, screaming.

Halfway to the ledge trail, Bianca yelled "Look! Down there, look!"

And there they were, a band of mustangs coming into the canyon far below. The stallion was a chestnut, reddish coat gleaming in the sun, his stance proud, watchful. His harem of mares and foals appeared healthy, bellies round, coats shiny.

Bianca's eyes grew wide, her chin dropped, and then she got busy with the video camera.

Evelyn squinted, muttered "They're ragged looking, scrawny. Not like real horses."

"But they're wonderful," Jessica whispered.

"I think they're sort of... ugly," Evelyn said.

"No way," Bianca said. "They're gorgeous."

And they were, no matter what Evelyn thought. But I was frowning. I'd seen this band before, knew the stallion. Counting the foals, there was now a total of seven animals. There'd been at least three additional mares the last time I'd seen this band. Maybe they'd been stolen away by another stallion, but this stud was in his prime, dominant. Maybe the mares had disappeared like many others.

Evelyn's gelding pawed the ground, and a rock tumbled over the edge of the trail, sending a cascade of dirt and pebbles down toward the canyon floor. "Oh!" Evelyn said, and then she jerked on the reins and shouted "No, stop!"

Below us, the mustang stallion's neck arched, he gave a snort, and all of them raced off in a cloud of dust.

Evelyn's gelding pawed once more and tossed his head.

"It's okay," I said. "Just loosen the reins."

"He's acting up," Evelyn said.

"Your reins are too tight, hurting his mouth." She was an experienced rider, but only in arenas. Very different from trail riding. She frowned at me and chewed her lower lip, but once she allowed more slack in the reins, the gelding's head lowered and he stood still.

"Will we see the mustangs again?" Jessica asked.

I looked at her and shrugged. Her eyes were teary.

"You okay?"

"I, uh…" she paused, sighed. "I'm fine. They're so elegant, so powerful."

"There's nothing like seeing mustangs running wild, running free," I said, "like the title of your song."

"This is what I wanted to convey, this magic. But now, seeing them… it's beyond words."

I nodded. All horses were special, but the wild ones ignited something deep within most people who saw them. The mustangs' connection with nature was both humbling and powerful. Knowing that Jessica was feeling much the same made me feel closer to her.

If the video from today's ride helped Jessica sell more songs, some proceeds might also help these very mustangs. Not such a bad deal. The rest of the way up was marked by the sound of horses panting. They were in decent shape, but still, Phantom was the only animal whose breathing wasn't labored. Exertion seemed second nature to the black mare. In the rugged land where she was born and ran free the first three years of her life, survival of the fittest meant more than a Darwinian slogan. At first, I'd felt a guilty about my instant attachment to the mare. She was only a mustang, after all. Maybe it was her dark good looks, her soft eyes or the way she whinnied and ran to me whenever I called, her black mane and tail feathering in the breeze. I loved each one of my horses, but Phantom combined heart and poetry.

I turned to Roy. "We need to pick up the pace, at least a faster walk," I said, loud enough for him to hear.

He nodded.

We hadn't trotted at all. I made much better time alone, but that was to be expected. Roy and I kept a watch out, and so far there was nothing to indicate fresh human footprints, nothing to raise the slightest suspicion.

All three women grew pale when they first saw the ledge trail snaking across the cliff, but to their credit, even Evelyn listened to my advice to take slow deep breaths, relax, hang onto the saddle horn if they wanted to. Sounded simple, but it gave people something to concentrate on besides fear. I reminded them to keep the reins loose enough so the horse could move their head and neck freely for balance.

We'd almost made it across the worst of the steep part when I glimpsed a dark mass to the side of the trail around a bend a ways ahead. Large black birds circled above, squawking. Vultures.

I looked down.

Something bright, out of place. On a rocky outcropping fifty feet below us, there was a swatch of red.

And a human hand.

# CHAPTER TWELVE

I LEANED OVER, peered down.

It was a hand all right, attached to a body sprawled face down on a narrow ledge. A man in a red jacket. Emblazoned across the back of it in big block letters was 'Rodeo Riders of the Rockies.'

I gasped.

Luke Barnes had a jacket like that. I turned, looked back at Roy.

He saw it too, mouthed the word, "Luke?"

"Hope not," I replied.

"What, Margo," Jessica said, "what's wrong?"

I opened my mouth, but nothing came out.

And then Bianca screamed.

I felt like screaming myself, but I was too numb.

"Oh my God, there's a… a body down there," Jessica said.

The women began chattering, all talking at once, firing questions at me. But I had no answers. Maybe it wasn't Luke, maybe it was someone else. There was no blood that I could see, but no movement either. I had to get down there. The trail was too narrow at this point for us to turn around, too precarious for the horses to just stand there for long.

I glanced back at the women. A wave of dizziness came over me, but I inhaled deeply to clear my head. The only thing I knew for sure was that I needed to see for myself who was on the ledge, what had happened. First, though, the women and the horses needed safer footing. Just before the bend where the vultures still circled, the trail widened. I untied the loop of rope I always keep on my saddle, took my feet out of the stirrups and slipped off Phantom on the uphill side. I patted her rump and clicked my tongue. "Go on, Girl, go on now," I said.

"What!" Jessica said, her voice squeaky with panic. "What're you doing?"

"It's okay," I said, watching Phantom walk away, Hawk and the other two horses close behind. This wasn't the first time I'd asked the little black mare to lead others by herself. I knew she'd understand I meant for her to wait for me where the trail widened. She was in charge of the other three horses now, and Roy brought up the rear.

"Follow Phantom," I told the women. "Stop and wait where the trail widens. Don't go any farther."

Jessica nodded, then frowned. "What about you?"

"I'm going down there, and Roy will help me."

I squeezed myself flat against the uphill side until the horses and riders passed by, asked Bianca to hand me the video.

Once the women and their horses were ahead and just out of hearing, I turned to Roy.

"There's a good chance that the dead horse is not far ahead, and I didn't want them seeing it yet."

He nodded. "Let me repel down."

"No, it's better if I do it. You can easily pull me back up," I said, securing the video camera to the back of my belt. "I'll repel down to the ledge."

Roy was actually the one who taught me to repel safely, but he was too heavy for me to effectively pull him back up. Made more sense for me to go.

This was one of the skills needed for traveling in the back country, so the first time I'd taken the plunge was over a decade ago under the casual eye of an instructor, a woman in form-fitting Lycra named Lee Ann who delivered a pep talk and then pushed me over the edge. I about peed in my pants on the way down, and I've been leery of women with an over-abundance of muscles ever since. Later on, though, the skill came in handy a time or two, and after Roy helped perfect my technique, it became less nerve-wracking except for times like this when I dreaded what I was about to see.

Bouncing down some sheer cliff with a death grip on a rope would never be my idea of fun. It did nothing to lessen my fear of heights, for one thing, and every rock I encountered was as hard as it looked, for another. Some people did it for fun, I did it only when there was no alternative.

Like now.

Roy kissed me before I grabbed the rope and held on tight. Another reason I always wear riding gloves. The rope we carry is sisal, strong and stiff. The initial drop-off was steep, the rocks slick, although it helped a lot to know that Roy was guiding my descent, giving just enough slack.

Looking down made me dizzy, so I concentrated on pushing the soles of my boots against the rocks, leaning my upper body back, easing myself down a few feet at a time. Almost anything was do-able, broken down into small steps. It was about fifty feet to the ledge.

And whoever was attached to that hand.

The ledge was maybe two feet wide, five or so feet long. The body took up most of that space, but I managed to plant my feet on what felt like secure rock. Before I saw his face, I knew.

This was Luke.

The lean body, the dark hair… it was him, all right. No signs of life. I slapped a hand over my mouth and groaned. Time raced in reverse as I remembered highlights from the years we'd known each other. Luke Barnes was an okay guy, a former lover, a character, a friend. Tears started to blur my vision. I blinked, willing myself to stop.

"Doing okay, Margo?" Roy's voice carried concern.

I looked up at him, nodded. "It's Luke, dead."

"Sorry," Roy said, nodding.

I felt sorry for Luke, but even worse was the all too fresh memory of losing Bow. Caught in a tangled and dangerous web of family secrets, she was found at the base of Rim Rock Cliffs last year, a place distant from here but now refreshed in my mind. The only parallels between Bow and

Luke were the fatal falls. That and the fact that both of them had been dear to me, Bow as my foster mother, Luke as a good friend.

"Need me to come down, Margo? I can anchor the rope up here."

I shook my head. "No. No room."

I knelt down, peered at his face, brushed my fingers against his cheek. Cold skin, pale, but no head wounds visible. I pressed two fingers into his neck, feeling for a carotid pulse, knowing there would be none. With an effort, I rolled his shoulder up as far as I could, felt around on his chest. There didn't seem to be any blood on his jacket, at least on the side near me. Nothing in his pockets. Couldn't tell about the rest of him. I picked up the hand that'd been hanging over the ledge. Scrapes crisscrossed the stiff palm. Maybe he'd reached out, frantic to try and break his fall. No telling how long he'd been dead. Only a forensic pathologist could estimate the time of his last breath. I unhooked the video camera, ran it a few minutes over the body, the ledge, the cliff leading up to the trail.

I slipped the video back on my belt and looked up again. This much of a plunge would've killed anyone. But Luke Barnes was an experienced outdoorsman. It seemed unlikely that he'd just tumble off a cliff. Besides, he didn't hike out here, he rode. Maybe he'd dismounted for some reason, peered over the edge of the trail, lost his footing. Which meant his horse was either still out here somewhere or had made its way home. He lived closer to the northern portion of Soda Creek Cliffs, up near Sagebrush Canyon. Sometimes he rode here from his ranch, other times he trailered into the Indian Springs Trailhead. If he'd driven, his truck and trailer would still be parked up north.

"You ready to come back up?" Roy's voice was soft.

"I... uh," I paused, staring at Luke. It didn't seem right to leave him here, but there was no other option. I felt obligated to do something, help him. He was beyond earthly assistance, though. I hoped he'd died quick, hadn't suffered in pain on this ledge, waiting for help. We'd have to call for a rescue team to remove his body. I looked around again, down toward the canyon floor, up to the trail and beyond that toward the portion of the cliff top visible from here. Nothing caught my eye except this body. If he'd seen something worth getting off his horse for a closer look, that something wasn't apparent now. The only possibility I could think of was that he'd seen something related to a dead horse.

"C'mon, Margo." Roy said. "Let's get you up. Grab the rope."

I grabbed it. Within minutes, Roy had me back beside him. The first thing he did was pull me close for a long hug. He understood, knew I was sad not only about Luke but also about Bow. About loss.

"I saw a glimpse of something around the next bend," Roy whispered. "Maybe an elk or a horse."

I nodded. "I'm glad you're here," I whispered back. I could be brave when I had to be, but it felt good to have Roy's help.

The women's horses stood like statues a few yards ahead. Phantom had proven herself every bit as reliable as expected, leading the others forward a ways, then stopping. The women remained in their saddles, all three turned around, watching. Jessica had one hand over her mouth, Evelyn chewed her fingernails, Bianca looked grim.

Roy pulled the satellite phone out of his saddle bag, called the sheriff.

It'd take a while for a helicopter to get here, not that there was much hurry. I recoiled the rope, squeezed past the women's horses, gave the video camera back to Bianca, and reached Phantom. I always kept a small bag of horse cookies in my cantle bag, and I retrieved several and fed them to the little mare. She deserved that and more.

The women remained silent, but I knew they were bursting with questions. They'd heard at least some of what Roy and I had said, knew the guy on the ledge was dead. "He was... a friend. Worked for the BLM, loved horses. A good guy," I finished, choking.

"Oh Margo," Jessica said, "I'm so sorry."

"Me too," Bianca agreed.

Evelyn blinked, said nothing.

"No idea yet what happened to him. They'll come as soon as possible with a special rescue stretcher and get, uh, his body," I said. "Meantime, I need to warn you. Roy got a glimpse of something around this next bend. Maybe the dead mustang."

Evelyn gasped and shut her eyes tight. The others just stared.

"Brace yourselves," I told them.

I was right about one thing. Just around the bend, there was a dead animal by the side of the trail. It was a horse, too, but it was no mustang. This animal was a large bay, sprawled on its side, saddle and bridle still in place.

This was a Quarter horse, a familiar one.

I'd raised this animal, named him Spirit, trained him and then sold him to Luke Barnes almost ten years ago. He was Luke's favorite mount, the one he used for trail riding, steer roping, rodeoing. Blood, dark and clotted, marked a large wound on the animal's side, right over the heart.

The horse was dead, no doubt about that. I sat on Phantom, knowing I should dismount, check things out, but I was frozen, unable to move or even think.

"Oh no, no," Jessica said.

Someone began sobbing, maybe it was me.

# CHAPTER THIRTEEN

I RUBBED MY eyes, found to my surprise that they were dry. Bianca was the one sobbing. Could've easily joined her. But no, I had to get a grip, figure out what the hell happened.

I slipped off Phantom, looped her reins on the saddle and crouched down over Spirit. Near the gelding's body, almost underneath him, was a rifle, possibly Luke's. Not far away was a shell casing. I'm no authority, but the horse's wound looked like it might've come from this rifle. Luke's horse, Luke's rifle. And the man himself, back there on that ledge.

I touched the tip of the gelding's ear, rubbed his neck as though providing comfort. I squeezed my eyes shut, feeling dizzy. This must be a movie, a horror flick. This was wrong, it couldn't be real. But I made myself open my eyes, looked up toward the circling vultures.

I stepped back, took a deep breath, and then Roy put his arms around me, pulled me close.

"What the hell!" I sobbed.

Right away, though, I could just imagine someone declaring that Luke had shot his own horse, then jumped off the cliff to his death. Suicidal, they'd say, just as they'd said at first about Bow. But I knew better. Luke Barnes would never kill himself or his horse. I wasn't sure who had jurisdiction out here. The Bureau of Land Management was a Federal Government agency, so maybe things here were out of local hands.

The women were watching me and Roy. I glanced at them, shook my head. Bianca dismounted and brought the video camera over, handed it to me without a word. I nodded, took it and began filming, starting with a heart-wrenching close up of the fatal wound, then everything in general. The dusty ground close to the horse's body held only a handful of clearly outlined boot prints, all large and similar as far as I could tell. I zeroed in on them just in case. When I finished, I loosened the blood splattered girth but left the saddle and bridle on, for now. I was torn between freeing Spirit from his tack and leaving things alone. Luke and his horse… this was a crime scene. There'd be an investigation, either by Sheriff Plackmon or someone else. The BLM would want to look things over too, in some capacity. So I left things the way they were, didn't touch anything except that girth. But I'd be back, and soon. Before I stood up, though, I took out my pocketknife, cut off a hunk of Spirit's mane and stuffed it into my shirt pocket. Luke would've wanted his gelding to be remembered.

This wasn't the same horse the Pennsylvania coeds had seen. They would've surely mentioned a saddle and bridle. Somewhere else here was a dead mustang that'd also been shot. I still needed to check for that animal, but Luke Barnes and Spirit took precedence now.

Jessica and the others looked horrified and exhausted. I wanted to send them back to the trailhead alone, wanted to stay here with Roy at least until someone came for Luke's body, wanted to stay here until my head cleared. But the women needed guidance, needed someone to ride with them in case of problems. I considered asking them to stay here, too, but the sun was heating up and there was little shade. They weren't used to rigors like this, they were capable of entertaining crowds all evening, exercising their lungs and their hips. They had stamina, but of a different kind. Besides, the rescue crew would come by helicopter, and even my calm horses wouldn't do well close to all that commotion.

I looked at Roy. "Can you take the women back?"

"I'm not leaving you out here alone, Margo. We can't do anything for Luke or for Spirit."

"I know."

"We can stay here as long as you need to," Bianca said.

"Thanks, but we need to have the horses in a safer place when the helicopter arrives, for one thing."

"Best that we all head back," Roy said.

I nodded.

Many of the trails at Soda Creek Cliffs formed large loops through canyons and over hills, making it possible to travel one way out, another way back. The six miles we'd ridden were less than half-way around one of the loops, so retracing our steps was the fastest way back. On a normal ride, two things were good about that. First, going back always seems faster, and second, traveling in the opposite direction provides a different perspective of the same scenery.

This was no longer a normal ride. For the first few miles, Roy rode beside me in silence, understanding I was waging war against tears and too many thoughts of too many people and a fabulous horse gone too soon. I was so preoccupied that I didn't hear Jessica bringing Hawk up beside Phantom. "Do you want to talk?"

I shrugged. There wasn't anything to say that could ease the pain.

"I didn't know Luke," she said, "but he must've been a great guy."

"Yes. We dated for a while, before Roy."

"I remember you telling me a little about him."

"Luke was, well, he got around," I said, smiling. "Not the marrying type, but a good friend."

"What about the horse?"

I shook my head. "Raised him," I said, choking.

"I thought so."

"How'd you know?"

"Just a hunch. The way you looked at him, stroked the neck."

I didn't fully remember doing that. When I realized who it was, I'd felt stunned, devoid of rational thought. I wanted to replace reality with something else, something less awful. "His name is... was... Spirit," I said. Finding the horse made Luke's death so much worse. I did remember cutting off a chunk of his mane, stuffing it in my pocket.

"Did you name him?"

I wiped my eyes, nodded. "I was there when he foaled. He was smart, easy to train."

"I bet you say that about all your foals."

"Huh-uh," I said. "Some of them are little spit fires. But Spirit progressed so well that I didn't want to sell him." I bit my lip, choking again. "Luke was good to him. They were a team."

"I can verify that," Roy said. "Luke was a good soul, loved Spirit."

If we didn't change the subject, I'd start blubbering.

"Speaking of teams," I said, "you and Hawk are doing okay."

"This little guy is doing all the work," she said. "I'm just hanging on."

"Give yourself credit. You've ridden well today."

She smiled. "Thanks to you."

"Margo is almost as patient with humans as she is with horses," Roy said, winking at me.

"Thanks, I think."

"Seriously, yes, I do owe you," Jessica said.

"So when can I collect?"

"Um, we'll see if I can stay in the saddle until Hawk gets me all the way back."

I smiled at her. Our friendship was worth salvaging. I guess it was kind of a good thing that Jessica had gotten me to talk a bit. We rode on in silence until a rhythmic thumping sound signaled the nearing helicopter. They'd have to land a ways from the steep trail, but the rescuers would be experts at challenging terrain. Admirable daredevils. Even though this would only be a retrieval, the risks they took were the same as if their target was alive.

My horses had seen and heard helicopters from a distance before, and since landing would occur well away from them, there should be no problem.

By the time we reached Cougar Spring, the worst sections of trail were behind us. I urged Phantom to approach the spring and drink her fill. She pawed the water with one front hoof, raising wet sprays that shone like crystals in the sun. The other horses came one by one.

"Anyone need to dismount, rest for a bit?" I asked.

"We're okay," Bianca said, and the others nodded.

Evelynn looked somber. "I'm... uh, sorry."

"We're all sorry," Jessica said, nodding.

I sighed. What good was sorrow, though. Soon there'd be a funeral, tears, grief. Luke had a lot of friends, all of them casual. He didn't socialize much, except for brief flings with women. Sometimes he'd drop a name in conversation. I recalled a Becky, a Susie, an Ava. And those were just the ones he'd happened to tell me about. No doubt there were others. Luke Barnes loved women, and they loved him back. I didn't know much about his family. He had a sister somewhere in Montana, a brother in Texas. Hadn't spoken much about either one, at least not to me. I knew nothing about his parents.

In the end, everyone faces death alone. Most of us avoid thinking about death, as though if we ignore it, it will forget to come for us some day, some way.

We'd no sooner left the water when something moved behind a scraggly pinyon pine. The only part visible at first was a tall oval ear, flicking back and forth. Soon the mule deer it belonged to stepped into full view, caught sight of us and froze. Two others, much smaller, peeked in front of the larger one. A doe with twin spotted fawns, soft brown eyes assessing us. The little ones weren't yet old enough to fear humans. They took several steps toward our horses, but whirled around and raced after the doe, who knew enough to be wary.

"Wow, awesome," Bianca said. "I used to see deer all the time in the woods near where I grew up. Hated hunting season."

"Speaking of that," Jessica said, "do you think some hunter shot Luke's horse by mistake?"

"Huh-uh," Roy said. "For one thing, it's not hunting season."

"That was a rifle on the ground though."

"Probably Luke's," I said.

"This is just so awful," Jessica said.

"Yeah." I could already imagine the nightmares.

Roy gave me a look that said he'd be there, for the nightmares, for whatever came. I smiled at him.

We were looping over Rock Creek Trail when Jessica spotted a band of mustangs. Only five in this group including the black and white pinto stallion. They were grazing halfway up the north side of a hill, tails sweeping back and forth against flies.

"Beautiful," Jessica said, "just look at them."

Bianca worked the video camera.

The wild horses saw us, of course. But we were far enough away that they didn't consider us a threat, although the stallion kept watch, neck arched and ears flickering. There was a foal who appeared to be a miniature version of his colorful father, right down to the two-toned tail, although the foal's stubby appendage had only wisps of hair instead of the flowing banner to come. The little one ducked under the mare to suckle, then raced in a circle on spindly legs.

When I'd last seen this stud and his harem, there'd been at least two other mares, both round with foals. Which pointed to possibly more unexplained disappearances. What was left of this band appeared as robust and healthy as the group we'd seen earlier. Other stallions claimed territory to the north and west in this vast range, but I feared that numbers were decreasing in all sections.

The value of wild horses varied according to who was talking. The places relegated to mustangs were rugged, inaccessible to most people. The majority who professed a love for mustangs were content to read about them, see them on TV or simply know they existed. Jessica and Eric had written their song far from actual horses, but it was still good.

Although the BLM offered regular adoptions of what they deemed excess horses, relatively few animals found new homes this way. Nor did adoption fees begin to cover the expenses of round-ups, now called gatherings. Thousands of unwanted horses languished in remote corrals, a crowded and miserable limbo. Official policy kept wild horses out of slaughterhouses. Many ended up there anyway. Those unfortunates who were slaughtered brought little profit, according to claims. At any rate, ever since the atrocities of previous years, a series of checks and balances safeguarded against wholesale slaughter. Supposedly, anyhow. Wild horses cost taxpayers far more than what was recouped. And when human greed factored in, mustangs suffered.

Still, horses don't disappear into thin air. There had to be a good reason for the dwindling herds at Soda Creek Cliffs besides those the BLM removed. Good reasons were often financial.

Money speaks, always and everywhere.

Luke would've done his best to find out what was happening. Random blood samples taken from mustangs in the spring hadn't implicated health problems. I hadn't spoken to Luke for a few weeks because I was so busy getting ready for Jessica's visit. Maybe he'd come up with something and gone out to check for himself.

Maybe someone followed to shut him up.

Permanently.

# CHAPTER FOURTEEN

When we got back to the trailhead, Roy and I untacked the horses, tied them to steel rings spaced around the long sides of my trailer. I grabbed a grooming tote. Jessica and the other two held out their hands for brushes and began rubbing sweat marks off their horses' backs. Jessica moved as stiffly as an eighty-year-old, which made Bianca tease and giggle. Evelyn joined in too.

Roy brushed Mutt and picked out the gelding's feet, then helped the others.

After the horses were cooled down and loaded in the trailer, we hung nets stuffed with a flake of grass hay by each animal. Usually, a ride like this was relaxing, fun. But now all I felt was trepidation, knowing that more trouble was ahead.

The women drank lemonade and munched energy bars before climbing into the truck and easing themselves gingerly onto upholstered seats. I pulled the satellite phone from Roy's saddle bag, scooted my backside on a trailer fender and dialed the sheriff's office, but they said he'd planned to go out with the helicopter crew, but had to deal with something in town and sent a deputy instead.

I needed answers. Next call went to the BLM. As the head honcho of the local field office, Joe Gannon wielded enough power to stretch or bend any rules he didn't agree with, maybe profit from under-the-table deals. Joe knew about Luke and his horse by now, of course, having been alerted by the helicopter crew. This time, he came on the line without delay.

"My God, what happened?" He sounded stunned.

"Wish I knew."

"I can't believe it, can't believe Luke is dead. And his horse. This is awful. Just awful." Either his concern was genuine or he was damn good at pretense.

"Did Luke say anything to you about going out to check on the herds?"

"No, not a word. He didn't say one thing about going out there. I knew he did that sometimes on his days off. Could've ridden out there Saturday or Sunday, who knows. You found him?"

"Right. We're still at Soda Creek Cliffs, at the Coyote Canyon Trailhead. So who has jurisdiction out here?" I held my breath, expecting him to get defensive, but he didn't.

"I do, for the most part," he replied in a calm but authoritative tone. "One of my men handles law enforcement. Local authorities get involved too, depending on circumstances."

Like deaths, for one, I was certain. Meaning Sheriff Plackmon would remain involved.

"I'll need an official statement from you, but for now please tell me what you saw."

"Luke was face down on a rocky ledge," I began, my recollection all too vivid. "About fifty feet below a steep section of Upper Deer Trail."

"You had a close look?"

"Yes, I repelled down."

"You did?"

"Uh-huh."

"Any blood, wounds?"

"Not that I could tell, just scratches on the palm of one hand. But there wasn't room enough to turn him over." I didn't mention the video camera. I might, later.

"Such a shame, such a damn shame."

"Yeah."

"He was a good person. Not ambitious, but okay. Moody type, but likeable." He paused, sighed. "The helicopter crew just arrived with his body. He's, uh, over at the morgue. I haven't been there yet."

"His horse…" I began, rubbing my free hand over the chest pocket which held the clump of Spirit's mane.

"That's the odd thing," Gannon said. "That his horse was shot too. And Luke's rifle was there on the ground."

I didn't say anything.

"That right, Miz Richards?"

"Yes."

"Hope you didn't touch that rifle."

"No."

"You knew Luke pretty well."

"We were friends."

"He's been moodier than usual around the office," he said. "You notice that?"

"Haven't spoken to him for a while."

"Think he'd shoot his own horse?"

"Never!"

"Any chance his horse was the one those Pennsylvania hikers saw?"

"Not a chance. Spirit… his gelding, was still saddled, bridled. Besides, the mustang was shot a few days earlier." I could've added that the mustang was either a mare or a stallion while Spirit was a chestnut gelding, but why bother.

"The rescuers took photos, of course, brought the rifle in. The coroner will determine the cause and time of death. The animal is another matter. That part of the range lies in Sheriff Plackmon's jurisdiction."

"What about Luke's family? Have they been notified?"

"Not yet," Gannon said. "I… do you know them?"

"I spoke on the phone to one of his sisters once or twice, a few years ago, first name is Donna. Lives in Montana on a sheep ranch. I didn't keep her number."

"I'll have my secretary obtain information. The sister might appreciate hearing from you, as long as you're not calling in an official capacity."

"Uh, maybe," I said, immediately regretting it. Talking to anyone about their dead brother sounded dreadful. Saying this to someone that I barely knew sounded even worse.

"All right, then, good." There was palpable relief in his voice. His job entailed few deaths, few conversations with grieving relatives. "Mary Lou will call you when she has the information. Please let me know when you've spoken to the family."

"Wait just a minute," I said. "Aren't you planning to call the family too?"

"Well, as I said, since you know the sister..."

"I didn't say I knew her. I spoke on the phone with her once or twice, and that was a few years ago. So I don't really know her. I don't even know how many sisters or brothers he has."

"Just give the one sister a call, and I'm sure she can notify the rest of the family."

Luke was the only one in his family who remained near Meeker, a rugged little town with cow and sheep pastures in spitting distance of the short main drag. The streets were wide but free of traffic jams, the people tough and the population even less than Pinedale Springs. The town's namesake was a Government Indian Agent whose attempts to 'civilize' the Utes by turning them into farmers lead to the infamous 1879 Meeker Massacre. Neither Nathan C. Meeker nor any of his employees lived to tell about this last major Native American uprising in Colorado, but the Utes didn't benefit either, ending up ousted from their homelands, forced onto reservations.

In recent years, another claim to fame, at least in some circles, centered around the annual Meeker Classic Herding Championship, a September event that temporarily swelled the local population with people from all over America, Canada, and even Britain. Top Border Collies and Australian Shepherds were the stars, racing across huge fields upon command from human handlers, gathering and then corralling recalcitrant sheep. Horsemen posted at the far end of the field assisted with sheep control. Luke, always riding Spirit, was usually one of the horse people. Like most others in this part of the country, he owned several Aussies, non-competitors. But he enjoyed watching the best of the best in action. I'd gone with him a few times, back when we were dating, and was amazed at the spectacle. Some of the dogs weren't much to look at, in show dog terms, but those animals oozed smarts. My own choice of border collies as canine companions and occasional horse-herding assistants was largely due to Luke and the Meeker event.

Luke was a product of his environment, a tough but gentle cowboy. I'd come close to marrying him, but so had lots of other women. I smiled to myself and sighed, and then I noticed Jessica watching me. I nodded and raised my hand in a half-hearted wave, got up and checked on the horses, secured all the doors and latches, climbed into the truck beside Roy.

"So what did Gannon have to say?" Roy asked as he steered the rig down the dirt road toward the highway.

I shrugged. "He seemed shocked. And asked me to call Luke's family."

"That's his job."

"You think he actually ever does anything?"

"Touché."

Roy's truck, an apple red dualie one-ton we called the Beast, had the same goose-neck set up to pull my six-horse slant-load trailer as easily as my own behemoth truck did, and Roy was a careful driver. Felt good to just relax and leave the driving to Roy today. The three women fit nicely in the back seat and were either appreciative of the comfort or simply exhausted, because before long, they dozed off.

"Poor Spirit," Roy said after a long silence.

"I was thinking about him, too," I said. "We need to ride out there again soon, try to bury him or cover him up."

"Yes, sure, let's do."

"So, can you really bury that horse out there?" Jessica asked, yawning.

"Not exactly. We can protect him, cover him with rocks and branches."

"So, uh, what happens when one does die, like at your ranch?"

"Depends," I said. "Horses weigh half a ton or more, but we do bury them, have a marker with their name. It's like... well, like losing a family member." I knew she didn't want specifics about the front end loader used to scoop out a grave, didn't want to know details. A dead horse wasn't easy to bury. I dreaded the emotional farewells more than the grim labor.

"How do you stand it?" Evelyn asked.

I turned around, saw that Bianca was the only one still dozing now.

"You do what you have to," I said without mentioning the sleepless nights, the taunting memories.

"Can we go back out there with you?" Jessica asked.

"We'll see," I said. And then, to change the subject for my sake and theirs, I told them how proud I was of them. "You all rode well today, really well," I said. I'd told them that earlier, but repetition didn't hurt. It was true. They'd surprised me, especially Jessica.

"Thanks to your horses," Jessica said. "It was great to ride again, and I love Hawk! But I wish we'd found Luke and Spirit alive."

It was time for evening chores when Roy parked the rig by the barn.

Everyone helped unload the horses. We led them to pasture, and all five animals ran into the grass, tossing their heads, happy to be home. Phantom and Hawk sank to their knees and rolled, legs kicking up and over, wiggling back and forth for a good back scratch. Wind Song and Flash sank their heads down for mouthfuls of green instead, and Mutt also seemed intent on grazing right away.

"You must all be starving," Roy said as we walked toward the house. "C'mon in, I'll put something together."

"We could go into town," Jessica said, but her comment was met with frowns.

The contents of the refrigerator were paltry, but Roy heated a big pot of water on the stove, added rigatoni noodles, thawed frozen meatballs and added them to a pot of spaghetti sauce. While all that was cooking, he chopped lettuce and green peppers into a big bowl, dribbled salad dressing over it, then topped it off with parmesan, pine nuts, and croutons.

I sort of did my part by distributing glasses of lemonade, and then Jessica and I set the table.

Frank called, said he'd have to stay another night in Oklahoma arranging for the Parker Company's next gig.

While we waited for the food, Mary Lou called, even though it was way past time for her to be working. The BLM secretary told me how sorry she was to hear about Luke, provided two phone numbers. One was for the Montana sister, the other for a woman named Rosie Garcia.

"I don't know anyone by that name," I said.

"Neither do I, really," Mary Lou said, "but she's called the office quite frequently the past few weeks, asking to speak with Mr. Barnes."

"Oh."

"He always seemed glad to hear from her."

"Oh, okay," I said. Must be his latest squeeze.

"She called again this morning, right after Mr. Gannon told me about, his... uh, accident."

"What did you tell her?"

"Nothing. I didn't know what to say, so I just said that Mr. Barnes was unavailable."

So now I not only got to try and console his sister, I also had to inform his latest lover that Luke Barnes would never again be available.

After we filled up on spaghetti and salad, I placed a call to Montana. Luke's sister had heard from Sheriff Plackmon, who found her contact info on Luke's phone. She was predictably shocked. She managed to assure me that she'd contact the rest of the family before catching her breath and beginning to sob in earnest. I gave her my phone number as well as one for the BLM office and left her to grieve.

It took only seconds to ascertain that, yes indeed, Luke had been intimate with Rosie Garcia. I didn't tell her right away why I was calling, wanted to find out what her agenda was first. After assuring her that I wasn't 'after' her man and was merely an old friend, she chattered freely.

"He's so hot, good moves... well," she said, laughing, "you wouldn't know, being just a friend."

I did know. The man's sexuality sizzled. Hot indeed. It'd been years, but the remembering could still bring tingles. In my opinion, though, Roy was not only hotter, he was exclusively mine.

Rosie rambled on. She'd known him for only a few weeks, but according to her, the two of them were already planning a long future together. He hadn't proposed yet, she admitted, but she figured he was about to. I had to smile at that. Luke was always about to propose to one woman or another, but commitment wasn't his nature.

"Oh yeah, now I remember," she said. "Luke did mention you once or twice. You're Margo, his horse trainer friend."

"Right," I said.

"He planned a trip out to that Soda Creek Cliffs place after he heard about some dead horse. Not sure when he went."

"He didn't tell me he was going out there," I said.

"He told me," Rosie said. "Tells me everything. And he said something about needing to get there before anybody else, clear the way or something."

"What else did he say about the mustangs?"

"Not much. He seemed awful worried about them, though. So anyhow, why are you calling?"

I took a deep breath, told her.

She cried.

I sank into a quicksand of guilt. I ended the call, covered my face with both hands, lowered my head.

Roy pulled me close, and I melted into him. Neither of us said a word. At times like this, I wondered how I ever managed by myself when he was gone.

"Those weren't easy calls to make," Jessica said.

I nodded. But what was gnawing at me was the guilt. "I should've kept in closer contact with Luke, should've known sooner about the dead mustang and his plan to go out there."

"He might not've even told you," Roy said.

I leaned back, looked up at him. "Maybe not, but I relied on Ruth Dunn for information instead of going straight to the one guy who heard mustang news immediately."

"Even then, what could you have done?"

"If I'd known he was going out to the Cliffs, I could've ridden with him, maybe helped prevent him and Spirit from riding straight into danger."

"He had his own reasons for going out there alone," Roy said.

I shrugged. "If I'd been a better friend, Luke Barnes might still be alive."

"Either that, or you both might be dead," Roy said, stroking my hair, hugging me again.

# CHAPTER FIFTEEN

I EXPECTED THE sheriff to call anytime now, but he drove up instead. Jessica and the others sat nearby, ready to listen in.

"Now about that BLM guy," he said, nodding at us. "I heard you and Roy found the body out there."

That BLM guy, indeed. Luke Barnes was much more than a government employee. By now, his sister had spread the bad news to the rest of his family. I imagined the shocked exclamations, the tears. And then there was Rosie, who'd expected marriage. Other lovers would be saddened, too.

Sheriff Plackmon was watching me, his expression neutral. "Joe Gannon told me some of what you saw out there. He also told me that Luke Barnes was a moody sort."

I shrugged.

"You knew him a long time?"

"About ten years," I said.

"Friends, or, uh…"

I squinted at him, but the question was a valid one. Irritating, but valid. "We dated for a while, before Roy and I got together. We stayed friends." I paused before adding, "Nothing more."

"When was the last time you spoke to him?"

"It's been several weeks."

The sheriff nodded. "So you wouldn't necessarily know if he was out of sorts, maybe depressed or some such when he rode out to the Cliffs?"

"He wasn't suicidal," I said, my voice rising, "if that's what you're getting at." It was the same thing he'd brought up when Bow, my foster mother, died last year. And once again, I supposed it was a valid question.

"No need to get riled. I'm covering possibilities, that's all."

I folded my arms across my chest and braced myself for the next question, remolding my expression as close to neutral as I could.

"We can continue tomorrow if you prefer," he said, his voice gentle. There was something grandfatherly about him at times, disarming. He wore a gun, of course, but I couldn't imagine him drawing a weapon, much less firing at someone. You never know, though.

"Now is okay," I said.

"Not easy talking about the death of a friend."

I wondered if his wife advised him on interrogation techniques. Hard to picture him in bed with the beautiful blonde Courtney, much less taking advice from her. She looked like a trophy wife, was considerably younger than her husband, but their bond seemed genuine.

"I understand that he rode a lot."

"He did," I said, nodding. "Loved horses, especially Spirit, the one that was, uh, shot."

"Yes, a shame," the sheriff said, tsking. "Joe Gannon told me about that too. What's your take on it?"

"I don't know. I suppose it was Luke's rifle there on the ground."

"We'll run ballistics, of course."

"Luke loved that horse," I said. "I can't imagine what happened."

I hadn't seen the video taken out there yet. I hadn't mentioned it to Gannon, nor did I mention it now, even though I trusted the sheriff more than Gannon and the BLM. I'd have to look at it first, decide whether or not to reveal it and to whom.

"I sent my deputy out with the rescue crew to get the body, and of course the rifle."

"Will you be going out there too?" I asked.

"Joe Gannon and I plan to take a chopper out tomorrow. A few things don't add up. The horse, for one."

"That's for sure," I said. "I need to go out there too. Any way we can join you and Gannon?"

He frowned. "This is official business. It wouldn't be appropriate for you…"

"One way or another, I'm going again."

"We were the ones who found Luke and also the horse," Roy said.

"You should leave this to official channels."

"I need to look around again, get Luke's saddle and bridle. Besides, I could show you the exact ledge, explain more of what I saw."

The Sheriff rubbed his chin. "You do have a nose for asking the right questions."

"Uh… thanks," I said.

"But you're not a detective, Margo. Still, I suppose it couldn't hurt to have you along." He paused, turned to Roy. "I suppose you want to go too?"

Roy smiled. "Sure. I should keep Margo safe."

Sheriff Plackmon grinned, on the verge of laughter, but not quite. "Sure, why not. But from what I can tell, Margo takes care of herself awfully well."

Roy laughed at that. "Understatement of the year."

"Well she may need help handling Gannon. I hear he's not particularly fond of your wife."

Roy grinned too. "Huh! How shocking!"

"Seriously, he'll be even testier than usual. But I'm in charge of the helicopter, so I make the decisions on who to bring. At least you two know better than to expect answers on the spot. It takes time to piece things together."

Roy and I both nodded.

Between the sheriff's office and the BLM, there'd be several trees sacrificed for a mound of reports from the initial helicopter retrieval crew, coroner, and of course the BLM and Sheriff's department. Most all of it ended up secure online systems, of course, but paper records still counted. Eventually, there might be useful answers in all that information.

"Thanks, Sheriff," I said. "I'll try to behave."

"I'll look forward to that," Plackmon said. "All right, then, meet me at the airport by 6am." He tipped one finger to his hat and left.

"I don't suppose I should ride along tomorrow," Jessica said.

"No, that wouldn't be good. Besides the helicopter has limited capacity. You and the others can stay here, though."

One of the beefy stagehands stationed himself outside for night duty and told Jessica he'd patrol up and down the road and all around the ranch. The other said he'd stay in the vehicle parked by the entrance. They acted like bodyguards, looked the part, but beyond the tight black shirts, their skills didn't hold up.

Eric and Damian arrived soon after the sheriff left. Eric, casted leg and all, was on crutches, but maneuvered quickly over to Jessica and their kiss was on the warm side of friendly. No one except Roy and me seemed shocked. Knowing Jessica, I shouldn't have been surprised.

After introductions all around, everyone settled on the front porch.

"What are we going to do now?" Bianca asked.

"I'd like to get my hands on this guy who is stalking Jessica, for starters," Eric said, settling down close to her.

"What a day you ladies must've had," Damian said.

"The ride started out so nice," Jessica said, yawning.

"Speaking of our ride, why didn't you tell the sheriff about the video we made at the Cliffs?" Bianca asked me.

"I need to see it first," I replied. A partial truth, but enough for now.

Damian and Bianca began kissing, hands roving. Finally, at least their lips parted and they stood, moving as one toward the door. "Later," Damian said, and Bianca gave a little wave. "C'mon, Evelyn," she said, "we'll drop you off."

As soon as the others were gone, Jessica and Eric went off to the guest room. Hard to believe Frank didn't know about them. He was no fool.

Once everyone was gone, Roy and I watched the video.

After we'd seen it twice, I turned to Roy. "Nothing makes sense."

He nodded. "Luke doesn't appear to be wounded. No obvious blood."

"I know," I said, "but I couldn't turn him over. That ledge was narrow."

"Maybe someone wanted it to look like Luke shot his horse and then jumped."

"Gannon told me Luke had been moody, off-kilter," I said. "But

Gannon never liked Luke because he was always trying to save the mustangs, talk Gannon out of doing the roundups."

"Yeah, we need to do some checking. Speaking of that, what do you think about Jessica and her friends?"

"When it comes to Jessica, I'm biased because we grew up together and were very close all through college. She's always been a drama queen, always pushes to get her way, but she's never done anything illegal that I know of. No one is perfect, though."

"You're perfect, Margo," Roy whispered, pulling me close.

After a few lingering kisses, I sat back, said "what's it gonna be, business or pleasure?"

"Both! Finish giving me your take on the women, and then we'll move on to the pleasure portion of the evening."

"As you wish," I say, smiling. "Ok, so Bianca is easy to read. She's friendly, open, and likable. I don't think she's the type to have hidden agendas. On the other hand, Evelyn is standoffish, seems to feel superior to others. She's more the type to spring surprises on us in some way. Then again, someone hit her, knocked her flat the other night."

"Yeah. The question is, who did that and why?"

I nodded. "Also, was she the real target? Seems likely the intruder was Jessica's stalker."

"Possible. Evelyn and Jessica do look somewhat alike."

I nodded again. "They do. Their hair is the same color, same style."

"We have a chaotic chain of seemingly unrelated events going on."

"For sure. We need to sort it all out, take one thing at a time."

Roy took my hand, pulled me close. "I couldn't agree more. But enough business."

We were both tired, but not too tired for the pleasure of love.

# CHAPTER FIFTEEN

THE HELICOPTER ROSE, smooth but noisy. The local airport and the town of Pinedale Springs spread out below us and soon shriveled away. Joe Gannon seemed less than thrilled to have Roy and me along even after Sheriff Plackmon explained that our observations might prove useful. That was how I'd convinced the Sheriff last evening, but now he sounded like he'd invited us rather than been pestered into allowing our presence.

Gannon's attitude sunk even lower when I hit him with my idea. It occurred to me in the wee hours before dawn. Although I usually arise without benefit of an alarm clock at 5a.m. for morning chores, I'd woken up this day at the miserable hour of half past three. Pitch dark, too early to do anything useful, too late to get back to sleep. Roy was sound asleep beside me, so I just laid there quietly, thoughts wandering.

And somehow, it came to me. Flying over Soda Creek Cliffs in a helicopter was an opportunity too good to miss. Not only could I get another look at the ledge where Luke had landed and at his gelding, Spirit. It'd also be a perfect time to count as many mustangs as possible, get a more realistic idea of just how much numbers were decreasing. And maybe, just maybe, Roy and I could spot the dead mustang, see where it'd fallen. I didn't expect Gannon to be so opposed. Matter of fact, I thought he might've been planning this himself. But no.

"Waste of time," he said.

"We'll be right there," I said, trying to reason with him. "If you have a look now, it'll save sending someone out later."

"She's got a point," Roy said.

I squeezed his hand, kissed him.

"All right by me. We can easily stay up a bit longer," Sheriff Plackmon said.

I could've kissed him too.

Finally, Gannon gave in. Not that he really had a choice. He did have to submit an annual head count on mustang numbers to state BLM headquarters over in Denver and also to the Washington D.C. honchos. He usually delegated the actual one-two-three to underlings. Luke had always been the first volunteer to get out there for counting the mustangs or any other reason. Gannon was not happy about the opportunity for doing this himself.

Not that I cared. But the more I thought about it, the more I wondered why he wouldn't want to survey the entire Cliffs area. After all, he was obligated to file a report on the horse that'd been shot as well as volumes on the demise of one of his own men on BLM land.

Where would civilization be without paperwork and online documents.

Or video cameras. The one Bianca used on yesterday's ride was quite compact. She'd left it with me last night, so I tucked it into my fanny pack today. Gannon looked a little startled when I pulled the camera out the first time. "Good way to document the animals, study them," I said.

He made a face, shrugged.

Roy brought his best binoculars, and scanned the land below us.

The chopper landed a ways from Upper Deer Trail, and the pilot stayed with his machine while the four of us hiked up the steep section. We stood looking down at the ledge where Luke had fallen. Sheriff Plackmon and Gannon asked Roy and I a bunch of questions before we proceeded on to Spirit's body.

Joe Gannon grunted and shook his head. "Whoever did this knew where to aim."

I thought about Spirit falling and felt nauseated. All I could do for him now was remove his tack. As soon as the official questions and search of the area ended, I undid buckles, lifted the saddle and placed everything off to the side.

Sheriff Plackmon watched without saying anything, just stood still for a minute, squinting. After I finished, he walked over to the horse, crouched down and ran his hands along each of the animal's legs, front first, then rear. "I'm no vet, but it feels like a big lump back here," he said, probing around Spirit's left rear hock, the one closest to the ground.

"So what?" Joe Gannon said. "That rifle is what killed him."

But I understood what the Sheriff was thinking. "What do you think, Margo?"

I bent down, felt Spirit's legs. "Can't tell. There is a lump, so maybe the bone is broken. Could've happened after the horse was shot, leg twisted as he fell."

Roy had the video camera now, and he recorded views of everything, zoomed in now.

"Maybe," the Sheriff said.

"What're you two getting at?" Gannon asked.

The Sheriff stood, brushed himself off. "It's possible that this gelding broke his leg so bad he couldn't walk. So bad that all the rider could do was put the animal out of his misery."

"Damn," Gannon said.

I shook my head. It was possible, of course, I had to admit that. The trail was rocky, the footing uneven. A horse just might trip on a protruding stone, take a fall.

"Horses stumble sometimes," I said, "but a broken leg is highly unlikely unless this animal was moving fast, took a bad spill. Luke wasn't the kind of rider who'd race over this type of terrain unless it was a matter of life and death."

"Maybe someone was chasing him," Sheriff Plackmon said.

Roy and I exchanged glances.

That seemed farfetched. I doubted that Spirit had been galloping at all, doubted his hock was badly injured. I knew where the Sheriff was headed with this. He'd asked last night about moodiness, depression. And before he verbalized it, I knew that Sheriff Plackmon had a theory which was wrong. He figured that an already moody Luke, despondent over having to shoot Spirit, threw himself off the trail, fell to his death.

Gannon blinked, turning from Spirit back toward the ledge, eyebrows rising as he realized what the Sheriff was implying. "Good Lord. I mean," he paused, shaking his head. "Moody is one thing, but jumping…"

The four of us stood there, silent. High above, a golden eagle circled, outstretched wings dark against the cloudless sky. Perhaps Luke had gazed up at this same magnificent raptor a few days ago.

"Well, I don't know," Joe Gannon said, stroking his mustache, "but I'll have to get some men out here, clean up the trail."

I glared at him. God forbid that a dead animal should spill blood on BLM property.

The Sheriff reached over to me, put a hand on my shoulder, looked me in the eye.

"No." I said, shaking my head. "There has to be some other explanation."

"And maybe there is, Margo. We'll have to see."

But seeing was the problem, because everyone's vision differed. Sheriff Plackmon saw an injured horse, a suicide. Joe Gannon saw a lot of paperwork, a mess on his precious BLM trail, and maybe regret that one of his employees had died out here.

If Luke faced having to put his horse down, he'd be torn up about it, for sure. He loved his animals, Spirit in particular. He wouldn't have left the saddle and bridle on, for one thing. And I couldn't imagine him jumping off a cliff.

It was at least a hundred feet from the horse's body to the part of the trail Luke had fallen from. The body was around a bend, the ledge not clearly visible from here.

I didn't know much about rifles, had little interest in guns. I felt apologetic about the handgun I carried in my cantle bag on long trail rides, resented the thing's power and hoped to never have to aim it at anything other than paper targets. If it hadn't been for Roy's belief that some humongous mountain lion was waiting to attack me out here, I would've locked the damn thing up in a drawer somewhere. Better yet, I wouldn't have it at all. Not that Roy doubted my ability to take care of myself. He and I both grew up around nature, were aware that mountain lions and bears demanded respect and a wide berth. But we also knew that humans were more capable of atrocities than any wild creature.

I'd looked at the wound in Spirit's side, and Roy filmed more, including the horse's legs.

The Sheriff remained next to me and Roy. He'd grown up around horses, admired them.

I turned toward Roy. "Is it possible to tell how far away the shooter was from the horse?"

He nodded.

"How would it look if that shot was taken from a long way off?"

"Different, at least to detailed ballistics."

"For God's sake," Gannon said, frowning, "This is a dead horse. Dead is dead."

I ignored him, still thinking about the bullet, about differences. And then it struck me. I crouched down beside Spirit, close to all the blood.

"What in the world are you looking for?" Gannon asked.

"How the bullet entered."

"We're doing ballistics," the sheriff said.

"It's not that," I said, "not matching the bullet to the gun. What if the shooter was, say above the horse somewhere up there," I said, pointing in the general direction of numerous overlooks that jutted out along the crest of the cliff.

The men looked up.

"Well," I continued, "the angle of the bullet hole would be different than if someone shot straight on."

"For Pete's sake," Gannon said. "I told you she'd be a pain in the butt."

Sheriff Plackmon and Roy ignored Gannon and crouched down beside me.

"What do you think?" I asked.

"Does seem a bit angled, from the look of it," the sheriff replied, peering close. Need a tissue sample to send to Grand Junction for forensics. I brought two collection kits, just in case."

He removed a small package from a bag he was carrying, pulled on rubber gloves, produced a plastic-handled scalpel and went to work.

I stood up and turned away, and Roy stood too, pulled me close. The thought of cutting into flesh that'd been intact over a wonderful gelding's beating heart not that long ago made me gag. I took deep breaths, concentrating on working my lungs, in, out. I was tempted to ask the Sheriff to be gentle, even though that didn't matter, not anymore. Still, I felt like apologizing to Spirit for what was being done to him.

"Is this necessary for a dead horse?" Gannon asked.

I could've kicked the man.

"May provide some answers regarding Luke Barnes," the sheriff replied.

"Let's hope so," Roy said.

At least the door wasn't slammed shut on possibilities. Besides, whoever fired that shot didn't have to be up above. They could've been anywhere. If testing could provide a definite angle, it could point to a shooter other than Luke himself.

The Sheriff finished quickly and slipped the tissue sample out of sight, into his bag.

I wished there were some way to give Spirit a proper burial even though rituals are for those left behind, not for the dead. Roy and I gathered what little brush was available, intending to cover him.

"What now?" Gannon asked, sounding exasperated.

"Leave them be," the sheriff said. "She raised this horse."

We layered sagebrush, the biggest rocks we could carry and whatever else we could find to place over the gelding's head and neck, and also covered the open area the sheriff had made. It didn't take long because there wasn't enough loose plant material to cover his entire body. I stood and brushed myself off. My aim was leaving the horse in dignity. The result wasn't great.

Sheriff Plackmon helped Roy and me gather Spirit's tack while Joe Gannon stood watching, silent and sullen. Nor did he help us lug the saddle and bridle back down the trail to the waiting chopper.

Soon after lift-off, first one band of mustangs and then another appeared below us, racing away. I filmed and Roy used the binoculars. One stallion was the black and white pinto that the women and I saw yesterday.

"Fine looking animals," Sheriff Plackmon commented, looking down.

The other band appeared robust, but just like the groups that Bianca had videotaped, the numbers seemed diminished from springtime counts.

Joe Gannon made marks on his clipboard, and I kept detailed count in my own notebook in between running the video. Within half an hour, we saw several other bands, all with less members than previously documented. I glanced over at Gannon. but his head was turned away, facing down. He appeared to be counting too, but maybe he was just sulking.

We flew northwest toward Far Canyon, a place less frequented by hikers, but accessible by a rough seasonal road which ended at Indian Springs.

"Not much up here," Gannon told the pilot. "Let's turn back, more likely to see mustangs in Rollins Canyon."

He was wrong. Maybe he didn't know his own territory. With the exception of a box canyon in about the middle of this vast range, the other canyons connected in a series of twists and turns.

The terrain up north was more rugged than the other sections, but Far Canyon opened out onto a huge sagebrush flats near Indian Spring, and mustangs frequently grazed there not far from half a dozen drilling rigs that'd been recently approved by the BLM.

The pilot began turning the chopper away, but I touched Sheriff Plackmon's shoulder. "I think I saw a couple horses up there." I didn't, but I might, if we flew far enough north.

"You did?" He glanced at Gannon, who was scowling. "We'd best check it out, long as we're here."

"Waste of time, I tell you," Gannon said.

But the sheriff motioned to the pilot, and the chopper changed course.

Gannon didn't seem all that interested in a total count of the mustangs. But I was, and I gave him a don't mess with me look meant to say that if I had to stuff a cork in his mouth and fly the damn chopper myself, I wasn't about to lose this opportunity.

He scowled some more.

I scowled back, and we had a little contest to see who'd blink first.

I won. Roy grinned, and the sheriff shook his head and almost smiled.

This was the first time I'd ever ridden in a helicopter, and I much preferred riding horses. Every time the pilot banked sharply, I wished I hadn't eaten breakfast.

We hadn't seen the dead mustang, but I doubted it'd be up this far. Those coeds hadn't hiked anywhere near far enough to reach this area. We might spot something on the way back. We still had lots of territory to cover. Not that we'd see everything. This was much quicker than trying to cover the range on horseback, but it was still just an overview.

We flew north without seeing movement other than a dust cloud from a driller's truck on a rough road down below, and Gannon turned to me. "This is ridiculous. Like I said, there are no horses up here."

I shrugged. And wondered why he was protesting.

The sagebrush flats were spreading out below us. Sure enough, scattered horses grazed in the distance not far from the drilling rigs. They raced off at the sound of our approach, but I filmed them, counting eighteen mature animals, half a dozen foals. They separated into three bands, each with the usual lead mare, the stallions driving their harem from behind. I wasn't as familiar with these horses as the ones who ranged to the south, but someone from Freedom Forever had claimed that the three groups up here totaled over two dozen mature animals just this spring.

That meant at least six mustangs were unaccounted for.

"Okay, there they are," Gannon said. "Now turn this thing around," he told the pilot.

But I saw something in the distance. This time I wasn't pretending. "Wait, up there. Look!" I yelled.

"Now what?" Gannon said.

"Is that fencing?" Roy asked.

"You're imagining things," Gannon said.

"Nope, I see it too," Sheriff Plackmon said.

Off to the side of Indian Spring was a V shaped area of fencing.

"Up there, fly up there," I told the pilot.

"It's nothing," Gannon said, clearing his throat. Either it was my imagination, or he sounded nervous.

The BLM gathered what they deemed to be excess mustangs, trucked them away to sites all over the country and put them up for adoption. When a gather was planned, a long funnel of temporary fencing leading into a sturdy corral was set up. Helicopters were used to bring bands together, and then a Judas mare took over. Wild horses naturally follow a lead mare, a wise older animal who knows the way to safety. A Judas mare was a trickster, a domesticated animal trained to led the mustangs to the funnel, into the corral.

Away from freedom.

This next planned roundup was several weeks away, and roundups were not planned for this portion of Cliffs. We were flying near the northern entrance, seldom used because the road leading up to it was rutted and challenging even with four-wheel drive. The driller's trucks used a different route. This is where Luke might've entered the range, but his truck and trailer wasn't in sight, which wasn't unusual. He sometimes left the rig at home, rode Spirit all the way in.

Some corrals were permanent structures for use by the BLM. But there had never been corrals or any fencing at all in this area. Official BLM protocol stated that fencing could only be erected when a 'gathering' was imminent.

"What the hell?" Gannon asked. "Who put up this fence?"

On the far side of the corral, tire tracks were evident. Fresh tire tracks. I filmed the fencing, zoomed in on the tracks and the inside of the corral. the ground appeared churned up.

"Someone's been here, not long ago," the sheriff said.

"And no one is authorized," Gannon said. "No one should be driving in here, putting up fence. These horses are government property."

Indeed. It was hard enough for the BLM to find adoptive homes for mustangs. What had happened to the horses who were rounded up into this corral? Where were they taken, and why? On behalf of the Forever Free group, I had alerted Joe when herd numbers began dwindling, and so had Luke Barnes. Why hadn't Gannon been out here to check things himself? And why had he seemed so reluctant to have the chopper fly up here? The answers might point only to his dislike of mustangs, to his generally disagreeable nature.

Or something more.

# CHAPTER SEVENTEEN

GANNON SAID THE right words, acted appropriately upset over the fence, the unauthorized intrusion on BLM land. He wasn't a politician, but he talked like one when he wanted to, maybe did favors for someone. Like looking the other way while someone stole mustangs under his very nose.

Even though their badges originated with different agencies, Joe Gannon and Sheriff Plackmon were comrades of a sort. The two of them began a heated discussion about who held jurisdiction over this area, whether or not to land the helicopter.

"Now look here, Gannon," the sheriff finally said. "This is my department's helicopter, therefore I am in charge. Part of the land below us may be in BLM's control, but this entire area is also my concern." He turned to pilot. "Land this thing, now!"

Roy listened intently to them, saying nothing. I sat silent too, thinking dark thoughts, wondering if Gannon himself was somehow behind mustang disappearances.

And that wasn't all. Dead horse, dead friend. Who shot the horse? Who did what to Luke?

There were plenty of ranchers who stood to benefit if Soda Creek Cliffs was cleared of mustangs to provide more land for livestock grazing. Millie Dickson, for one. And many landowners around here saw dollars headed their way with increased drilling permits. No wonder so many people considered me the bad guy, the one who stood in the way of their greed.

Last but not least, there was the matter of Jessica's stalker. The guy was escalating, the danger growing. I'd been thinking of ways to smoke him out, force him to reveal himself. I needed to act, and soon. My thoughts whirled with questions, possibilities. We didn't know who had jimmied the bolts on Jessica's stage the other night. For all we knew, even Jessica's stalker was somehow connected to the mustangs.

Roy and I exchanged looks. We had a lot to consider.

The chopper landed not far from the corral. When we got out and approached closer, it was obvious that a large number of horse hooves had churned up the ground.

"Could be cows," Gannon said.

"No! Horses!" I said.

Sheriff Plackmon nodded. "She's right."

Gannon looked at me, scowled. "Well what are you doing with that damn video?"

"Documenting," I said, taking images of horse's hoofprints and also closeups of tire tracks.

Sheriff Plackmon did the same, but with his iPhone.

"No animals around now," Roy said after we'd looked all around.

"Let's head back," the sheriff said.

The chopper rose and angled south. The sheriff told the pilot to change course, and we flew low over twisting canyons punctuated by pinyon pines that, from above, resembled ragged green pom poms. We'd covered much of the eastern areas, then headed down along the western part of the range. A trio of hoodoo spires provided rocky perches for golden eagles and a huge nest clung to the side of one crevice. Just beyond Badger Gulch, the Mustang Hill Trail wound its way down to connect with Canyon Trail.

Then came our first glimpse of Wild Box Canyon to the east, a spectacular place where the lushest grasses in the range beckoned summer grazers. A bottle-neck opening led to a sheltered but dead-end enclosure surrounded by steep cliffs. We flew closer, saw that no horses lingered inside Box Canyon, and were about to head south again when Roy spotted a large brown lump on a little rise beside Canyon Trail.

"There, down there, must be the mustang," he said.

The pilot did a slow circle.

"Sure enough," the sheriff said, "a dead horse."

Gannon grunted. "Well, these mustangs do die, you know."

Everyone ignored him.

The coeds had said the trail was steep, but then again, they were new to Colorado, they were inexperienced, they were from sea level. By the time they stumbled upon the horse, the least little hill probably looked and felt steep to them, for one thing. For another, the shock of seeing a dead animal no doubt played havoc with their memories.

"Can we get down there, have a look?" I asked, turning to the sheriff.

"Yes, let's do," he replied, spoke to the pilot. "Can you get us down?"

"Looks tight, but yeah, sure"

Within minutes, we were out of the chopper again. As interesting as the flight had been, as awesome and different the scenery from above, I vowed to never climb aboard another helicopter, at least not right after breakfast. It wasn't that I questioned the pilot's skill. As far as I could tell, he was a pro. I just wasn't suited to travel in these things. I didn't really like planes much either, but the chopper's sudden dipping and swaying rattled me. My cowardly attitude might've been due to the fact that my parents died in a plane crash back when I was twelve. But I'd never cared for high places. Steep trails were about as much height as I could handle, and even those brought near-panic at times. Clients on my wilderness pack trips thought I was just kidding, putting them at ease when I said I hated heights. It was no joke.

We had to walk a ways to the body. The closer we got, the stronger the stench of rotting flesh, the smell of death. Overpowering but strangely humbling. Despite the dust to dust, ashes to ashes chants, many humans try hard to prolong the inevitable. As if the flesh and bones are immortal in some way. Like ancient Egyptians, some dearly departed are still embalmed and preserved, encased in elaborate containers but then hidden away underground or behind stone mausoleums.

Remembered, but out of sight.

If a bird flew into a window and dropped dead to the ground, people scooped up the broken body, disposed of it. Soon forgotten, but again, out of sight.

Nature took a different view. A spent butterfly, its wings shredded, melts into its surroundings along with autumn leaves. That sight might elicit a human sigh, maybe not even that.

A spent horse, hooves still, melted away also if left where it fell, but leaves came and went more than once before the earth claimed the animal completely. That sight was guaranteed to elicit at least a human sigh. To most, it would seem sad at first, then increasingly grotesque, and, much later, nearly unrecognizable.

Instead of embalming fluid, nature provided beetles and maggots, microscopic organisms. Fellow creatures large and small. Abhorrent, perhaps, but efficient, necessary. I refused to let myself think about all that happening to Spirit's flesh, but at least I hadn't known this mustang personally.

"The thing's been there awhile, that's for sure," Gannon said, covering his face with a handkerchief. "Damn. Worse than skunk."

Large black birds with red featherless heads flapped wide wings and lifted up as we drew nearer, circling overhead, resenting our intrusion. Vultures.

"Best let me have a look, you're not gonna want to see this," Sheriff Plackmon said to me.

"I agree, Margo," Roy said.

In a way, I appreciated their attempt at chivalry. In another way, I resented it. "It's okay," I told them, smiling a little.

Gannon glanced at me and raised one eyebrow. Didn't have to say a word. It was obvious what he was thinking.

I delivered a look at all three men. Challenge accepted.

The horse had been dead awhile, all right. Still recognizable as a bay, though, and a mare. I'd been afraid this would be that gorgeous bay stallion. In my opinion, he had the most impressive conformation of any studs out here. Straight legs, good stout cannon bones, short back, powerful hindquarters. He was well proportioned and had kind, intelligent eyes. I'd feared the loss of his contributions to the mustang gene pool. Even though the sight of this dead mare saddened me, I also felt relief.

Then again, according to the coeds, this horse had been shot.

No telling where the bullet hole was, not anymore. But vultures wouldn't be likely to devour the lethal metal. Not far away, there were a few old branches lying on the ground beneath a scraggly tree. I picked up a three foot piece and carried it over to the body, holding my breath. I'd have to breathe, of course, would have to inhale the stench of death. Gingerly, I began poking around with the stick.

"What the hell she up to now?" Gannon asked. "Geez, the woman is flipping crazy!"

"This horse was shot, right Joe?" the sheriff asked.

"So I'm told. College girls from back East found it. Doubt they knew what they were talking about. Animal probably died of old age."

"One girl's father is a hunter," I said without looking up. "She's seen dead deer, bullet holes."

"That a fact," Gannon said.

I was in danger of contributing the contents of my stomach to the mess in front of me. Movies and those crime shows on TV leave the gross stuff to viewer's imaginations. Reality doesn't hold back.

Roy picked up a long stick of his own and knelt next to me. "Not finding a thing," he said after a while.

"Me neither," I said. Sometimes bad smells sort of fade after they're inhaled for a few minutes. This wasn't one of those times. Breathing through my mouth helped, but not enough.

Gannon had backed away a few feet and stood watching us, grimacing.

"Take a lot of luck to come up with a piece of metal in that mess," the sheriff said, "if there is one. Maybe not much point in finding it anyway."

I twisted around and looked up and him. "Why do you say that?"

"Can't trace a shooter by a single bullet. Need a gun."

"Give it up," Gannon said, his voice muffled. He still had a handkerchief over his nose and mouth.

I didn't bother replying to either of them. But I looked at Roy, shook my head. We weren't finding anything. Roy stopped probing and leaned back. I was about to do the same when my stick clunked against something small, solid. Might've been quick to reach in there with my bare hand, grab the thing. But the thought of that made me gag even more. Took a couple minutes, but I managed to ease the object to the surface without contaminating my hands.

A bullet. Looked like it came from a rifle.

"Well what d'ya know," Sheriff Plackmon said. He pulled a small plastic bag from his pocket, bent down beside me and slid the bullet inside the bag.

"All right," Gannon said, frowning "you're persistent, that's for sure. Now let's get the hell out of here."

I turned to the Sheriff. "You have another tissue kit?"

"Sure do."

"Could we take a bit of, uh, material, have someone check how long this mare's been dead."

"Why would you need to know that?" Gannon asked.

"Might be useful information," the sheriff said. "Experts can tell a lot by the life stages of these maggots." He produced the kit and handed it to me. I used the stick to ladle a small mess of flesh inside, maggots and all. Forensic pathologists must have strong stomachs.

"Good job," Roy said, nodding at me.

"Yeah, but I don't think I'll ever forget this odor. I'm still…" I paused, made a face, "gagging. I felt sick to my stomach the entire time."

Roy nodded some more. "Me too."

Back up in the helicopter, I looked down at the dead mare one more time, felt bad for her. I not a church-goer, but I believe there's an afterlife and it's not only for humans but also for all creatures, with a special place for horses. We saw one more band of mustangs, and the wonderful bay stallion was down there, in charge and in great form. I watched him, my eyes moistening.

Roy pulled me close. This day would've been so much harder without him.

Joe Gannon was watching too. "Okay, several more, then," he said, jotting a note on his clipboard. "Brings the total to eighty seven. So numbers aren't declining."

I'd counted the same number. "They are. If you don't count this year's foals, the total drops alarmingly."

"Bullshit," he said.

"Your office reported a total of one hundred and six mares and stallions last year. And there were twenty in the last roundup, which would leave eighty-six mature mares and stallions."

Gannon grunted.

"I counted thirteen foals today, which leaves only seventy four mature horses. Twelve less than last year, and the only carcass was that mare. What happened to the others?"

"Can't say," Gannon said, scowling.

"What about the fencing and those fresh tire tracks in Far Canyon?" Roy asked.

"I'll look into that," Gannon replied.

Roy and I would be looking into that too. Maybe the publicity from Jessica's song would help in some way. She wanted to ride out here again, now that Hawk, the gentlest gelding ever, had helped overcome her fear of falling off. Good thing she and the others hadn't been along today, though. They'd seen enough yesterday as it was. Sometimes, ignorance really is bliss.

They were off practicing dance moves for their next concert and reviewing the arrangement for "Running Wild, Running Free." With any luck those lyrics would be familiar before long. People would listen to Jessica Parker sing and imagine wild horses galloping across a green meadow, manes ruffling in the wind, powerhouse legs propelling a poetry of motion. Sweetness and light, carefree horses, that's what many people wanted to imagine, what Jessica's words would help them see.

A dream world.

Joe Gannon and Sheriff Plackmon had both been at her concert, heard her new song. They began chatting about her as the chopper headed back to town. When the Sheriff mentioned that Jessica was my friend, Gannon turned to me.

"You know her?"

"We grew up together."

"You don't say," Gannon said. "When she brought you up on stage after that three-ring circus with the horses, I thought she was just being nice because they were your animals."

"She is nice."

"Talented, too," Roy added.

I nodded.

"Think you could introduce me?" Gannon asked.

"Yeah, I suppose. She's married, you know."

He shrugged. "So am I. Makes no difference. I'd just like to, you know, say hello or something."

"I'll see what I can do."

I suppose he clapped along with the crowd after Jessica sang "Running Wild, Running Free," but his behavior confirmed that he considered mustangs more of a nuisance than a treasure. As head of the local BLM district, he interpreted and implemented government guidelines for managing the animals we'd counted today, but he wasn't obligated to like them.

Sheriff Plackmon seemed more sympathetic towards the mustangs, but had no official say over them. His jurisdiction only extended into BLM areas in cases of human incidents, like Luke's death. Both of them were fans of Jessica Parker, though, along with most males who met her. The sheriff had practically drooled over her, even though his own wife was gorgeous. But Jessica was not only great looking, she was also a performer, a local girl who'd tasted the big time. And even if she was no longer a top-selling vocalist, her brush with celebrity translated into power. Part of the reason she and Eric wrote the song about mustangs was the broad appeal of horses, their mystique. Hopefully, her song would bring back old fans, add new ones, make them think about wild horses.

I didn't trust Joe Gannon the least bit. But I needed his stamp of approval in order to establish a rescue operation and save as many mustangs as I could from BLM lands. Maybe Jessica could sweet-talk this guy into cooperating.

# CHAPTER EIGHTEEN

THE NEXT DAY before lunch, I headed into town to finally scope out the stagehands, especially those who chewed tobacco, see if one of them squirmed, acted guilty. My thoughts swirled from one problem to the next, but it was high time to see if I could find out who hit Evelyn on the head a few days ago and if that guy might also be Jessica's stalker. I made myself take a deep breath, concentrate. There was so much going on. One thing at a time, though. My truck rolled down the dusty road, a behemoth of mechanical horsepower keeping me momentarily safe from demanding friends, from enemies known and unknown.

The driver of the truck used to transport stage equipment slept in the cab, but most of the crew stayed in a cramped motel. It seemed best to keep things relaxed, as though I'd just happened to run into them. I guessed that most of the guys would eat lunch at Rebecca's Pantry. It was close by, for one thing, and the best restaurant in town.

I parked the truck on a side street near Rebecca's and walked around to Main Street, ran into the drug store for some items and left with a small brown bag that might be of use, then went a few doors down to the restaurant. The place was packed. Ken Munson sat alone, sipping coffee. He was on the short side, medium build, gray-streaked mustache, a dragon tattoo pierced his left bicep, a heart pierced by an arrow on his right forearm. He drove the Parker Company truck and looked like the kind of guy you meet and then forget. He glanced at me, nodded without smiling.

"I'm Jessica's friend," I said, pulling out a chair and placing my small brown bag on the table. "I saw you at the concert. Remember me?"

"Yup."

"Mind if I join you?"

He shrugged. "Suit yourself."

I ordered a grilled cheese and iced tea, he asked for a hamburger and a coke. He'd driven rigs for ten years, he said, zigzagging from one coast to the other. Sometime last year he'd signed on to drive for the Parker Company, less road time. Grew up in Cleveland. Married briefly, no kids. He didn't seem to mind questions, but gave staccato answers. I asked what he thought of Jessica. He said, "She's hot," and smiled, showing tobacco browned teeth.

About the time our food arrived, Millie Dickson and Rose Montoya came through the door, chatting away. Millie's face froze when she saw me, and we exchanged cool stares. I hadn't yet figured out a way to prove if she was behind anything, but even if she wasn't, she irked me, brought out some primal need for flight or fight.

I turned my attention to food and the guy in front of me. I didn't know for sure what to think of Ken Munson, but he made me vaguely nervous. He seemed more pitiful than tough, one of those people who existed on the fringes, sat while others danced, lived alone and lonely.

After a while, I brushed the little brown bag with my arm, hoping it looked like an accident. The bag crumpled, and three tins of Skoal chewing tobacco rolled out onto the floor. "Oops," I said, leaning over. I retrieved the tins and sat them on the table. "These are for my Uncle John," I said. "He's chewed ever since I can remember."

"Bad for the teeth," he said. "Probably better to smoke."

But he didn't smell of cigarettes. His breath projected that stench of moist tobacco.

I put the tins back inside the bag. "So you don't chew?"

"Yeah, some," he admitted through mouthfuls of sandwich, "but I gotta stop one of these days."

I couldn't come right out and ask him if he'd stood around outside one of my bedroom windows with a wad in his lower lip.

I sipped iced tea. "Everyone is worried about Jessica."

He frowned, looked up at the ceiling before saying, "I could help her." His tone was flat, devoid of emotion.

"Oh, how so?"

"Watch out for her if they'd give me a chance," he said. "I'd be better than those big goons they're calling bodyguards."

"What would you do differently?"

He just shook his head, refused to elaborate.

"You ever been a bodyguard?"

He frowned, pushed back his chair, threw a ten dollar bill on the table and stomped out, leaving half his burger. So he had a temper, that much was clear. And he'd admitted chewing.

After he left, I took the rest of my iced tea and joined three other stage crew guys who'd just arrived. They were boisterous and talkative, buddies who hired on about a year ago, right after high school. Seeing the country, they said. They also thought Jessica was hot.

"Man, she sizzles," said Derrick, a skinny kid who hadn't yet outgrown acne.

"Too bad about that corral thing," the chubby one named Mark said in a high-pitched voice which the other two immediately mimicked. He blushed a bit, but only said "Aw c'mon, you guys, cut it out."

The third, Ted, appeared to be the leader, and answered most of my questions. None of them remembered seeing anything suspicious nor recalled strangers hanging around. "But we were all hustling," Ted said, "setting up stuff on the stage, loading stuff on and off the truck. No time to look around much."

The only one in that group who reacted when I again let the Skoal tins roll out of the bag was Mark. I couldn't tell about his breath, but his teeth looked brown. Derrick said that chewing was gross, and Ted claimed that he'd tried the stuff once, but it made him puke.

After one last glance at Millie, I left the café, drove down Main Street to the Aspen Market and was filling my truck with diesel when a tall guy walked up. I remembered him helping at the concert.

"Hi, aren't you Jessica's friend?" he asked.

I nodded. "And you're Jake, right?"

"You remembered! Wow, people don't usually notice me, much less know my name."

"You helped load up the corral pieces after the concert."

"Uh-huh," he said.

Maybe because of his freckled face, he looked like a teenager, but he told me he was in his twenties and had been on the crew over a year.

I reached into the cab, saw to it that my bag of Skoal rolled right out onto the asphalt. "Oops!"

"Hey, what're you doin' with that crap?"

"It's for my Uncle John."

"I hear it's addictive," he said with a big smile that revealed brown-stained teeth. "You're the horse lady, right?"

"I'm a horse trainer."

"I love horses. Used to ride when I was a kid."

"Ever have your own horse?"

He shook his head. "Nope. Not that lucky. So anyway, you like to ask questions." I shrugged. "Sometimes."

"Any answers about who caused all that ruckus with the corral?"

"Not yet," I said. "What do you think happened?"

"How should I know? Sounded like a bomb. But I feel sorry for Jessica. I mean, she needs somebody to look out for her more. I don't think her husband knows how lucky he is."

"What do you mean?"

"He's got Jessica. Every guy on the crew would like to be in his shoes."

"You think so?"

"Heck yes," he said, nodding. "I mean, she's so, well, perfect. Speaking of which, your truck is way cool too."

"Thanks," I said. By then, I'd processed my debit card, both tanks were filled with diesel, and I was waiting for the receipt to print. Almost requires a loan to refuel this truck.

Jake glanced at his watch. "Um, gotta get goin'. Nice seeing you, Miss, uh…"

"Richards," I said, "but call me Margo. Here," I said, holding out a tin of Skoal.

"I'm trying to quit," he said, giving me a boyish smile but grabbing it anyway before jogging off.

I chatted up other crewmembers I found outside the motel where they were staying. None of them had bad breath or discolored teeth. Everyone said 'hot' to describe Jessica, thought she was nice and knew their names.

They weren't quite as complimentary about Frank, although no one admitted disliking him. They said he was a demanding boss, knew everything that was going on.

No one had noticed any strangers or anything unusual.

Eric Jakowski earned a broken leg from his efforts to wave down my mustangs on-stage, but was released from the hospital and he'd spent the night with Jessica at my place. Tall and blond, the guitar player oozed rugged charm and an easy manner. I moved him to the bottom of my list of possible stalkers. His teeth sparkled white, his breath held no hint of tobacco. The only reason to keep him in mind at all was his relationship with Jessica, which could be volatile if Frank found out or already knew.

Virgil, a Texan with scuffed cowboy boots and a pronounced drawl, was missing one front tooth, but the rest of his teeth were white. I crossed him off of my list of chewers. He was the last guy I spoke with and his words summed up things in general when he finished denying that he'd seen anyone or anything. "Could have missed something."

Ken, Mark, and Jake were the only Skoal users I found, so maybe one of them had spit out the mound of stuff outside my house. All three were open about their admiration for Jessica, so if one of them was her stalker, they were adept at hiding it, but I'd sure keep them in mind. Then again, it was possible that the fanatic fan wasn't employed by the Parker Company.

Before I returned to the ranch, I pulled out the name and address of Jessica's ex-boyfriend. Dave Shipton still lived in Chicago, answered the phone himself, and within the course of the conversation, I decided Jessica was right. He wasn't the stalker type. Besides, the band he played with now had a nightly gig there in the Windy City, meaning that although he admitted seeing her several weeks ago, he had an alibi for the past few nights at least. He admitted using Skoal, said Jessica hated the smell. He answered questions without hesitation, asked some of his own.

"She's high-maintenance, but a cool lady, hot," he said. "Anything I can do, more questions I can answer, call."

The real question was, whose infatuation with Jessica Parker had gotten out of control, what came next, and did it tie in with the mustangs and my detractors in some way?

Back at the ranch, Louie jumped onto Jessica's lap, wagging his wiry stub of a tail, trying to lick her face. Eric had gone back to town, so Jessica and Roy were at the table, sipping tea.

"Louie is trying to remind me that he hasn't eaten yet," Jessica said.

Roy laughed, and I managed a smile. One reason dogs are good for us is they know when to entertain, how to make tension disappear. I love my border collies, love the way Zap consoles, the way Fetch entertains. Dogs are much more perceptive than they get credit for.

I shook my head, thinking about friends. One lost forever, Jessica here tonight but soon gone again. I wasn't often moody, but seeing Luke and also Spirit had shaken me, reminded me that death hovers ever near. Losing my parents happened so long ago that my memories of them grow ever fainter. I was only twelve, then, after all. But all the deaths last year were crystal clear. Losing Bow, and then the others still seemed more like a nightmare than reality. Loss is inevitable, they say. You grieve for a time, then find closure, they say. Whoever they are, they're full of shit. You grieve losses for sure, but those feelings don't stop and disappear as if closed inside a drawer or locked away somewhere. Yes, loss is inevitable, grief is too, but it changes you, becomes part of who you are. You learn to carry it, deal with it. But it never leaves.

Loss comes in many forms. Death is the worst, but loss of friendship isn't easy to deal with either. Jessica was here now, and it felt good to renew our friendship. Despite what she told me a few days ago about being tired, wanting to escape to a simpler life, I doubted she could give up singing, especially if "Running Free" became a hit. She was born to perform. Our relationship was destined to follow a pattern. We'd call each other often when she first left, she'd tell me what she was doing, I'd tell her about one horse or another. After a while, our talks would grow strained, the frequency would dwindle. I'd tell myself that our worlds were different, that it didn't matter.

I'd be wrong. It mattered. Losing Luke reminded me that friends were precious. He was gone before I knew it. Friendships were too precious to neglect.

My phone interrupted the musing. The caller's number wasn't one I recognized. "Hello?"

"Jessica please." The voice was male, polite, a bit muffled. I handed over the phone, guessing it was one of her crew members.

Jessica listened for a moment, and then her eyes widened, her jaw dropped. "Stop it. Leave me alone."

"What's wrong?" I asked, frowning. "Who is that?"

She grimaced and threw the phone on the table as though it'd bitten her.

I grabbed it, listened. The line was dead.

"Him, that guy," she said, rubbing her forehead.

"Michael Turner? How'd he know you're here right now? And how did he get my number?" I asked, knowing the answer. A town as small as Pinedale Springs seldom has a homegrown celebrity. Never mind that Jessica Parker wasn't world famous, the fact that she grew up here and everyone knew her memorable hit song sufficed. Also, right after the mustang incident on stage, Jessica had announced to the crowd that I was her friend. News stories followed. I tried redialing the number, but it'd been blocked.

Her hand remained over her face. "He... Oh God," she said, her voice muffled.

"What'd he say?" Roy asked, frowning.

She dropped her hand, shook her head. "Started with the usual. He is the only one who really cares about me." She paused, grimacing. "Said he'd be the best lover I ever had. Then came details, including the size of his..."

"What else?" I asked.

"He said judgment day is coming, a red-letter day... said he can't help it if anything bad happens." She began crying. "He said he has another knife just like the one he gave me."

143

"We'll find him," I said, hoping I was right.

Roy call Sheriff Plackmon and he was already on his way out to talk with us about the situation at Soda Creek Cliffs.

Roy and I met him at his truck. "Jessica's fanatic fan is escalating," Roy said as we headed to the house.

Inside, Sheriff Plackmon questioned Jessica, took notes. "We'll do everything we can to keep you safe," he said. He knew better than to make promises.

"Does your wife do any profiling?" I asked.

"Of stalkers, you mean?"

"Yeah."

"Courtney provides opinions for my department when needed since she is a psychologist, but deviant behavior is not her specialty."

Even so, it couldn't hurt to have a chat with Courtney Plackmon.

Deviant behavior wasn't my specialty either, but it sure as hell was my concern.

# CHAPTER NINETEEN

THIS WAS THE second day that my training schedule held nothing but cancellations. I checked my appointment calendar, prioritized the afternoon's tasks and made some phone calls to reschedule riding lessons. Several horses needed attention to stay on track.

I still kept tabs on Phantom and the other four mustangs who'd been onstage. Only the pinto filly still seemed skittish, so I set aside daily quiet time with her for grooming and conveying calm. Outlaw, who came from the Pryor Mountains, had the typical stout and well-muscled stature of those herds and was good-natured and great under saddle even though when he first came to me, I'd thought his name fit his disposition. I was wrong.

There were two yearling filly Quarter horses to gently work each on long-lines, followed by another short and uneventful ride on a four-year-old gelding that was sold and would be going to a new owner in a few days. Next came a five-year-old Thoroughbred mare off the track that was a bit too spirited for her new owner, so after working her in the arena, I took her out on the trails and other than some mild side-step shying, she did fine. I was brushing Hotshot and about to pick out his feet when Roy approached.

"About to ride?" he asked.

I nodded.

"How about some company?"

"Sure, great."

"Isn't that the gelding that bucked you off?"

"Yeah, but I can't really blame him for getting excited. He's doing fine now."

"That's good."

Within minutes, I was mounted on Hotshot and Roy was on Mutt, his fabulous cutting horse. We headed to the trails behind our ranch. The sky was blue, the ride was relaxing, but our conversation was not.

"Ok, let's break it all down," I said, plunging right in.

Roy nodded. "Yeah, there's so much going on, it's hard to keep up with all of it."

"It began with this little guy," I said, leaning forward to pat Hotshot's neck. "No doubt it was Millie Dickson or one of her clan who rudely disrupted my lesson plan with a big yellow ball."

"The Dicksons have never liked mustangs."

"True. The question is, how far will they go to stop me from establishing a wild horse rescue? I also suspect they cut my front fence and spray-painted several young mustangs, but I can't prove any of it."

"They tend to act dumb, but they're actually cunning and dangerous."

"Agreed," I said, "although I don't think Millie or her husband shot the mustang we saw yesterday, but their son seems capable of just about anything."

"Why would anyone shoot just one? I mean, if the intent is to get rid of wild horses, whoever did it would've killed more of them."

"I know, it does seem strange, unless maybe the bay mare was a lead mare. With her out of the way, a judas mare could more easily be brought in to lead a herd into catch pens. Anyhow, yesterday's helicopter trip covered the entire range, and we didn't see evidence of the other eleven missing horses. No bones, nothing."

"Right," Roy agreed. "Whoever shot the bay must've had a completely different agenda."

"Yes."

Roy shrugged. "Back to the disappearances."

"The mustangs that disappeared were taken alive, so they must be worth a lot to someone for some reason. But no matter why the horses are disappearing, Luke Barnes must've stumbled on someone out there who didn't want to be seen."

"Maybe someone shot Spirit using Luke's rifle so it would look like Luke planned to jump off that ledge to his death."

"That's more likely than what the sheriff brought up," I said, "but I need to find out more about what Luke knew before he rode out there."

Roy rubbed his chin. "Meantime, I don't see how any of that is related to mustang incidents at our place or at the concert."

"If the Dickson clan meant to warn us, they should know I don't scare easily. And in the end, I'll succeed in seeing their sorry asses behind bars."

Roy grinned. "I'm glad I'm on your side."

I grinned too, but I was serious. Anyone who threatened me or my horses would find out I wasn't a woman to be messed with.

We fell silent for a while, just took time to enjoy the ride. Roy could totally relax on Mutt, of course, while I kept alert for possible antics with Hotshot. So far, though, he was a little saint, absorbing calmness not only from me but also from Roy's horse. When the trail leveled out for a stretch, we cued the horses into a trot and then a gradual increase to a full-out gallop. Other than a few half-hearted crow-hops while transitioning from one gait to the next, Hotshot did fine. With a few more weeks of training with emphasis on maintaining balance and the right attitude, the smart little gelding would make a quirky but reliable and sure-footed ranch horse. Once we'd slowed back down to walking our horses on a loose rein, our conversation resumed.

"Let's review things with Jessica and her stalker." Roy said.

"Things began with cut up lingerie, progressed to a package with a large knife, then a package with bullets, but that last one might've been meant for me. Progressively more steamy phone calls led to this latest threatening one. The collapsing fence and my scrambling mustangs at the concert might be related to Jessica or to me."

"Or both of you. Those bolts had definitely been messed with. Someone wanted to make a mockery of the mustangs on stage for sure."

"I knew better than to put my horses in that precarious position."

"But you'd worked with them, exposed them to more noises, brighter lights than what they actually faced on stage. If the corrals had held, it could've been great publicity. Actually, even the chaos ended up on more streaming news and online write ups than if everything had gone as planned."

"Even so, no amount of publicity is worth traumatizing my mustangs."

"I know that's how you feel, Margo. But in the end, both you and Jessica came out okay. And thanks to Phantom and to your calmness in the midst of hellish chaos, none of the mustangs were harmed physically."

"Okay, but the intent must've been to make both Jessica and I look foolish."

"I agree. What else has Jessica told you about this stalker guy?"

"His calls started out 'sweet,' then gradually got steamier. Said his name was Michael Turner, but Jessica doubts that's true. The package with the knife came the night of the concert, marked a turn to danger."

"What about the box of bullets?"

"Jessica found them, and a note saying only, 'Mustang Mayhem."

"Which seems aimed at both of you."

I sighed, nodded. "Then I found Evelyn, unconscious on the ground in front of our house."

Roy nodded. "Probably the stalker, maybe the only time he's actually assaulted anyone."

"Yes. And from the huge wad of chewing tobacco, it appeared he stood around awhile. But how did he know anyone would come out?"

"Right, weird, and not really in character for a stalker. But who else would hang around in the middle of the night?"

We were nearing home, and Hotshot remained calm, taking cues from me and also from Mutt.

"Everything has escalated since the band arrived," Roy said.

I nodded. "Yes, and it must be one of the three stagehands who chew."

Roy nodded too. "Being a stagehand traveling with the band is a perfect way for Jessica's stalker to stay close."

"Whoever hit Evelyn could've easily mistaken her for Jessica from behind. Same hair color, same length. And that person must've been lurking around outside for quite a while."

Roy turned, looked at me. "Meaning maybe he'd been at our house before. He knew how to approach the house without being detected."

"Yes, the so-called bodyguards aren't all that effective. And we can't expect much help from Sheriff Plackmon because he doesn't have the manpower."

"What is Frank's take on all this? I've tried to talk with him, but he's tight-lipped when he's around, and gone a lot."

I nodded. "True. He manages everything from the current gig to the next one, which will be in Oklahoma City. He seemed highly agitated the night of the concert and also the next morning. Told me his priority is keeping Jessica safe. Told me there was another 'over-zealous' fan, but that one flooded them with chocolate-covered cherries, then suddenly faded away."

"What do you think of Frank?"

"He's a control-freak," I said, "egotistical, quick to anger."

"Does he know about Jessica and Eric?"

"Jessica seems to think he doesn't. I'd be surprised if he didn't know."

Roy frowned. "I agree."

"So when are you heading away again?" I asked as we rode up to the barn and dismounted.

"All too soon, I'm afraid. Meantime you do your thing, and I'll see what I can dig up on your stagehands who chew."

I nodded. "And I'll make an appointment for input on stalker profiles." Courtney Plackmon didn't look like a highly educated woman, but that changed when she spoke. In her case, looks were surprising.

In other cases, looks might be deceiving.

So far, I'd pegged Millie Dickson and her clan as culprits because they looked the part.

But what if the culprits were hiding behind respectable positions. What if they neither looked nor acted like danger.

# CHAPTER TWENTY

**AFTER OUR RIDE**, Roy and I groomed the horses and did evening chores.

"I have some work-related emails to answer, calls to make," Roy said as we headed to the house. "I hate to say it, but I have to fly to Idaho tomorrow for a quick trip, meet with managers of a huge cattle operation near Boise who're having issues with their pastures." I'm sorry, Margo."

"No need to apologize! Traveling is part of your job, and I can take care of myself. Meanwhile, I need to head into town, speak to a few people."

After Roy hugged me and told me to be careful, I washed my hands and face, ran a comb through my hair and brushed the worst dirt from my breeches.

Investigating could morph into a full time job that neither Roy nor I had time for if we couldn't find at least the beginning pieces of this interlocking puzzle that involved too many unanswered questions. The one woman who might fill in some blanks was Ruth Dunn, the silver-haired dynamo who'd called me about the dead mustang. She swallowed rivers of gossip, doling it back out in drips or torrents, as she saw fit. If something was worth talking about, Ruth knew, and she spoke more freely in person than on the phone.

I parked outside the B&D Tack Shop on Main Street. A row of saddles, half Western, half English, lined up in the display window. Inside were bridles and bits, halters and lead ropes, everything imaginable for horses and certain gems for riders. Best of all was the tantalizing scent of new leather that always tempted me to just stand still inside and breathe it in.

Ruth, dressed as usual in spotless Levi's, plaid shirt and her signature denim vest with bright red lining, was unpacking a shipment of shiny metal bits. She and I maintained a wary friendship, the type that deteriorated into uncomfortable formality all too easily. We exchanged greetings, and I asked what she'd heard.

"About Luke Barnes, you mean?"

I nodded. I was also hoping she'd gotten wind of that fencing up in Far Canyon. But I wanted to hear the scuttlebutt about Luke first.

"People are saying he shot his horse," she said, "then jumped off that ledge to his death."

"Who's saying that?"

She shrugged. "Most everybody, beginning with Joe Gannon. You found him. What do you think?

"Not sure," I said, although I was certain that Luke had neither shot Spirit nor jumped off that cliff. As certain as I was back when people were speculating that my foster mother, Bow, had died of suicide. "I'm just gathering information."

"That man never settled down, just bedded one woman after the other." Her tone dripped righteous indignation. "Maybe killed himself over some love affair gone bad. God save his immortal soul."

I was tempted to make a comment about her own soul, but I bit my tongue. She and I had our differences and besides, I mostly admired Ruth. But my purpose today was listening to whatever she knew, whatever she'd heard. Didn't matter if I disagreed. I leaned on the counter, stared into a display case with assorted riding gloves. "So, uh, there's talk about his love life."

"Certainly," she said, almost smiling. "Goodness knows he's had most of the single women in town, some of the married too."

I chewed on my lower lip, stayed silent.

She sat down on a stool behind the counter, arms folded against her bony chest. "If he didn't jump off that cliff, maybe some jealous husband pushed him."

Possible. Except that a man intent on killing a rival would be more likely to do the deed in a fit of anger, confront Roy in the act. Didn't seem logical that a jealous husband would follow his victim out to the Cliffs and push him off a ledge. And it was harder yet to believe that such a rivalry would make even the maddest guy shoot Luke's horse.

I straightened up, moved away from the counter. "Any specific husbands come to mind?"

Ruth shrugged. "Ellie told me the other day that Doris broke down in tears at last week's bible study, asked us to pray for her."

I frowned. "Doris Gannon? You don't think she—"

"Everybody knows Joe hasn't been happy since they moved here, maybe never. He got tanked up one night at the Riverside," she went on, "told the bartender that he and Doris slept in separate beds."

How in the world did she hear this stuff? Probably kept notes on everyone within a hundred miles of town. I wondered what Ruth Dunn knew, or thought she knew, about my life.

"Doris is a good ten years younger than Joe," she added, raising her eyebrows.

"Uh, yeah," I said, "but still."

"Maybe he has, you know, problems in bed."

"Hmm." Sexual prowess, or lack thereof, was not something I cared to consider about Joe Gannon. But if Doris was out searching for bodily pleasure around town, she didn't seem like Luke's type. She wasn't a bad looking woman, but I couldn't imagine the two of them having a conversation much less a sexual encounter. She admired bibles, he admired bodies. And besides, there was Rosie Garcia, who claimed she was about to become Luke's one and only.

"Heard anything else about Joe?" I asked.

"Other than the fact that he thinks wild horses are a nuisance, he is a good man."

"Uh-huh," I said. Good man or not, he seemed more shocked than saddened by Luke's death.

"Comes to church every Sunday," she said, giving me a look implying that the path to salvation began inside buildings adorned with steeples.

Religion was one of the topics I never discussed with Ruth Dunn. "So you know him well."

"Not really. Talked to him a time or two is all. Can't imagine him killing anyone. He runs the BLM office by the book. It's no secret that he didn't get along with Luke."

"True," I said. Luke wasn't the type to fit into the government politics or red tape. He often clashed with authority, especially when it came to laws regarding the mustangs. Surprising that Joe's predecessors hadn't fired him long ago.

"Did you talk to Joe about the dead horse?" I asked.

"Of course. Called him the same day I heard about it. He didn't have many details, said he'd send someone out to investigate when possible. Such a shame." She paused, shook her head. "This town's full of problems. Speaking of which, I hear your friend has herself a stalker."

I nodded. "What've you heard about that?"

"Nothing. Haven't heard a thing. What's this world coming to, anyhow? If more folks went to church regular like they should, they'd learn to love one another instead of all this shameful business."

I was mulling that over when the shop door opened. Ernie Martinez strolled in and asked if the Billy Cook saddle he'd ordered was in yet. Ruth nodded, disappeared into the back room and returned with a Western saddle, carrying the heavy leather with ease.

He pulled out a wad of cash from a weathered billfold, and the two of them bantered back and forth about cattle and fencing. Ever since Parkinson's disease had struck Ruth's beloved husband, Jim, robbing him of dignity and landing him in a wheelchair, Ruth assumed responsibility for running both their ranch and also ran the B&D Tack Store. Ernie and his wife, Edna, extended a helping hand whenever they could.

Many spreads in this part of Western Colorado bordered on the White River National Forest, where towering ponderosa pine and Douglas fir marched over hillsides while prickly but beautiful blue spruce cozied up to riverbanks. Much greener, vastly different than Soda Creek Cliffs which held drought tolerant pinyon pines and junipers. Rather than mustangs, the wetter forest sheltered elk and deer, along with echoes of Native American Utes. Deeper into the mountains, the Flat Tops Wilderness came as close to untrampled ground as the modern world allowed.

I left Ruth, thinking about the next person I needed to speak with. But it was too late to catch Mary Lou today. I'd have to call the BLM secretary in the morning. I also had to get out to Luke's house for a look around. The sheriff had surely done that by now, but I wanted to see his place for myself.

When I got back to the ranch, Roy was inside packing for his Idaho trip. Jessica and Frank sat on the porch, and before I got out of my truck, I could tell something was wrong.

"What happened?"

"The bastard did it again," Frank said. He had one arm around Jessica, and her head was on his shoulder.

So Michael Turner. Again.

"What now?"

Jessica shivered, hugged Louie tighter. She sniffed again, blotted her eyes with a tissue. "He's gonna kill me!" She shook her head, mumbled something I couldn't understand.

"Another call?"

"No, a letter, a horrid one," Frank said. "Ken, our driver, found it in the cab of his truck. This has gone too far. Way too far. I will find the idiot who's threatening Jessica and strangle him with my bare hands."

"What was in the letter?"

Jessica answered, her voice cracking. "Said that if he can't have me, no one can, so he'd rather see me dead." Louie sat at her feet, and she pulled the little guy onto her lap. The dog's tail flapped against her legs. "I can't take much more of this," Jessica said, beginning to cry.

Frank pulled her closer, stroked her hair. "I'll put a stop to this!"

"Have you told the Sheriff?"

"He's on his way," Frank said, "but what can he do? His resources in this little town are limited."

"Can I see the letter?"

"Whatever for?" Frank asked.

But Jessica reached into her pocket, handed me a piece of paper. "Here."

"I'd better not touch it in case there are fingerprints."

"Perhaps you read too many mystery novels," Frank said, wrinkling his nose.

"No, she has a point," Jessica said, "although you and I have both touched it. She held it up by the edges for me. It was immediately apparent what had frightened her the most. The guy asked if she'd kept the knife he'd sent, said he was coming to use it, which was bad enough. Huge uneven letters occupied the bottom half of the page. 'All my love, M.T.' was scrawled in what looked like bright red blood.

Michael Turner might've started out as a sweet-talking, love-stuck fan, but rage crept in. Except for that last part, the letter was typed. No spelling errors, the grammar correct.

Jessica wiped her eyes, sighed. "I can't stand not knowing who this guy is, worrying about when he might appear."

"I've been thinking about a plan," I said.

"I must ask you to stay out of this."

"No, Frank, I asked her to help," Jessica said.

"Margo is a horse trainer, my Dear, she's hardly qualified."

"Stop it Frank, just stop."

He rose and gave me a withering look. "As you wish, my Dear," he said, rising and stomping into the house.

"Frank is right," I said. "I can't promise anything, but I have a plan that might bring this guy out of hiding. Besides, there's a good chance this stalker is the one who sabotaged the corral, let my mustangs loose on stage, so besides putting a stop to your threats, I've got a personal score to settle with him." I peered toward the barn, scanned the area in front of the house, the long driveway curving between my front pastures. No one lurking, nothing alarming. The dirt road out front was quiet, devoid of telltale dust plumes.

"I'll need your bodyguard to back me up," I said. "Will Frank allow that?"

Jessica raised her hands, squeezed her fingers into fists. "I'll make sure he does."

Sheriff Plackmon came within minutes, and both Roy and Frank reappeared. The sheriff verified that the crime lab might be able to raise fingerprints from the letter. "We'll do our best to identify this person," he told us.

"Any idea how to bring him out in the open?" Frank asked.

"Stalkers like this fellow can be elusive, but sooner or later they all slip up."

It sounded like a bad idea to just wait until Michael Turner slipped up.

"I know what you're thinking," Sheriff Plackmon said, turning to me. "You're wanting this guy found right now. We all do. Michael Turner. Any idea what his real name is?"

Everyone shook their heads.

He asked more questions, made notes, then left with the letter, carefully placed in a plastic bag.

"Before this, the guy was just toying with you," I said, "but now maybe you'd be safer in town than out here."

"No," Jessica said, shaking her head. "No way. I don't want my life further disrupted by some crazy fan."

"I am doing my best to protect you, my Darling," Frank said, and then he turned to me. "And although I appreciate your willingness to help, I don't want you in jeopardy, either. You must stick with the animals, my Dear."

The way he said 'dear' sounded more menacing than soothing. Or maybe I was just paranoid.

"Sorry, Margo, but I side with Frank on this," Roy said.

I gave Roy a look that said he and I would be chatting later about this.

"Thanks for the concern, Frank," I said. I knew Roy meant well and I assumed Frank did too, but there was something about Jessica's husband that still bothered me. Maybe it was his chauvinistic undertone.

He kissed Jessica, told her he had to meet someone in Denver and would be gone a day or two.

"I just want to be normal, left alone to live my life," Jessica told me after Frank left.

But what was normal. At the moment, I knew what it wasn't. Not some crazed stalker. Not the dead mustang, the disappearing herds, nor my own horses bursting across a stage. Not the crazy stuff that happened on my own ranch, either. And certainly not the deaths of Luke and Spirit. Usually, my biggest worry was maintaining a training schedule, giving riding lessons and dealing with the BLM or a few disruptive neighbors who disagreed with my plans for a mustang refuge. Then more energy companies arrived, followed by my long-time friend Jessica Parker and her entourage, and everyone brought new problems.

I despised the drillers, loved Jessica, but both of them were in the mix that had turned my world upside down, inside out.

# CHAPTER TWENTY ONE

Roy left early the next day right after helping with morning chores and Frank also left on business. The Parker Co. people remained in town, so the house seemed deliciously relaxing with just Jessica and me at breakfast. One of the bodyguards patrolled on foot while the other occupied the big black SUV at the ranch entrance, but they never came inside the house unless we called them, and I had no plans to do that.

Jessica ate only half a piece of toast, but she nodded when I offered more tea. As I added milk and two teaspoons of sugar to her mug, my thoughts flashed back to college when she and I roomed together and knew each other's preferences. I still took tea black, she used milk and sugar, and we both gravitated toward Earl Grey. Sometimes, knowing the little things about a person renews friendship. Maybe now that Jessica and I had time alone together, our bonds could fully rejuvenate.

"I know Frank thinks he and the so-called bodyguards can protect me, Margo, but I'm not so sure. I'm scared to death. Tell me your plan."

"Okay, but I can't make any promises."

"I know, but I trust you," she said, sipping tea.

"Okay, then" I said, trying to sound more confident than I felt. "My perspective is different from pros like Sheriff Plackmon, which might be an advantage. I've tried to take a logical approach like I use in training horses; take one issue at a time, deal with it, move on. So first of all, let's go over what we know about this stalker."

"Not that much."

"Let's review the calls, the letters, the packages. You're keeping a log, right?"

She retrieved it and we reviewed dates and times, what was said and done. It was clear that the so-called Michael Turner maintained control by keeping his prey jittery, guessing. Taken as a whole, his actions looked calculating, planned. And escalating.

"It's time to turn the tables, make this guy reveal himself," I said, "and in order to succeed, we need as much insight as possible."

"Insight?"

I nodded. "The more we know about what makes this guy tick, the more it'll help us figure out who he is, how to snare him." I finished my tea, placed the mug on the kitchen counter. "Let me make a call."

Courtney Plackmon was at her office and answered the phone herself. Within several hours, Jessica and I were seated across from the area's only psychologist. Courtney herself ushered us in, as usual, and we settled into comfy chairs. She sat across from us, slender legs crossed, hands rested in her lap.

"Jessica Parker," she said, her smile wide. "It's such a pleasure to meet you. Your concert was wonderful."

"Thanks," Jessica said, smiling too.

I glanced from Jessica to Courtney, both serenely beautiful. Jessica wore skin-tight jeans, a red top that highlighted long mahogany curls and makeup only slightly diminished from her onstage glam. Courtney's long blonde hair, blue eyes, and sculpted cheeks made her look more like a model than a psychologist. Didn't seem like the type who'd pick Sheriff Plackmon for a spouse, either, but it was easy to see why the men in town signed up for counseling without protest. I'd met with her a handful of times after all that'd happened last year.

"Ben mentioned that you're having some problems with a fan," Courtney said. "How can I help?"

Both women looked at me.

I blinked, feeling stupid. Everybody does have a first name. Roy and

I had dinner with the Plackmons a few times, but I could never bring myself to address the sheriff as simply Ben. "Well, the sheriff, er, Ben, said that this fan might be, uh, crazy. Either that, or he's overcome with infatuation. If we understood more about him, it'd be easier to find him."

"Maybe so," Courtney said, nodding, "as you know, I occasionally do some criminal profiling for the sheriff's department, but my specialty is individual or marriage counseling. I'll do what I can, though. Begin by telling me everything that's happened, everything you know or surmise about this person."

Jessica did that, from the sweet calls and the cut-up lingerie that seemed almost comical to the knife that signaled increasing danger. Then came this latest letter, even more sinister. In the exchange that followed, Courtney Plackmon verified that Michael Turner's escalation from admiration to obsession followed a classic pattern. She agreed that the name was certainly bogus, and she went on to say that he was probably nearby, closer than suspected.

"Maybe a member of the stage crew?" I asked. I already considered that. Several of the crew used chewing tobacco, for instance, and I had found that fresh wad of Skoal under our ponderosa the night Evelyn was hit on the head.

"Quite possible," she said.

"Then he knows I have pretend bodyguards," Jessica said "and he knows they're not professionals, but they are big and tough."

"True, but don't be complacent," Courtney said. "Stalkers are persistent. And as you already realize, dangerous. Also, as you've surmised, this is certainly a male."

Jessica chewed her lower lip.

"What turns someone into a stalker?" I asked.

"A subject of some debate, but one plausible theory says these people either have a personality disorder or some other mental instability. They tend to have low self-esteem, live in a fantasy world. They feel rejected, isolated, don't relate well to others. Some present as charming, many are quite shy. They're often obsessive, but may be bipolar or even have some type of schizophrenia."

I nodded. "There's information on the internet that mentioned some of that. So how do you tell the difference?"

"It's not obvious, at least not initially. In any case, by the time things get out of control, jealousy often leads to rage. They have a need for control, for a sense of power."

"You're saying their logic is different from most people?"

"For sure," Courtney said, "but remember that we're talking generalizations. No one fits an exact mold. Take the three of us. We're women, about the same age, slender, American, English speaking. We're all in relationships. These similarities fit, and yet they're not sufficient to distinguish us one from the other."

"So how can we figure out specifics about this guy?"

"Look for patterns, details. Study the log you've made. Do you still have his letters?"

Jessica nodded. "With the exception of the last one, which the sheriff, uh, your husband, has."

"It can't hurt for the two of you to think things over repeatedly. Gives you some feeling of control, of doing something rather than just waiting for the next wave of terror. You may come up with one small but useful detail you've overlooked, so try to examine all angles, go beyond the obvious."

"I'm thinking we can trick him into revealing himself," I said.

"That might work," Courtney said. "But it could also backfire, make him more determined to carry out whatever ultimate plan he has in mind. Don't underestimate this person. He has a goal of his own, one that seems logical in his particular view of things."

"On the other hand," I said, "the longer this goes on, the more risks this guy takes. No plan will be perfect."

"Be very cautious," Courtney said as we left her office.

Once we got outside, I called Joe Gannon's office, and Mary Lou said he'd be happy to meet with Jessica.

"So you want him buttered up, right? But why?"

"To start with, he hates mustangs, and I need his approval to establish a refuge."

She nodded. "Ok, I get it. I'll tell him how wonderful mustangs are, how wonderful you are."

"Might be better to start off telling him you actually dislike mustangs to get him to talk freely about them. And don't mention me at all, not right away at least."

Everyone in the office stood up when we entered. They seldom even looked up when I went there alone.

Mary Lou spoke first. "Your singing was wonderful!"

Jessica smiled. "Thank you."

One of the guys whose name I didn't know approached us. "Could you sing for us?"

"Well, I…" Jessica began.

"Now settle down, everyone," Mary Lou said. "Jessica is only here to see Mr. Gannon. If you'll come with me, please, Ms. Parker."

Jessica gave everyone a thousand-watt smile and disappeared into Gannon's office, leaving me standing near the door.

She emerged in about fifteen minutes, followed closely by Joe Gannon himself. "I'll think about what you said, Ms. Parker."

"Thanks, Joe. And please call me Jessica."

"All right then, Jessica, and come back soon," Gannon said, his face flushing bright red. He didn't look my way, no doubt didn't notice me at all.

"So how'd it go?" I asked when we were outside.

"I see what you mean about that guy. He's… well, I get a bad vibe. I wouldn't want to spend much time around him."

"I know, but it looked like you charmed the heck of him. He was practically slobbering over you."

"Don't remind me. But I managed to compliment him on taking care of mustangs, even though I said those animals are scrawny and just not very useful. Next, I said he looks like the type who knows how to manage money. Then I mentioned how much his department and the entire Federal government could save by removing some mustangs to private refuges rather than the costly holding pens."

"Great! What'd he say?"

"Not much. He just kept smiling. He didn't disagree with anything I said."

"No, I bet he didn't."

"I told him it was terrifying to see one of his men, the one named Luke, dead out at Soda Creek Cliffs. And his poor horse, too. I asked if he knew what'd happened, and he said he was personally investigating."

I shook my head. "As if. But thanks, you did good. If he agrees to let me establish a refuge, I'll owe you big time. So are your backup singers staying in town again?" I asked as we strolled down the street.

"Uh-huh, which I'm happy to say gives you and I more alone time."

"Good. And Courtney's input gave me confidence in my plan."

"Exactly when will you tell me the details?"

"Soon."

We stopped, waiting for a truck to go by before crossing the street. Jessica turned to me. "Hey, Margo, you're frowning. What's up?"

"I don't know. I mean yes, my plan sounds good, I suppose. But can I really snare the guy?"

"I'm sorry, Margo. I don't want you doing something dangerous."

"But I live for danger."

"Uh-huh, sure you do."

I shrugged. "I'm just worried, that's all. We'll recheck your logs, look again for patterns. Meantime, as long as we're in town, let's stop in and see if the sheriff has any news."

Sheriff Plackmon looked up as we entered his office. "Good afternoon, have a seat. We found several fingerprints on the letter sent to you, Jessica."

Jessica and I leaned forward.

"Your fingerprints and also Frank's, as expected. And a third set, belonging to someone else."

My eyebrows lifted. "And?"

"I have no idea who, not yet. But we're running those unidentified prints through every available system. It'll take a while, but if your stalker has any priors, we'll get a name. Meantime, you two be careful. Don't be doing anything dangerous, Margo."

I grinned. "Who, me?

"Well, that was disappointing," Jessica said after we were in the truck.

I nodded. "One more stop for pizza, then back to the ranch."

"Sounds good. I'm hungry."

Harvey's Pizza Parlor sat near the outskirts of town. The place featured mismatched wooden chairs and a general lack of décor, but it was clean, the aromas were first class and so were the pizzas. Thick crust, exquisite sauce, selections of any topping you might want and some you'd never thought of, mounds of mozzarella.

We got out of the truck, and a small crowd descended on Jessica. She paused for autographs and smiled for smart phone photos in front of Harvey's. To locals, she was a homegrown celebrity. What struck me was how much Jessica seemed to enjoy the attention, the celebrity treatment. She'd said that she wanted to stop performing, slide into obscurity. Attention turned her into someone different, someone in her element.

We finally got inside Harvey's, and while we waited for pizza, I asked if she had wigs.

Jessica laughed. "Yes, but I don't know why you're curious about that. Still, if anybody can untwist what's going on, it's you."

"Uh, well, thanks," I said.

"I've always had confidence in you."

I gave her a half-smile and hoped her confidence wasn't misplaced.

When we got back to the ranch, we sat on the front porch eating pizza. Zap, Fetch and Louie settled at our feet, hoping for handouts.

"I do have a plan," I said, "and it unfolds tonight."

"Tonight? Okay, how?"

I pointed to a little brown orb weaver on a web by the porch railing. "See the spider?"

She made a face. "This some sort of riddle?"

"You bet. I'll be the one spinning a web, luring the stalker in, entangling him."

# CHAPTER TWENTY TWO

"Courtney Plackmon advised taking another look at everything about this guy."

Jessica nodded, got up and gathered her logbook and the letters.

Once again, we went through everything and once again, we came up empty-handed.

"The answer is here, but it's hidden."

"I know," Jessica said, sighing.

"Did you recognize this guy's voice at all, ever wonder if he was a former boyfriend?"

"His voice was always muffled, disguised."

"Ok, so that still points to him being someone you know or someone always nearby."

"I can't imagine it being a former boyfriend. How about a crew member?"

I nodded. "Exactly. And I found only three crew members who chew tobacco: Ken Munson, your truck driver, Mark Hanson, and Jake Campbell, both stage crew. One of them might've lingered around outside this house, probably waiting for you to... I dunno what, come out and talk to him or whatever, but he hit Evelyn on the head instead." I paused. "The question is, what was his intent that night?"

"Who knows?"

"You and Evelyn do look alike, especially your hair. So he could've mistaken Evelyn for you."

"Yes. People comment on that all the time, ask if we're sisters."

"She could serve as your double."

Jessica frowned. "Don't even think it. You can't put her in danger!"

"I don't intend to. I asked about wigs earlier, right?"

"You did, yes. Why?"

"Because later, when it's dark, you're going to dress me up, secure a wig on my noggin, and then I'll look at least passably like you."

"So you'll go out and catch this guy with your bare hands?"

"Not with my bare hands, but I will be the bait that brings him in."

Jessica sighed. "I don't want you getting hurt, Margo."

"I don't intend to be hurt. And I do know how to take care of myself. Tell me what you know about these three with the tobacco chewing habit: Ken Munson, Mark Hanson and Jake Campbell."

Jessica tilted her head to one side. "Not much," she said. "I mean, they're all just average guys. Ken is quiet. Guess you could say he's a bit odd. I don't know Mark all that well, but he's never caused any trouble. And Jake is a really sweet freckle-faced kid who looks a lot younger than he is." She frowned. "I can't imagine any of them being a stalker, except possibly Ken."

"Have you noticed any changes in the way any crew member treats you lately?"

"I don't think so. I've never spent much time with either Ken or Mark. Now Jake, there's a talkative guy."

"I noticed," I said. "He came up to me at the gas station, just started chatting." I pulled out my list of names. "And Mark, he's the chubby one with a high-pitched voice."

"Uh, yes," Jessica said. "He hangs out with two or three other stagehands."

"There are a few guys around Pinedale who chew. One guy at the feed store always has a wad of the stuff tucked between his teeth and lip. The only other one I'm aware of is Nick Dickson, Millie's son. He's a big guy, ex-marine. But he's lived on the Dickson ranch for a while now, so I can't imagine how he'd be able to cut your lingerie when he wasn't anywhere near you until you arrived."

"Ok, let's not even put him on the list."

"I agree. The letters always have perfect spelling, correct grammar. There's a certain level of sophistication."

Jessica nodded. "Good point."

"The only way we're going to find this guy is to make him come to us."

Jessica frowned. "And that means putting you in danger?"

"Yeah, a little. We need for him think you want to meet with him, talk things over. So I typed up a letter yesterday, wrote: 'Important, for Michael Turner,' gave it to Derrick, asked him to pass it on."

"What if he isn't one of the crew?"

"That's possible, sure," I said. "But my gut instinct says our little deviant has been taking paychecks from the Parker Company."

"What a thought."

"For sure. But otherwise how would this guy find out that you're staying with me? And if he is a stranger, how would he manage to slip by the stage crew and place boxes or letters in the truck?"

"Do you think Ken put things there himself? I mean, he even sleeps in the cab of that truck."

"Possibly," I replied.

"I really hate to think that it's somebody on the crew. The Parker Company is a small group, friendly and supportive."

"All it takes is one oddball."

"What else did your letter say?"

"Just said where and when to meet and that you wanted to talk. That's all."

"I don't like this."

"I'm not terribly fond of it myself, but he's escalating and needs to be stopped."

I asked her for any information the Parker Company had on the families of Ken, Mark and Jake. Then I picked up the phone. Mark's mother was a soft-spoken woman with two other sons, and in the course of conversation, she readily admitted that Mark was the one who worried her. He'd been kicked out of high school shortly before graduating because he had, in her words, an unfortunate tendency to harass the girls. I asked for specifics, but the mother clammed up and then ended the call. Harassing girls could mean a lot of things, and the fact that the mother even mentioned this might point to something on the serious side of 'harassing.'

Jake's father claimed that his son graduated high school near the top of his class. Almost an honor student, almost a saint according to this proud dad, who went on to say that Jake was working to earn tuition money for college.

Ken remained an enigma. Although he'd provided the Parker Company with the phone number of an ex-wife, the number was no longer valid. Maybe she'd moved. Maybe she never existed.

The bait letter was short and to the point. A bit flattering, a plea to 'just get along' and specifying a meeting at 9PM tonight near the Fairgrounds where the concert was held.

"He won't come," Jessica said. "He'll know it's a trap."

"Maybe. But he'll be excited by your invitation, hopefully hyped up enough to overlook the downside. This guy is persistent but probably wacko, so this could work."

"Frank will be gone a few days, but I thought you said Roy is due back any time."

I nodded. "Yes, told me he'll be home tomorrow."

"That's good, Margo. Roy can help keep you safe. This could be very dangerous."

"We need to do this before Roy returns. He's too protective. I want one of your bodyguards hidden nearby. If and when the guy appears, the big guy and I can restrain him."

"How about the sheriff?"

"I'll call him as soon as we have the guy, not before."

Jessica rubbed her forehead. "So much can go wrong. I'm... I'm scared for you."

"This is our best chance to nab this guy before he escalates even more. You asked me to help, Jessica. So give tonight's plan a chance, okay?"

"I guess."

"Good. And don't tell anyone a thing about this."

"But the stage crew will already know! Gossip spreads fast."

"Sure, and that's just what we want. If anyone calls you, say Eric, Bianca, Evelyn or whoever, act totally shocked."

Jessica nodded.

"All right. Meantime, how about a nice relaxing ride?"

"Seriously?"

I nodded. "I have someone coming to look at a few Quarter horses tomorrow morning, so I need to bring them in from pasture, put them through their paces."

Jessica's eyes widened.

I smiled. "I'll put you on Hawk."

She put her hands over her chest. "Okay sure. Hawk."

"We'll tell the bodyguards right before we get things rolling."

"Right. And how do we know that one of those two aren't my stalker?"

"We don't, not for sure. But neither of them chew, so that's good." I had no intention of admitting to Jessica that tonight's plan was more of a shot in the dark than a sure thing. But it was better to be doing something instead of chewing our fingernails and wondering what would happen next. This way, we had at least the semblance of taking charge of the situation.

Jessica brought Hawk in from pasture while I brought Toby and Big Red. They were four-year-old Quarter horses I had in training for potential buyers. After helping Jessica get Hawk tacked up, I saddled Toby, and we all had a short and uneventful ride in my arena. Big Red came next. This chestnut gelding had a temperament similar to Hotshot's. Unlike the mustang, Big Red was handled properly as a foal, but he still regarded humans as adversaries. More heavily boned than a mustang, but just as fiery and athletic. He was reasonable at a walk and a trot in the confines of my arena, although cantering still presented some balance issues. Trail work would help.

Late afternoon was my favorite time to ride. The spring sun eased to the west, casting a soft glow and less heat than earlier in the day. As always, Hawk moved through the forest with ease and patience. Big Red wove side to side a bit in the way of all green horses, but he seemed relaxed and amenable to cues this day.

A slight breeze waved through ponderosa branches and fluttered aspen leaves that would be turning gold in a few short weeks. A stellar jay squawked from the top of a nearby tree, then swooped in front of us, a sudden flash of blue. Big Red's neck rose, he shied sideways. Nothing much. All I did was sit deeper in the saddle and he settled right down.

My mind drifted, wondering if tonight's little scheme would work. The trees gave way to a small meadow, more or less even ground with tufts of grass interspersed with bluebells. All of a sudden, the gelding spooked again, whirling this time and then taking off as if in a race. I automatically sat back and attempted to circle him, but he'd caught me off guard, so it took more effort than usual to persuade him to circle, slow down, turn some more. Finally, he stopped, but he was panting, tossing his head. "Easy now, Fella," I said, "what was that all about, huh?" He snorted. And then he threw his head up, darted forward a ways, lowered his head and starting bucking like a rodeo bronco. Agile beast. And determined to get rid of me. He didn't manage it on the first buck, nor the second, but the third was a whopper. I lost first one stirrup, then the other. There's no good way to fall off a horse. I'd fallen before, of course, it's inevitable now and then. Always happened fast, but at the same time felt like a long way to the ground. And the landing was always hard.

Jessica brought Hawk beside me. "You okay?"

I nodded. "Just keep Hawk right here until I have the gelding."

The big chestnut had moved only a few yards, lowered his head again, this time to graze. I eased myself up, brushed off, and took one step, then another. All my parts seemed to be in working order, although my butt already hurt. I knew from past experience that the stiffness would worsen in a few hours, and I'd feel double my age by tomorrow. Now, though, I began making my way slowly toward Big Red. The snot saw me, of course, but he kept on munching, nonchalant. If I approached too fast, he'd run, possibly all the way back to the barn. I couldn't allow him to get away with that, so I began talking to him in a soothing tone. His ears twitched, his long silky tail moved side to side.

Patience is essential for anyone who works with horses, especially young ones. Fortunately, I'd been in this situation before, which gave me the advantage. It took only a minute to catch the gelding. He stood still while I checked the girth and remounted. He offered no additional problems on the way home, at least not until he stumbled. We were at the property line, the barn in sight when his right front hoof slipped on a rock. His next step and the one after that were lame ones, so I dismounted and lifted his leg. No rocks embedded between the inner rim of his shoe and the shock absorbing frog in the middle. I put the leg down, led him forward a few steps. He remained off just a bit, putting partial weight on the right front, not fully lame. Probably a mild stone bruise. I always carried a rubber Easy Boot, but he didn't seem to need it.

Jessica rode while I led the gelding back to the barn. We unsaddled and groomed them, let Hawk out to pasture, put Big Red in the round pen for the night with a generous flake of grass hay. Chances were he'd be moving fine by morning. Meantime, best to keep him confined rather than letting him run out in pasture.

My cell rang with the special chime I'd programmed for when Roy called.

"How're things in Idaho?"

"Not bad, but I miss you. And you sound upset. What's up?"

"I'm tired, that's all. Just got bucked off Big Red."

"Damn him. He's a handful, that's for sure."

"Tell me about it. And I've got a prospective buyer coming tomorrow."

"Do you think Big Red is ready for a new home?"

"Actually, no. He demonstrated that today. So I'll show the buyer some others instead. They're looking for large boned Quarter types."

"Okay, but tell me the truth, Margo. Are you hurt?"

"No, I'm really not. You know how it goes. I'll just feel a little stiff and sore by morning. And Big Red stumbled, probable stone bruise, so I put him in the round pen for the night."

"Who is there with you?"

"Just Jessica and her bodyguards."

"I'm sorry I'm not there. Have a nice quiet evening, okay?"

"Um, yeah, I'll try," I said, although my forecast for the evening ahead held anything but quiet.

# CHAPTER TWENTY-THREE

THE LAST THING I felt like doing after the hard fall I'd just taken was donning a wig and luring Jessica's stalker out of the shadows. But no way to back out now. Jessica arranged for one bodyguard to come with me while the other one remained at the ranch with her.

She dressed me up in her clothes, secured a wig, applied gobs of makeup and even false eyelashes. I protested that the guy would only be seeing me from a distance, but she seemed to enjoy transforming me into a glamour girl. I stowed my gun, a can of bear spray, and my phone in one of Jessica's purses.

"Wow! You look just like me."

I laughed. "If you say so." I grabbed two Aleve pills, washed them down with a glass of water.

At half past eight, the so-called bodyguard and I set out for the Fairgrounds. It had seemed like such a good plan, until I walked out to the designated spot. Now that I was here, I couldn't believe this was my idea. Despite the big guy posted out of sight but within shouting distance, I felt alone, vulnerable. Some investigator I turned out to be. I made myself sit still despite a temptation to keep looking behind me, and an even stronger temptation to just get up and go home, forget this insanity.

Each time I fell off a horse, it took a couple hours for the stiffness and aching to begin. This time was no exception, and sitting still on a hard bench didn't help. Dusk morphed into dark, and it looked like the guy was a no-show. Maybe he came, saw through my disguise and knew I was an impostor and this was a trap.

Seemed like I sat there for hours.

And then, behind me, footsteps.

I swallowed hard, goose bumps dotting my arms. Who the hell came up with the word goose bumps, anyhow. Fear bumps sounded way more accurate. My pulse transitioned from trot into full gallop, my breathing went shallow. Slowly, casual-like, I turned my head partway, just a glance over my left shoulder.

The footsteps belonged to what looked like a tall human. Too tall to be a woman. Too dark to see a face. It'd been my idea to meet away from streetlights, a decision I now regretted. Hell, I regretted being here at all! What was I thinking? Which one would it be; Mark the chubby one, Ken the loner, or freckle-faced Jake? Maybe all three of them were coming, one after the other. Maybe they all had guns, knives.

Which was worse?

The footsteps kept coming. Only one set of footsteps. So far.

While planning this seemed super smooth, the reality of being here right now felt like the stupidest damn thing I'd ever done. What the hell was I thinking? Ok, I wasn't thinking at all.

I was strong for a 5-foot-two female. I mean, sure, I can throw heavy bales of hay all around. But hay doesn't fight back, it doesn't have guns or knives. The chance I could wrestle a gun or a knife away from one guy intent on stabbing me was probably slim to none. If all three guys showed up, my chances lowered all the way from none to no effing way.

The footsteps kept coming, but slow, as if to further scare the shit out of me.

I inhaled, held my breath, considered getting up, running like hell.

But no, I stayed there, frozen like a deer in front of a speeding truck.

I wondered what it felt like to die, how long it took.

The fear bumps were snaking their way from my arms up to my neck. I tried to swallow, couldn't.

All of a sudden, other footsteps pounded nearby. I turned, saw the bodyguard.

"Hey you," he shouted, "stop right there, don't move a muscle."

I wanted to get up and run. I was barely breathing, just sitting there, immobilized by a crazy mixture of curiosity and fear.

"What the... Oh, please, I don't have any money," the guy said.

So the stalker thought he was being robbed. I almost laughed.

The bodyguard grabbed the guy from behind, immobilized his arms.

"My God, my God, please don't hurt me," the guy said.

This voice was familiar. Not at all what I expected.

I got up, moved toward him. And gasped. "Mr. Edwards! What're you doing here?"

This couldn't possibly be our stalker. The man was elderly, for one thing, and the kindest person I knew. He was a retired teacher, and many of the locals, including me, had scrawled algebra problems on the blackboard under his watchful gaze.

"Margo? Is that you? What's going on?"

"Let him go," I told the bodyguard, who loosened his grasp but didn't let go entirely. "We, uh, expected to catch someone here this evening."

"So you thought..." he paused, blinked. "Oh my goodness. I take a stroll here most evenings. Enjoy the solitude."

"I'm so sorry, Mr. Edwards."

"Never mind, my Dear. But I must keep moving, or I stiffen. Arthritis, you know."

"Yes, yes, of course. Have a nice walk, then."

The bodyguard returned to his hiding place and I reluctantly sat back down. I peeked at my phone inside Jessica's purse. The time was 9:03pm. The night air was crisp and cool, and I was getting even stiffer with every passing minute. What if the real stalker saw what happened to poor Mr. Edwards? But maybe the guy never intended to come.

Finally, about half past nine, I stood, sighed, and texted the bodyguard.

He joined me and we headed home, both of us silent. If he was disappointed, his face appeared void of emotion. I, on the other hand, felt weak with relief.

Jessica was sitting on the front porch and the other bodyguard was not far away.

She took one look at me. "What happened? Are you okay?"

"I scared myself to death just being there. And do you remember Mr. Edwards from high school?"

"Of course! He was so sweet. What about him?"

"Well, there were footsteps approaching right about nine. It was Mr. Edwards out for his evening stroll."

"No. Seriously?"

I felt like I deserved a celebratory Hershey's bar just for being alive. I went inside and grabbed a handful from my snack cupboard, gave one to Jessica. Then I sat down, unwrapped the last one and popped a sizable chunk into my mouth. Almost purred.

"I'm going down to check on Big Red," I said after a while, calling to my border collies.

On the way to the round pen near the barn, I had floodlights on, but I always took a flashlight in case my eyes didn't adjust quickly to the dark. Fetch and Zap ran ahead, as usual, chasing shadows.

The gelding seemed agitated, trotting back and forth on one side of the round pen with his neck high. He snorted as I approached. "Easy, Fella," I said. But as I drew nearer, I saw what was bothering him.

On the ground just inside the pen was a body, face up.

I ran the last few yards, knelt down and noticed a wet looking spot on the ground. I directed my flashlight there, saw that it was dark red. And then I shone the light on the bloodied face.

Jake Campbell, tall guy, freckled.

He was not just unconscious.

He was dead.

# CHAPTER TWENTY FOUR

I knelt down, pressed two fingers into his neck beside the Adam's apple. Cold skin, no pulse.

I kept current on basic first aid. Jake appeared beyond my help, or anyone else's, but starting CPR just in case is protocol.

The dogs cowered, sensing death, smelling it.

I grabbed my cell, put it on speaker, and without stopping CPR, I asked Siri to call 911 for the paramedics, then the sheriff, told both dispatchers I'd found a man down, appeared dead.

Took a while, but a high-pitched siren, faint at first but growing louder, signaled the ambulance's arrival with two paramedics.

"I couldn't detect a pulse," I told them, stepping back.

The paramedics nodded, resumed CPR where I'd left off, hooked Jake up to an EKG machine and portable oxygen, placed EKG leads. But when the tracing showed only a flat line, they sent the tracing to a doctor, looked up at me, shook their heads.

I hadn't seen Jessica and the bodyguards appear, but they'd heard the siren, of course.

I looked at them, shrugged.

Big Red remained on the far side of the pen. I haltered the gelding and led him inside the barn to a stall. Roy's voice was the only one I needed to hear. He answered on the first ring.

"Hi Sweetheart."

"I… oh Roy."

"What is it? What's wrong?"

"It's… Jake Campbell."

"Are you okay? Where are you?"

"I'm home. Jake is dead, in the round pen with Big Red."

"There's a red eye into Grand Junction. I'll be on it."

"I… yes."

"I love you Margo. I'll be there in a few hours."

I hung up, closed my eyes.

Jessica approached. "What? What's happening?" She came closer, stared at the body. "Jake? Oh my God!"

Before I could say anything, a siren blared as sheriff's SUV arrived and approached the barn. The siren ceased, but the blue and red lights kept flashing, painting the night sky with caution. Plackmon himself emerged from the vehicle, glanced from me to the paramedics.

"Total flatline," one of them said.

The sheriff turned to me. "You know him?"

I nodded. "Jake Campbell. He's one of the Parker Company crew members."

"Was there a horse in this pen?"

Another nod. I knew what he was about to say.

"Looks like this guy might have been kicked square in the face."

"I know." No disputing the fact that Jake's wound had a horseshoe shape.

"That's just one possibility among many," Sheriff Plackmon said. "We'll leave it to the coroner to determine cause." He pulled on gloves, leaned over. "What've we got here," he said, pulling a piece a paper from Jake's shirt pocket. Along with the paper came a tin of Skoal.

"There it is," I said.

The sheriff blinked at me. "What?"

"Skoal. The guy who hit Evelyn on the head left a wad of chewing tobacco buried under pine needles outside one of my windows. Jake was one of three who use the stuff."

The sheriff unfolded the paper, looked at it, frowning.

"What?" I asked, and Jessica crowded close.

He grimaced. "Starts out 'My Dearest Jessica, it's signed All My Love, M.T. Wrote that he only wanted to make her happy. Said he'd rather be dead than live without her. Apologized about rigging the corral at her concert so it pulled apart on cue, says he loves horses, was real sorry to do that." Still wearing gloves, he folded the letter, placed it in a plastic bag.

"Michael Turner," I said, catching my breath, "is... Jake Campbell?"

Jessica's eyes were wide, mouth open, but she said nothing.

The sheriff had more questions for me, and after he finished, I asked him why he was on call so late.

"Nighttime deputy injured his back playing tag football. Rest of us rotating night calls."

"Oh, I'm sorry."

His lips curled into a smile. "It's duty, that's all. Things always happen at night." He turned to Jessica and her bodyguards, had them follow him to a bench outside the barn.

The Coroner arrived, and after a while Jake was zipped into a black body bag just as Frank Stanza emerged from a car driven by Ken Munson.

"What in the world?" Frank said, rushing to Jessica's side.

She looked at him, frowned. "I thought you'd be gone until tomorrow."

"Well, yes, my Darling, but I missed you, so I flew back. Just arrived." He paused, looked around. "Now will someone please tell me what's going on here! My God! Is that... a body bag?"

Jessica just nodded.

Frank turned to me.

"Jake Campbell," I said.

"But what happened?"

Before I could say more, Sheriff Plackmon interrupted. "I'll need to know who you are and why you're here, for starters."

"I'm Frank Stanza, in charge of the Parker Company. I manage Jessica Parker and everyone from singers to stage hands. I'm also married to Jessica."

The sheriff's expression remained neutral. "Where have you been?"

"Arranging for our next concert, scheduled for Oklahoma City a few days from now."

"I was about to begin finger printing everyone," the sheriff said, "so I'll begin with you," he said, removing an ink pad and special paper from his pocket.

"But why? I just arrived."

"You're here, though," the sheriff said, taking hold of Frank's hand.

Jessica and the bodyguards lined up silently for fingerprints. I was the last, also silent.

Despite the evidence, despite the fact that he'd been on my short list of suspects, in death Jake still looked like the boy next door. The kind who helped old folks cross the street.

"There was a letter in his pocket," Jessica said. "He... he's the stalker."

"No! Really? But how can that be?" Frank asked. "When did he, I mean who found him?"

"Details will be in my full report," the sheriff said, "now please move your vehicle. I need this area clear to complete my investigation."

After the others left, I asked the sheriff if he wanted me to stay. He did.

The sheriff did a thorough search of the place, peered at tire tracks, footprints, photographing all of it. After that, he asked me to show him which horse had been in the round pen with Jake.

I led him inside the barn, flipped on the lights and proceeded to Big Red's stall. The gelding reacted to our presence by pinning his ears back and pawing the straw with a front hoof.

"This one looks too big for a mustang."

"Right," I said, "he's a young Quarter horse."

"Looks wild."

"He's a little hyper," I said, "but he's in training. He's just young and frightened. I rode him earlier today." I wasn't about to volunteer that this chestnut had bucked me off just hours ago and was every bit as feisty as the mustang called Hotshot.

Sheriff Plackmon peered in the stall. "This horse shod?"

I nodded.

"We need to have his shoes removed so we can test them."

"I can do that," I said. I relied on a farrier to shoe my horses, but kept a few tools for emergencies, like detaching loose shoes. I pulled on gloves and got to work. Before long, the gelding's hooves were bare and I handed over the four horseshoes. There was no obvious blood, at least non I could detect.

The sheriff accepted the metal shoes with gloved hands and placed them in plastic.

After finishing in the barn, he came up to the house and had a look outside there too. "The deceased had a horseshoe-shape facial wound. Question is," the sheriff said, "if the horse didn't kill the guy, then who did?"

Indeed.

By the time he left, it was after midnight. I was emotionally and physically exhausted. Jessica and Frank were in the guest room. I had no idea when Roy would arrive, but I stretched out on the living room couch to wait for him. The next thing I knew, Evelyn was standing over me, her hand on my shoulder.

"What? Oh, I guess you heard," I mumbled, rubbing my eyes.

Evelyn sank into a chair. "You found Jake?"

"Yeah," I began, pausing to yawn, "he was in the round pen."

"What was he doing there?"

"I have no idea. How well did you know him?"

"I... well," she said, "he was such a nice kid."

She appeared to be near tears. The Parker Company was relatively small, so everyone knew each other to a certain extent, they travelled together, worked and often played together.

"Did a horse really kick him in the head?" Evelyn asked, crying now.

"I'm not sure."

Evelyn dabbed more tears. "Awful, just awful. And he liked horses, too."

"You must've known him real well."

"Well, sort of. I mean, how could this happen? He is... was... such a nice kid."

Nice enough to cry over.

"Were you here when… it happened?"

"No, I came home and went down to check on the horses. That's when I found him."

"And he was dead?"

I nodded. "I called for help, started CPR. The paramedics came, tried resuscitation, but he was… gone."

"I can't believe it," she said, crying more. "This wasn't supposed to happen, you know?"

I just looked at her, didn't know what to say. "You're welcome to stay here tonight. I'll grab a blanket and pillow for you."

She blew her nose, nodded, and sat down on the couch.

When she was settled, I told her to come to my bedroom and wake me if she needed anything and also said Roy would be coming home in a few hours. I left her with a box of tissues.

Within less than five minutes, I fell into bed. Next thing I knew, Roy was leaning close, kissing my forehead. Half-awake, I told him some of what'd happened, then fell asleep in his arms. The one thing I remembered was thanking him for coming. I slept right through chores the next morning, thanks to Roy, who must've been just as tired as me. But he not only took care of morning feeding, he also made breakfast for Jessica and Frank as well as for Evelyn.

I was the last person out of bed, and after Roy made me an omelet and a steaming cup of tea, he sat down beside me while I ate.

"I don't deserve you," I said, leaning over to kiss him.

"That's not how I see things," he said. "But let's not quibble."

"I do love you so much."

"We'll, uh, discuss last night's excitement at length later, right?"

"Oh yes," I said, yawning. "Excitement."

He smiled, we kissed some more, and then he made a big pot of tea and served it to Jessica, Evelyn and me on the back porch.

"So your stalker is history," I said to Jessica.

"It's surreal," she said. "I spent so much time and energy worrying what he'd do next. And I thought he'd be someone bigger than life, ominous."

"Well, I just feel sorry for him," Evelyn said, looking like she was about to cry again.

"Yes, and his poor family," Jessica said. "Hard to believe that he was the one who caused all that trouble."

"He must've really been disturbed, but also really good at hiding it," I said.

Evelyn dabbed at her eyes. "This isn't right. This wasn't supposed to happen."

Jessica looked at her. "What do you mean?"

"I… well, just that Jake was the nicest kid on the crew. I can't believe he's dead. I mean, who'd kill a nice kid like Jake?"

I had a strange feeling about Jake, where he died, the way he died.

# CHAPTER TWENTY FIVE

FRANK JOINED US. He looked at Jessica with adoring eyes, leaning over to kiss her not once but several times. I smiled at his jokes, acted pleased at his compliments about how much he loved the peace and solitude here. But hardly anything he said seemed sincere. I'd been around Frank just enough to understand why Jessica yearned to be free from his controlling ways.

Finally, he glanced at his watch. "Well, ladies, I know you enjoy being together, but it is nearly time for rehearsal." He held a hand out to Jessica. "Bianca will meet us in town. And as for you, Margo," he continued, smiling at me, "Long-term friendships are quite special. I'm so happy that you and my lovely wife have gotten reacquainted."

"I'm glad too, Frank," I said, and that much I meant.

After they all left, I went inside to find Roy busy at the computer.

"Oh, don't tell me we're... alone, at last," he said, smiling.

"Oh, don't tell me you'd take advantage of little old me."

"Okay, I won't tell you, I'll just show you," he said, closing the laptop. He looked me up and down. "Is it getting hot in here?"

"Starting to," I whispered.

We shed clothes in record time, started out on Roy's desk chair, then spent the better part of an hour in the bedroom.

"How did I ever manage before you became part of my life," I murmured.

"So am I a big part or a little part?"

"Ummm, let's see… a substantial part, I'd say."

"But I'm not here when I should be."

"You're here now, cowboy."

"Seriously, though, I'll look for a different job, one that keeps me here with you."

"No way! You're in demand, Roy Holden, PhD. You didn't earn all those fancy letters after your name for nothing. People all over the planet rely on you to be a doctor for their land, their grass."

"Well, sure, I am Dr. Grass, and green blades everywhere get excited when I come to tenderly stroke them, solve their problems so they can happily grow tall."

"Are we still talking about grass? And should I feel jealous?"

"Possibly. That's up to you, my Darling. Some call me Dr. Poaceae or even Dr. Natural Resources, but they're just being fancy. Maybe you could travel with me sometimes."

"Yes, I should. I could make sure you don't get involved with the wrong type of grass. I know how slutty some greens grow."

"You'd be a valuable travel companion. You might not get in as much trouble if you were always under my wing."

"I didn't know you have a wing."

"Sure, although I keep it hidden. I'll show you sometime. Meantime, spill it. What the hell happened here yesterday?"

I sighed. "It started out with a plan to smoke out Jessica's stalker before things escalated way more."

"Let me guess. You got all dolled up to look like Jessica, set yourself up as a decoy."

"Yeah. But the plan failed spectacularly. All I 'caught' was Mr. Edwards, my old math teacher who was out for a stroll at nine in the evening. Nearly scared him to death. Then, when I came back home, I went down to check on Big Red, who'd acted up earlier, bucked me off, then slipped on a rock and hurt a hoof so I put him in the round pen." I paused, shook my head. "The guy I'd hoped to catch earlier ended up in the round pen, dead. Turned out that Jake Campbell seems to be the stalker."

"Seems to be?"

"There's something off about this whole thing. I'm not sure what, but Evelyn seems way too upset about Jake Campbell's death. I mean everyone thinks he is a nice kid, but there's something more Evelyn knows."

"So we're not done with the stalker thing."

"It's just a hunch, so far. But finding Jake dead in Big Red's pen seems like a weird coincidence. There's still something about Frank that bothers me, too."

"I know what you mean. I started a computer search on him, haven't come up with anything interesting yet, but I'll continue. What about Luke and his horse? And the dead mustang. Any news there?"

I shook my head, but before I could say more, the doorbell rang.

Fortunately, we'd gotten dressed by then, but we were still lying in bed. I stood up, ran a comb through my hair, pulled it into a ponytail, and hurried to open the door.

It was Ruth Dunn. She was all of five feet tall, dressed as always in stiffly pressed Levi's and a red-lined denim vest over a western style plaid shirt with pearl buttons. She turned seventy not long ago, but she had more energy than most people half her age.

"Hi Ruth, c'mon in. How about some iced tea?"

"Yes, sounds fine. Left Sara in charge of the store for a bit. Got wind of some things you'll want to hear."

"Okay. Have a seat and I'll get the tea."

Ruth knew just about everything worth sharing in Pinedale and the surrounding area. If it was important, she could scope out what time every person around here crawled out of bed, what they ate for breakfast, lunch and dinner. Maybe she tapped our smart phones somehow or had hidden surveillance cameras here and there, although she relied more on local gossip than the latest tech. She was somewhere between clairvoyant and a well-informed busybody.

I came out of the kitchen with a pitcher of tea and three glasses just as Roy emerged from the back of the house.

Ruth smiled at him. "Howdy, Roy. How was Idaho?"

"Uh, just fine. How're you these days?"

"Good, thanks to our Lord who looks over us all."

I poured tea, handed everyone a glass.

"People say the young man who died right here at your place last night might not be the real stalker."

I nearly choked on the tea I was sipping.

Roy glanced at Ruth. "How interesting."

Ruth turned to me. "I thought so too. But you went and scared poor Mr. Edward last night, Margo."

"Uh, yes, but how do you know all this so quick?"

"How was Mr. Edward feeling when you dropped in on him this morning?" Roy asked, smiling.

Ruth squinted at Roy. "What makes you think... oh, never mind. He seemed fine." She sat silently then, sipping tea.

"So what else is new, Ruth?" I asked after a few minutes.

"Nothing as dramatic as a death. However, Agnes Vigil came into my store just before closing yesterday, said Doris Gannon broke down in tears at Bible study."

"Really," I said.

She nodded. "I didn't go, although I do hate to miss. Jim was feeling poorly, couldn't leave him alone."

Managing everything Ruth Dunn did seemed amazing to me. It'd been nearly ten years since her husband became an invalid. Last time I saw Jim, he could barely hold his head upright.

"Is he better today?"

"A bit," she said, blinking rapidly as though she had dust in her eyes, or maybe tears. "Parkinson's isn't an easy thing. But his nurse is with him today."

"That's good," I said. "So about Doris..."

"As you know, Doris was raised on a ranch near here, so she was thrilled to come back when Joe got assigned to this section of BLM. Naturally, we welcomed her back, too. But Agnes says that Doris has been a wreck, says Joe doesn't love her anymore. Such a shame." Ruth checked her watch, sipped more tea. "I hear that Millie Dickson has been spending time with Joe." She paused, stood up. "Well, then, must be going."

"Wait," I said. "What else about Millie and Joe?"

"I haven't personally seen them together." She sat back down, sipped more tea. "Although as everyone knows, Millie has always had a... well, a reputation. Of course, I don't know everything."

"Right," I said. What Ruth didn't already know, she would soon hear from the stream of people who dropped by the B&D Tack Shop to shoot the breeze.

"Jessica Parker's concert was lovely. She can certainly carry a tune."

"Yes. We grew up together, you know."

"Of course. You two even shared a dorm room all through college, as I recall. Anyhow, Margo, you'd both best be careful."

"That's what I keep telling her," Roy said.

Ruth stood up again, nodded at me, and this time she did leave.

"What a character," Roy say, laughing.

"She's one of a kind," I said.

"For sure. So what do Joe and Doris Gannon's marital problems have to do with anything?"

I shrugged. "Maybe nothing. Then again, it might be good to know what's going on between Joe and Millie. We also need to uncover what role the BLM and the energy companies could have in all this. Might have some bearing on the mustangs' disappearances and on Luke's death. And somehow we need to figure out if Jake Campbell was really Jessica's stalker. The sheriff found a letter in Jake's pocket proclaiming his love for Jessica."

"Someone could have killed Jake and then planted the letter there."

I nodded. "What if we're looking at everything all wrong? Maybe every single issue is linked together. What if Luke and Jake were killed by the same person?"

Roy drew me close. "What if we're getting carried away with crazy theories?"

"All we need to do is unwind things, look at each segment separately, then link them together."

"Sounds simple."

I winked at him. "I do my best to keep things simple so I don't scare you."

# CHAPTER TWENTY SIX

ROY WENT BACK in his office to finish searching about Frank Stanza and anything at all on Jake Campbell. I type fast, but I think more freely with a notebook and pen, so I headed to the dining room table and began jotting notes.

Key people most likely to be involved with the disappearing mustangs included Millie Dickson, Joe Gannon and Juan Gomez. Millie represented certain local ranchers, Gannon managed the local BLM, and of course Juan Gomez wielded control of a major energy company. A powerful trio, especially if they had some sort of joint effort underway. One thing stood out. With these three, it was certain that greed was a prime motive.

Millie Dickson and her clan's large cattle operation had ever-expanding needs for grazing permits, which were granted by the BLM. At the same time, Juan Gomez was certainly on the lookout for more drilling permits, again from the BLM and, of course, Joe Gannon.

With less mustangs, the Dicksons could graze more cattle and Gomez's companies could expand drilling operations. I wasn't sure exactly what Joe Gannon stood to gain, but it was most likely money under the table. What we had to find out was how far into illegal territory one or all of them were willing to reach.

Ruth Dunn's revelation about Joe Gannon's unhappy wife might be meaningful. Doris had always been religious, and so had Ruth, which meant the two were friends. I didn't yet know what to make of Ruth saying that Doris was so upset with Joe.

Roy appeared just as I was about to turn my attention to Jessica and her situation.

"Well, I've come up with an enormous blank regarding Frank Stanza," Roy said. He leaned down to kiss me. "And so far, Jake Campbell seems like a choir boy."

"Somehow I'm not surprised," I said. "Frank undoubtedly keeps a tight control on all personal info."

Roy nodded. "But what about the dead kid?"

I shrugged. "I have a feeling that Jake was simply as nice as he seemed."

"So maybe he wasn't the real stalker?"

"Maybe not," I said, "but Evelyn was upset and crying last night and still teary before she left this morning. She's never so much as mentioned Jake or shown any interest in him that I've seen. I need to ask Jessica if I'm missing something. I'll call Jake's mother later. She'll be grieving, of course, but I wonder if she'll have anything surprising to reveal."

"Ok, and let's not forget your personal incidents."

"No doubt I have the Dicksons to thank for all that. I can just imagine Millie laughing when Hotshot bucked me off, and Nick, her brute of a son could've easily thrown the rock through our living room window. He's the type who would've enjoyed cutting my fence and spraying the young mustangs, too."

"What we need is proof."

"I'm sure that all those incidents were supposedly scary messages from the Dicksons, so proof won't change anything. Besides, I don't scare easily."

Roy grinned. "No kidding. You're tougher than you look."

"I'll take that as a compliment. Besides, even if we can prove everything the Dicksons have done, all the sheriff could do is slap their wrists. I'm more interested in finding out what happened to Spirit and Luke Barnes. And also who shot the bay mustang mare."

"Everything is likely connected, don't you think?"

I shrugged. "That'd be handy." I glanced at my watch. "I have horses to train, several people coming for lessons this afternoon."

"How about a bite to eat first?"

I stood up, put my arms around Roy, gazed up into his eyes. "Um, sure, cowboy. Did I ever tell you that you're the best lover I've ever had?"

"Oh, we're not talking about food now, right?"

"I'll take whatever you've got," I whispered.

"Did I ever tell you that you scare me sometimes? I mean, I try to keep up, but—"

I grinned. "You're doing fine, cowboy."

"Good to know. Now, madam, if you'll wait here in the main dining area, I'll rustle up some gourmet grub."

I sat back down. "I'll be right here where I can watch your moves."

After lunch, I hustled to the barn. The rancher who'd brought three young mustangs, to me for training was coming by to see if I was still in one piece and having any success with Hotshot, Lady, and Trooper. I'd assured him on the phone that training was going well, although I thought that all three animals needed another month or so. Just prior to his arrival, I led the three into my round pen, groomed them, and saddled Hotshot. The rancher's name was Ted Stewart, and he was one of the richest, most successful breeders of Angus cattle on the western slope. Ted built a mansion for his wife and a fancy barn for his horses. He was smart enough not to care what other people said or thought about him, which is why he chose mustangs as well as Quarter horses for riding.

"I chose the right name for this gelding," Ted said after I finished a demo of Hotshot's skills in the arena. "What do you think of him?"

"He's smart, and once he settles down some more, he'll make a great horse for you. But he'll always be a bit unpredictable."

"Just what I wanted to hear. I don't want boring. I'd like to ride him for a bit." I adjusted the stirrups, checked the girth, and turned the chestnut over to his owner in the arena. This day, Hotshot was quiet as a lamb until a sudden spook at something only he perceived, whirling around, even snorting. Ted sat deep in the saddle to ride it out, then laughed. "I like the little turd," he said when he dismounted.

I rode Trooper and Lady one after the other, and just as I expected, both of them were much mellower under saddle than Hotshot. Ted didn't ask to ride these two, but he opened his wallet, handed me another wad of cash, told me to take my time with his horses, tipped his hat and left smiling.

Next on the agenda was Melody, the most spoiled little twelve-year-old I'd ever run across. Her obnoxious mother, Babs Kingbury, brought Melody for every lesson, blabbing the whole time about her precious little princess.

Before they arrived, I outfitted Hawk with an English saddle similar to the one Melody used and tied my little pinto near the arena.

Their new truck and fancy horse trailer arrived right on time, and I went over to help Melody unload her bay gelding, a stunning and well-trained eight-year-old Dutch Warmblood. I'd tried to talk Mrs. Kingbury out of such a spirited horse, but she had more money than sense. The gelding came with a fancy name, but Melody called him DD, shorthand for Doodley the Dutchman. I helped tack up DD and Melody led the gelding to my arena.

"Mount up and walk DD around to warm him up," I said.

Mrs. Kingbury approached. "How is she doing?" It was the question she asked every single week.

"Melody is making progress," I said, "but I can't tell if she really wants to keep riding."

"Oh, sure, of course she does. She looks forward to these lessons."

I smiled at Babs Kingbury, then entered the arena. "Ok, Melody, go ahead with a posting trot."

Melody made a face. "Oh, but DD is so lumpy."

"You're on the wrong diagonal, Melody. Sit two beats, then post again."

"This saddle hurts my butt."

"Okay, bring DD down to a walk, then halt." I approached her. "You say the same things every week, Melody. Do you enjoy riding?"

She looked behind her, saw that her mother was out of hearing range. "I love horses," she said, "but I don't know if I love this one."

"Okay, how about if I ride him for a few minutes and you go right outside the arena and watch how he moves."

"Whatever," she said. "I mean, sure, okay."

I adjusted the stirrups, checked the girth, then mounted. One problem was DD's size. He was 16.2 hands, and since Melody was under five feet tall, it wasn't a good physical match, to begin with. I began with a posting trot, then halted near Melody. "I want you to watch and call out what gait we're doing, okay? Tell me all about each gait from walk to trot to canter."

Melody grinned. "Okay, fun!"

I began at a walk, then a sitting trot alternating with a posting trot. And for once, Melody seemed to be enjoying herself.

"Trot, two beat, a pair of legs."

"Excellent." I cued DD into a slow canter, and Melody correctly said that canter is a three-beat gait which pushes off from one of the hind legs.

After that, I took the gelding over several jumps.

Melody clapped her hands. "Wow! DD looks so good!"

I halted near her again. "He's gorgeous, don't you think?"

Melody shrugged. "I guess."

I dismounted, slipped DD's bridle off, halter on and tied him to a secure fencepost. I motioned for Melody to follow me over to her mother.

"Is it all right with you if I put Melody on Hawk, the cute little pinto? It's often very good for students to ride various horses. Helps with confidence, with everything."

"Well, I—"

"Please Mommy, please?"

Mrs. Kingbury nodded.

Melody was an entirely different kid on Hawk. She trotted in perfect rhythm, moved between posting and sitting trot with ease, then transitioned to canter. She took him over close to her mother. "Oh, I just love Hawk!" she said, grinning.

"Yes, Dear, I can tell," her mother said, then turned to me. "So what is the point of this?"

"Did you see how relaxed Melody was on the little pinto? She enjoyed him, partly because he is the right size for her at this point, and also because he's very calm. When she grows taller, she'll be more suited to taller horses like the lovely Dutch Warmblood."

"So you think I bought the wrong horse for her?"

"It is too soon for her to have such a large horse, and even though he is well-trained, he's too spirited for Melody at this point."

"So what do we do? Sell the warmblood, get some little pony?"

"No. But what I'd like to do is put Melody on several different very calm horses each time she comes. Hawk will be the main one. Melody will appreciate DD when she is also more experienced. Riding different horses will build up her confidence and her enjoyment. And speaking of enjoyment, I'd like for her to take a trail ride with me next week. I'll put her on Hawk and we'll ride for about an hour on the trails behind my property. I can provide a horse for you too, if you'd like. Does that sound okay?"

"I suppose so, but now that she loves this… this pony, I don't know if she'll ever enjoy a real horse."

"Hawk is 14.2 hands, so he just meets the height benchmark for a horse, not a pony. Bring her the same time next week, but no need to bring DD."

"Well I… oh, all right."

I let Melody ride Hawk for a while longer, and she didn't complain about one single thing. Even when I put her back on DD, she was visibly more relaxed and still smiling when the lesson ended, and Mrs. Kingbury looked, well, not totally unhappy.

My next student was Gina, a talented sixteen-year-old who was a pleasure to teach and had an older Quarter horse gelding she loved. Gina was tall enough and confident enough to handle Melody's Dutch Warmblood, so maybe I'd ask Babs Kingbury about a year-long lease of her fancy gelding and in turn lease one of my quieter horses to Melody for a year. I had several horses in mind, but not Hawk. He was altogether too valuable. Melody could ride him during lessons if she wanted to, but I was too fond of Hawk to let him out of my sight.

My last lesson was a monthly with Adair, an accomplished adult rider who enjoyed everything from trail riding to stadium jumping and had an off-the-track thoroughbred gelding who was as enjoyable as his rider. Today's emphasis was on jumping, and the goal was preparation for the next show over in Grand Junction to which I'd be taking ten riders of all ages and abilities.

It was late afternoon by the time I called Doris Gannon and arranged to meet her at Rebecca's Kitchen for pie, so I cleaned up and headed into town.

Doris Gannon perched on the edge of her chair at a table for two near the back of the restaurant. Slender, conservatively dressed, even I noticed that her chin length hair lacked style, like maybe she cut it herself. I should know, I've wacked the ends off my own hair every now and then. Something about the way she sat there made it obvious she'd avoid saying 'shit' if she landed in a pile of it.

She smiled, I smiled, we put in our orders, and then I got down to business.

It didn't take much to make her cry. Not my intention, but after the third question about Joe, her eyes grew moist and she reached into her purse for tissues.

"Uh, gee, uhm, I'm so sorry," I stammered.

She dabbed at first one eye and then the other. "Never mind, Mrs. Richards, it's not your fault."

"Please call me Margo."

She nodded.

"So about Joe," I said. "You started to say something."

She dabbed some more and sighed. "Well, greed is one of Satan's tools, you know."

"In what way, Doris?"

"We never have enough money. At least that's what Joe says. I think we should just spend less, but he thinks we need a new truck, he even insisted on renovating the kitchen. I asked how we could afford that." She shrugged, sipped some coffee. She hadn't so much as glanced at the blueberry pie the waitress placed in front of her, but I'd already shoveled in half of mine. Blueberry anything at Rebecca's was my fav.

"But Joe has a great position at the BLM," I said. I didn't need to add that his salary was probably higher than that of many locals.

"He used to be content," Doris said. More tears, more dabbing.

I waited, hoping she was on the verge of revealing something useful. Meantime, no sense in wasting the rest of my pie. Umm, blueberry.

"I rarely open the bank statements," Doris said. "Joe handles all the finances, you know."

I nodded, trying to look sympathetic while enjoying the pie.

"But last month, I looked at our savings account, just a peek, you see." She closed her eyes and shook her head. "There was so much money in there. Why, I tell you, I was just flabbergasted."

I swallowed and put down my fork. "Why was that, Doris?"

"Well, Joe, he's been making odd comments lately."

"Is that so."

"About horses, of all things. I mean, he doesn't even like them. I just worry he's involved in something. All I can do is pray, of course."

"Of course." I said, wondering if Doris would let me have her untouched pie. It'd be a shame to let something so yummy go to waste.

"He's a good man, you know. An excellent provider. He fixes dinner most of the time, too. I'm not much of a cook, myself. But Joe, he loves to barbecue. Funny thing, though. He thawed some steaks the other night, said they were special. But they had a… I don't know, a different taste."

I felt my jaw begin to drop, forced myself to bring my lips together, keep my face neutral. "You don't say," I managed.

"Joe said somebody, a hunter I suppose, had given him the meat, he said it was sort of like venison."

"So it tasted gamey?" I asked. I've never eaten venison, had no desire to roast Bambi. But I had a feeling this meat might be something very different than venison.

"We eat venison quite a bit," Doris replied, verifying my suspicions. "and it didn't taste like that at all. I just didn't like it. Joe kept trying to tell me it was good, seemed a bit miffed that I wouldn't eat more than a bite. He said we could get hold of more."

I stopped listening, overcome by a wave of nausea despite my cast iron stomach. Suddenly, even Doris's untouched pie lost its appeal. I was tempted to just come right out and ask Doris if she had any idea that the steaks her loving husband brought home might come from one of the very mustangs he was supposed to be protecting. But if she suspected as much, she'd be unlikely to admit it. I picked up my mug of tea and sipped so that I wouldn't have to say anything for a while.

Doris signaled the waitress for more coffee, and then she looked at me, tried to smile.

After I finished my tea, I put down the cup. "So has Joe brought home any extra, uh, steaks, then?"

"Yes, he has, unfortunately. They're in the freezer. And it's a sin to waste food, of course."

"Uh, I'd love to have some," I said.

"You would? Oh, wonderful."

"I could drop by your place right now, pick it up."

"Yes, fine, Margo. And perhaps we can get together again soon. I've never gotten to know many local people. Of course I know Ruth and some others from when I lived here before. You would've been just a girl back then, but you seem so nice." She smiled.

I did too. But I was imagining how her smile would fade when she found out that I planned to use that frozen meat as evidence rather than food.

# CHAPTER TWENTY SEVEN

I PICKED UP the meat from Doris, and casually asked if she and Joe spent much time with Millie and Hank Dickson. She said no, but judging from the look on her face, she at least suspected there might be something going on between Millie and Joe. She mentioned that Millie's son, Nick had seemed quite enthralled with the strange meat.

Nick Dickson was discharged not long ago from the Marines. Dishonorably, according to Ruth Dunn. A beefy guy who favored aviator sunglasses and black muscle shirts, he'd been at Jessica's concert, and I'd seen him talking with Evelyn afterwards. Later on, I found out that they'd dated a few times while the band was playing near Camp Pendleton when Nick was stationed there. If Evelyn wanted to flirt with him, that was her call.

The next name that Doris Gannon mentioned was the one that got my attention. "Joe keeps inviting Juan Gomez over to dinner. I have nothing in common with the man, and I've told Joe that I'd rather socialize with my church friends, but Joe says it is important to know the right people."

"Interesting," I said. "So what do Joe and Mr. Gomez talk about?"

She shrugged. "I don't really pay much attention. It might be more interesting if his wife were in town, but I understand that she lives in Texas. Did you know he has his own private jet?"

"No, but wow."

"I fear he is a bad influence on Joe."

"How so?"

"For one thing, he's very rich. He flew Joe down to his place in Texas one time. Joe came back raving about this huge ranch, said the Gomez family lives in a mansion. Joe has always been, well, there's that old saying about wanting champaign on a beer budget. We're not poor, but we're far from wealthy."

We were sitting in the living room, and I had a clear view of what looked like a brand new kitchen. "So you already did some remodeling?"

She smiled. "Isn't it lovely? I just hope we'll be able to pay for it. Joe handles the bills, though, and he says not to worry about money."

I asked Doris not to tell Joe that I'd been there for some frozen meat. I left with renewed questions not only about Joe Gannon but also about his relationship with Juan Gomez and the energy companies. Gannon was in a position to do a lot of damage. He had seemed shocked about that fencing in Far Canyon. Maybe he didn't put it up himself, but he might've known about it or agreed to overlook it. Maybe he was a darn good actor. The big question was his true involvement with the dwindling herds and the truth about why he kept rejecting my plans for a mustang refuge. No doubt he'd formed an alliance with the energy companies. It was no secret that the BLM favored drilling. That in itself was bad enough, because BLM land also held most of America's wild horses. Even though the laws Congress had enacted to protect the mustangs decades ago were under constant attack, the official propaganda was that drilling and mustangs could co-exist. I'd hoped that drilling would lessen with the increase in climate change, but that hadn't happened so far.

I shipped the meat in an insulated express package to the vet department at Colorado State University in Fort Collins with a request to verify whether or not it was equine.

While it was obvious that Joe Gannon didn't have much regard for the horses under his care, it couldn't hurt to have him admit that and record it with a smart phone. If anyone could get him to open up even more than he first did with Jessica, the glamorous singer whom he'd already met once was the one.

To me, Jessica was a friend, but to most men, she was a hot babe.

I arranged a time for her to meet Joe the next morning, and before we headed to the BLM office, I explained the plan. She'd heighten her supposed dislike of mustangs, even though her latest song was about them. She could say she was afraid of them, whatever it took to get him to admit his own feelings about horses in general and mustangs in particular. And who knew what else he'd say once she had him under her spell. Maybe he'd invite her to a barbecue, grill up some of that strange meat.

She pulled on skin tight jeans and a snug knit top that displayed plenty of cleavage, slathered on makeup and did something fancy to her eyelashes and hair. She'd have Joe panting like a puppy.

"I'm so glad the stalker thing is over," she told me on the way into town, "but guilty too. I mean, I'm not happy that Jake is dead. He seemed like such a sweet kid."

I nodded. "I know. But Evelyn sure seemed upset."

"I noticed," Jessica said. "But they never spoke all that much as far as I know."

I dropped her off at the BLM office and lingered over tea at Rebecca's Pantry until Jessica texted me.

"Criminy, what a sleaze," Jessica said when she was settled in my truck. "Even worse than the first time. Didn't take much for him to say he'd be happy to get rid of all the mustangs at the Cliffs." She handed me her smart phone. "It's all here, every word."

"Great," I said, "you only had to breathe to reel him in, charm him out from under his slimy rock."

"He also said that some Europeans have the right idea. What'd he mean by that?"

"Quite a few countries do eat horse meat, from Japan and China to Switzerland and Germany, Mexico too."

"How could anyone even think of eating... oh, sick."

"Yeah, gag me," I said. "But different cultures have varying food sources."

"Sure, okay, but still," Jessica said, scrunching up her face. "You think Gannon has ever eaten actual horse meat?"

"There's no law against it," I said, "but that isn't the question. I need proof that he's involved in profiting from the mustangs he's supposed to protect."

"How can you get that?"

"I'm going to have a chat with someone at the bank and then visit Sheriff Plackmon."

"I can't stand the thought of any more of those beautiful animals out there disappearing. You've got to put a stop to this, Margo."

"I will."

Sue Barton graduated from high school with Jessica and me. She and every other employee and customer at the Bank of Pinedale Springs were thrilled to see Jessica Parker entering the establishment. After the hometown singer smiled through a round of autograph signing and photos, we took Sue aside and sweet talked her into revealing approximately how much money the Gannon savings account held. Sue couldn't reveal an exact amount, of course, but she told us it was 'very high' six figures. So way more than enough to renovate Doris Gannon's kitchen.

Jessica's exit from the bank caused a bigger stir than her entrance, beginning with a cameraman and a guy who shoved a microphone toward her and said "Grand Junction TV news, Ms. Parker. We understand the man stalking you was found dead last night."

Jessica produced an automatic half-smile for the camera, said "I, uh, have no comment at this time."

The guy glanced from her to the camera, "This is an exclusive, folks. Sources revealed that the stalker was one of your stage hands. Frightening. You must be relieved that this is over."

Jessica blinked at him, wearing her public face, and said "It's always regrettable when someone dies."

"Of course, most definitely," the guy said, nodding. "But still, your fans are worried."

"I appreciate everyone's concerns," Jessica said. "My fans are simply the best, and it's so great to visit Pinedale again." She blew a kiss toward the camera and we made our way to the truck.

"How did they hear about Jason so soon?" I asked.

Jessica shrugged. "Evelyn must've called them."

"She does believe in publicity, doesn't she?"

"I think she gets carried away with it, but Frank insists the exposure is always good." We stopped by the Sheriff's Department, located in a small brick building toward the north end of Main Street. Sheriff Plackmon had grown up around horses in Oklahoma, still rode occasionally. I wasn't sure how he felt about mustangs, but I'd never heard him complain about them the way certain locals around here did. He didn't seem to like Joe Gannon very much.

"You do tend to overstep, Margo," he said after I'd presented my suspicions. "But the possibility that anyone could be killing mustangs for meat is disgusting. It's also illegal if they're selling the meat."

I nodded, but said nothing more. I turned to leave, but he held up a hand.

"Wait, Margo. I'm afraid I have some bad news."

"Bad news?"

"Sit down a minute."

I sank into a chair, folded my arms against my chest, Jessica next to me.

"Coroner finished his report on Luke Barnes," he said. "There were no bullet wounds on the body."

I'd checked as best I could myself, found none.

The sheriff sighed. "He died from the fall, broke his neck, massive internal injuries."

He was building up to something, I could tell by his tone. I unfolded my arms and leaned forward, gripping the arms of the chair.

"Also got ballistics reports, and therein lies the problem. We confirmed the bullet that killed his horse was fired from the rifle found beside the animal. Only fingerprints lifted from it matched Barnes. No surprises there." He paused, sighed again. "Thing is, the other bullet, the one you extracted from the bay mustang, that one came from the very same rifle."

That made no sense. I frowned. "Seriously?"

"The lab had a look at tissue from that mare. They estimate she died a week ago, approximately last Saturday according to the microbes present."

I was too stunned to say anything.

The Sheriff nodded. "I know this is hard to hear, Margo. I checked with Joe Gannon. Barnes didn't miss any days at work until right before you found him. I called his roping partner, checked around with a few others who might've known his whereabouts during the days in question, talked to a woman name of Rosie Garcia too. She spent a week ago Friday at his place, but left early next morning to visit her sister in Durango."

"Did she tell you he was worried about the mustangs?"

"Sure enough. He told her that he planned to ride out there, check on them. Didn't know when he was going. Seems he didn't share his plans with many people."

"He kept to himself," I said. Except for the womanizing. I wondered if Luke knew that Rosie's own plans included marriage. Wondered if she knew how many other females would mourn his passing. I was one of them. I'd gotten over loving him long ago, but I still cared about him. There'd never be another friend like Luke. And he was my only connection with the BLM.

"No one saw him or was with him on the weekend in question," the sheriff added.

I hung my head. Obvious where this was heading. Jessica put her arm around my shoulders.

"Looks like he rode out to the Cliffs twice," the Sheriff continued, "the first time was about the time that bay was shot."

"No, no," I managed to say.

"Facts don't lie," the Sheriff said, "and everything points to the conclusion that for some unknown reason, Luke Barnes shot that mustang, then rode out there again a few days later, shot his own horse, jumped off that ledge."

"That can't be," I said. "Luke wouldn't do any of that. Never."

"He's not around to answer questions," the Sheriff said. "I showed Doc Wilson the photos of Luke's horse, and he agreed that the rear leg might have broken. Luke might have put the animal out of its misery. Maybe same thing happened with the mustang."

"No way. Like I said when we were out there, Spirit's leg could've broken when he fell, after he was shot."

"Sorry, Margo. But what I'm telling you is not just opinion."

I leaned back, rubbed my chin, stared at the ceiling. "The angle of the bullet I removed from that bay mustang indicated it was shot from a long distance, right?"

"Yes, that appeared to be the case."

"That takes a certain amount of skill."

The sheriff nodded. "True, but lots of people around here know how to handle a rifle, Luke Barnes included."

"You're right."

"Joe seemed shocked too," the sheriff said. "Looks like Barnes descended from moodiness into full-blown depression. I checked with Courtney, not because she's my wife. She understands human emotions, how the mind influences actions. She said it sounded possible."

"Possible," I repeated. "Circumstantial evidence. That's all."

"That's often the case," he said. "We can only work with situations as presented. In this instance, everything points to this conclusion."

"There must be something missing."

"I always consider any evidence that comes to light," he said, sounding weary. He heard this a lot, the questioning, the protests.

I'd given him plenty of grief when he'd said my foster mother's death initially looked like a suicide last year. Turned out he was wrong about how my beloved Bow died, and he had to be wrong now too. Still, I felt sorry for him. Law enforcement was a tough job. But I felt much sorrier for Luke Barnes. The sheriff had considered Luke's death a possible suicide right from the beginning.

"I understand," I said, without adding that I knew better.

I stood and walked out, followed by Jessica. My mind whirled with questions, possibilities. Somehow, I had to clear Luke's name.

Easy to say, harder to do.

# CHAPTER TWENTY EIGHT

JESSICA PLANNED TO meet Frank in town, so I left her, leashed the dogs and strolled to the B&D tack shop for a chat with Ruth. Zap and Fetch were happy to get out of the truck and even more excited to see Ruth, who always kept a bag of treats under the counter. Before she even said hello to me, she grabbed a dog bowl, filled it with fresh water and placed it down for my tail-wagging boys.

"So hello, Margo," Ruth said as she handed treats to my happy border collies.

"Hi Ruth, do you have time for a few questions?"

"For you, certainly. C'mon, let's sit," she said, leading the way to the table and chairs in the back room with Zap and Fetch crowding close to her.

Ruth opened the small refrigerator, poured two glasses of lemonade and brought them to the table.

"Thanks," I said, sipping. "You told me a while ago that Nick Dickson was a sharpshooter in the Marines, right?"

"Yes, indeed. Millie goes on and on about it. She's so proud of her son. But she never mentions the fact that he was dishonorably discharged."

"Really! Do you happen to know why?"

"Not directly, but my grandson was a marine who served with Nick.

He'd know all about it, I'm sure." Ruth took a piece of paper, wrote down a name and a number, handed it to me.

"Thanks, Ruth."

"Why are you interested in Nick?"

"I'm not, particularly. I'm just searching for info on anyone who might know something about the bay mustang that was shot."

Ruth squinted at me. "It's no secret that the Dickson's dislike mustangs."

I nodded.

"Still. I don't know why Nick would go out there and kill that mare."

"I'm not accusing him of anything, but he might know something."

Ruth shrugged. "Maybe." She handed more treats to the dogs, whose tail wagging accelerated.

We sipped lemonade in silence for a bit, then discussed the tack store, which Ruth said was doing better than ever. On the way out, I ran my hand lightly over a few saddles and inhaled the intoxicating scent of new leather that always permeated the store.

Roy had already started evening chores when I got home. He stopped and walked over to my truck. "How are things in town?"

"For starters, the sheriff says the bullet used to kill the mustang came from the same rifle that killed Luke's horse. He brought up the possibility that Luke died of suicide."

"Oh no, not again." Roy drew me close for a hug.

I clung to him, trying not to cry but knowing I would. This was out of the same playbook as last year when the sheriff thought that my foster mom had died of suicide. It'd taken a while, but I'd proven him wrong. Now I had to do it again. Different person, different circumstances, and I couldn't blame the sheriff because suicide was one possibility.

It was just the wrong possibility.

"I'll be here, I'll help," Roy whispered.

I pulled a tissue from my pocket and dabbed my eyes and wet cheeks. "Don't ever leave," I whispered, leaning back to gaze into Roy's sky-blue eyes.

"Okay, we'll build a twelve-foot high wall around our entire place, dig a twenty-foot deep moat and top it all with a drawbridge that opens only with a secret code."

I nodded. "Do I get the code?"

"Hmmm… we'll see."

I sighed. "It's okay long as you're here. I used to feel just fine alone, but I rely on you now."

Roy grinned. "You needs your man. And speaking of—"

An earth-shattering bray drowned out all speech, all thought.

I laughed. "Maynard wants us to know that we're exactly four and a half minutes late with his food."

"Oh no! We must hustle!" Roy grabbed my hand and we ran to the feed room.

Even though our very loud donkey was out with the others on lush pasture, everyone got a small daily helping of either grain or pellets in the evening. And woe be to us if we didn't ladle out Maynard's ration at the precise time he expected. He possessed an internal stomach alarm that was accurate and formidable because it connected directly to his larynx. Any donkey's bray can be heard up to two miles away. Maynard's most earnest efforts carried even farther.

When Maynard and the other donkeys as well as all the horses were cared for, we went up to the house. As soon as I got inside, I knew what Roy had in store for dinner. The aroma of lasagna made my stomach rumble. All of Roy's cooking was fabulous, but his lasagna reigned supreme.

We cleaned up and within minutes were seated. Roy dished out equally large portions for each of us.

I stuck my fork in, blew on it and savored the first bite. "Umm, yum."

"So you do like lasagna. What a surprise."

"Where's the box this came in? City Market, right?"

"Yeah, but I might attempt to make it from scratch some time."

I grinned. "Oh, could you?" Actually, my cooking cowboy had devised his own recipe for what I called his royal lasagna.

"Anything for you. So what else did the sheriff say?"

"Not much, but I did stop and chat with Ruth. We already knew

Nick Dickson was a marine, but Ruth said he was dishonorably discharged. She doesn't have details, but she gave me the name and contact info of her grandson who served in the same unit as Dickson. I plan to call him after dinner. Meantime, would it be terrible if I ate this entire pan of lasagna?"

"Not for me. I'll call the doctor after you finish."

"Ha! Haven't you ever seen me make a pig of myself?"

"Your words, not mine, darling."

"Ha again! I might not eat the entire thing after all, but just know that I could."

"Right."

Ruth's grandson was named James after his grandfather. I put the phone on speaker mode and punched in the number for the marine corporal.

"Call me Jim, Ma'am. Grandma Ruth told me you would call," he said in clipped tones that made me wonder if he was standing at attention. He verified knowing Nick Dickson, said they'd served in the same platoon.

When I mentioned dishonorable discharge, Jim's tone changed.

"That's correct Ma'am. Unfortunately, three other marines and I observed the incident and had to testify. Mr. Dickson shot four stray dogs that weren't bothering anyone. Some of us tossed scraps to them. But one evening, the dogs were sniffing around a dumpster. Dickson was at least five hundred yards away, shot one after the other right through the heart. He was laughing, seemed to enjoy it."

"That's awful. Sounds like he was a good shot, though."

"Yes Ma'am. He was a sharp shooter, one of our platoon's best marksmen, but a guy like him does not belong in the United States Marines."

"I see. Thank you, Jim."

"Yes Ma'am. Did Mr. Dickson do something else?"

"Not that I know of."

"I'm out of the marines now, Ma'am, and I... I adopted two rescue dogs."

"That's very good of you," I said.

"Thank you, Ma'am."

Roy sat silently until the call ended. "Interesting."

I nodded. "What if he was the one who went out to the Cliffs and shot that mare, then went back and shot Spirit, pushed Luke off the cliff."

"Speculation. We need proof."

"Yes. And motives. Hating mustangs is one thing, shooting them another. If Nick shot Spirit and pushed Luke to his death, I'll deal with him myself."

"Easy, Margo."

Luke and Spirit died several miles from the trailhead, and the mustang mare was miles in another direction. Nick didn't seem like the type to hike long distances even though he'd been a marine, and besides, he would've needed some way to pinpoint where his targets were. Mustangs don't stay long in one location, and Luke would've been riding too. Although Ruth said that Nick owned at least one Harley, no motorized vehicles were allowed on that range with the exception of limited access for driller's trucks which traversed the far northern sagebrush flats. If someone was up to no good, they'd go right ahead and take a motorcycle or better yet, an ATV that could negotiate the Cliff trails.

The helicopter ride Roy and I took with the sheriff and Joe had afforded an expansive view. The only tire tracks we'd seen were around the northern entrance. Doris Gannon had linked not only Joe and Juan Gomez together, but also Millie Dickson. If Gomez was wealthy enough to have his own jet, he'd have access to a helicopter too. Nick Dickson seemed like the type who wouldn't pass up a chance to demonstrate his sharpshooter skills. The local BLM honcho and one of the area's most powerful energy executives would probably not stoop low enough to shoot horses or kill a BLM employee themselves.

But they might've hired an ex-marine to do it for them.

# CHAPTER TWENTY NINE

**THE FINAL RIDE** Roy and I took with Luke was late last fall. The aspen stood bare, but brilliant leaves lined the trails and sparkled against the forest floor like gold coins. The sun's warmth embraced us on one of those Indian summer days made all the more special by the possibility that fickle winds could bring dark clouds the next day, or the one after that, but soon for sure. Then snowflakes would fall, covering the leaves and clinging to blades of grass. A bittersweet time of year, one day summer, the next winter.

Luke was on Spirit that day, Roy on Mutt and I rode Phantom. Our horses were in shape, so we kept a good pace at a walk, with trotting or cantering where the trail allowed, covering close to thirty miles all totaled. We stopped for lunch, unsaddled the horses and tied them within reach of grasses. We always found plenty to chat about, most often something to do with horses. Luke had a knack for storytelling, embellishing facts, eliciting laughs.

Now, it was only a few days since we found his body. It still felt unreal that he and Spirit were dead. I'd suspected right from the start that the official word from the coroner would point to suicide. I knew better right from the start. I'd spoken to Rosie Garcia. Didn't sound like Luke told his lover much about the mustangs or his plans.

The one person we hadn't yet spoken to was Luke's roping buddy, Harold Price. He and his wife lived on a small place less than a mile from Luke. Harold and Luke traded off caring for each other's animals when one of them was away. Now, Harold would be making sure that Luke's dogs and livestock were tended to as one last favor for a fallen friend.

Harold himself was an old time cowboy, wrinkled face, stooped shoulders, shiny silver belt buckle accenting a lean waist. At least seventy, maybe older. Like many ranchers in this area, he grew up on horses, felt more at home in saddles than rocking chairs. "Dang shame 'bout Luke," Harold said when I called him. "Way too young to die, that's for certain."

"Yes," I said.

"Any idea yet what happened out there?"

"That's why I'm calling, to ask for your help."

"Already spoke to the Sheriff, but whatever I can do."

Within an hour, Roy and I were at Harold's place, showing him our video of everything from Luke's body to both dead horses.

"Awful grim," he said, shaking his head.

"Yes."

"That isn't Luke's rifle."

Roy and I leaned forward and spoke in unison. "What?"

"That rifle out there, the one by Spirit's body. Wasn't Roy's."

"Seriously!" Roy said.

"Not a doubt. His dad and I hunted together many a year, and after that, Luke and me. He favored a softer recoil pad on the butt end of his guns. Used to tease him about it something fierce."

Roy nodded. "Did the sheriff ask about the rifle?"

"Nope, and he didn't show me any photos, or I would've set him straight. But every last one of Roy's rifles is fixed the same way. That one in your pictures has a stock recoil pad, different color."

"You need to tell the Sheriff," I said.

"You bet I will. And another thing. That dead mustang, the bay, I know her. Not much left in your pictures, but the odd-shaped white marks all down her face still showed up. I've seen a good many horses over the years, but never with a face like that. She was older, over ten at least. Smart mare."

"So she was a lead mare. I thought she might've been."

"That's right," he said. "Now why would some fool go and kill her?"

"I might know that," I said. "You've heard about the disappearances, of course."

He nodded. "Luke told me a while ago that something wasn't right."

"We have reason to believe that mustangs are being illegally rounded up, mostly to get rid of them, but also to profit by selling them to foreign gourmet markets."

"Gourmet? You mean—?"

Roy nodded. "Some of the Cliffs mustangs are possibly ending up on restaurant menus in faraway places."

"Well, shit," he said, frowning. "But not that bay mare."

"No," Roy said, "and probably because she was too smart, meaning she'd do her best to guide the others to safety."

"Oh, I see what you two are getting at."

"Uh-huh," I said. "The bay mare interfered with the Judas mare that was planted by the thieves."

"Yup," Harold said, "Judas mares are trained to lead the wild ones straight into a corral trap. Same method been used for many a year. But what fool shot the bay and Spirit too?"

"We don't know yet," I said. "But ballistics tests indicate the same rifle was used on the bay and then on Luke's horse. Whoever shot the horses might have pushed Luke off that cliff."

"He must'a seen something he wasn't meant to."

"Something incriminating," Roy said.

The three of us drove the short distance to Luke's place. The house was small, the décor lacking, but right away we saw three of his rifles, each with a distinguishing yellowish recoil pad.

"We'll take all three in to the sheriff," I said.

Harold nodded. "Yes, and I'll go with you."

Luke's home office was a blizzard of haphazard papers and books almost obscuring a laptop. Harold and I leafed through a stack of papers and notebooks. Nothing interesting. Roy fired up the computer, but didn't get much out of it either.

"Doubt what we're after is in this stuff," Harold said. "But somebody must've broken in."

I frowned. "I thought so too. But did he have a safe?"

"Yes, a portable one, for important papers."

I looked at him, my eyebrows elevated.

Harold shrugged. "Never said exactly where he kept it. Back of a closet, maybe."

The safe turned out to be in the bottom of a dirty clothes hamper. The only reason we looked there was that I stubbed my toe on the thing. It seemed far too heavy for just clothes, so we unloaded skivvies, crusty jeans and smelly socks to find a small metal safe. Roy and Harold freed it from the hamper, and Harold pulled out Luke's key ring and opened it.

Along with insurance data and other personal information, the prize was a notebook with detailed accounts of BLM activity at Soda Creek Cliffs, beginning with sanctioned roundups, numbers of mustangs gathered, any injuries. Then came theories about the dwindling herds, specifics about which mustangs disappeared and when. Luke included suspicions that Joe Gannon and Juan Gomez, the energy company honcho, were somehow implicated in the disappearances. He also noted that Nick Dickson was a sharpshooter in the Marines and that he'd seen Nick hiking at the Cliffs more than once with a rifle sticking up from his backpack. Luke lived closer to the remote north entrance rather than the main Coyote Canyon, so he would be more likely to see unauthorized fencing and associated tire tracks right away. The last note was about the dead bay mare found by the college girls and Luke's plan to ride Spirit out there.

"Okay, let's all go and talk to the sheriff," I said.

Harold nodded and picked up Luke's rifles. Roy grabbed the notebook and the laptop.

Sheriff Plackmon was outside, about to leave for the day, but when he saw us approaching with three rifles, he ushered us right into his office. He listened to everything the three of us had to say, then pulled on gloves to accept Luke's three rifles, the notebook and the laptop.

"I intended to get out to Luke's place soon myself," the sheriff said, "but this new information changes things."

I nodded. "So what about Nick Dickson? Can you run ballistics on his rifles?"

"Maybe. But it's important to proceed legally. I need just cause to impound anyone's weapons."

"Damnit. I was thinking about just sneaking onto the Dickson place and lifting one or two of Nick's rifles from his truck."

"That would be burglary, and you know it, Margo!"

I bit my lip, spoke softly. "I didn't do it, though."

The sheriff sighed. "It's never easy to lose a friend. I get that. But if Nick Dickson is implicated in some way, he and his family will lawyer up and I guarantee the first thing any lawyer does is sniff out improprieties and use them. Taking Nick's rifle would complicate things and land you in my jail."

Roy frowned at me. "I'll make sure she behaves."

"Good luck with that," the sheriff said.

I chewed my lip some more, thought about the orange jump suits, the little cots, the bars.

Worst of all, no Roy to cuddle with, and not a horse in sight.

"So what happens now?" Harold asked.

"I'll have the deputy take fingerprints from the three of you now for comparisons and elimination, then we'll lift fingerprints and do ballistics on Luke's guns and compare results with the ballistics from the rifle found out there, see what we've got. That, coupled with the information in Luke Barnes' notebooks may point to Nick Dickson, for one, and possibly to Joe Gannon as well."

"Thanks, sheriff."

"Well, you're welcome, Margo. And please remember that I'm not the enemy. I will confiscate Nick Dickson's rifles as soon as I find just cause."

"I know, and I do appreciate how hard your job can be."

He actually grinned. "You're pandering, but I hope you appreciate what law enforcement jobs entail."

"We do," Roy said.

Harold nodded, and so did I.

"Is there any news on Jake Campbell?" I asked.

"Not yet," the sheriff replied, "but I'll let you know when the Coroner's report is available."

We took Harold home, then began chores, but Maynard's insistent braying let us know that his dinner was late. Good thing the donkey couldn't talk, although his displeasure was clear enough.

Roy fixed sandwiches and salad for dinner. As usual, my contribution was setting the table and pouring lemonade.

Halfway through dinner, my phone rang. I bit down on my already sore lower lip, afraid it'd be Millie Dickson for some reason. But it was Luke's sister. I'd never met Donna, had only spoken to her by phone several times, most recently to tell her about Luke's death. She asked about the funeral, wondering when to arrange for his family to come. She and her husband planned to drive down from Montana, which would take a day or two. I gave her Sheriff Plackmon's number, told her he'd know when Luke's body would be released. I also invited her and her husband to stay with Roy and I, and she accepted gratefully.

Later, Roy and I sat on the porch with Fetch and Zap to watch a colorful sunset, but our discussion was dark, centered on the deaths of Luke Barnes and Jake Campbell.

# CHAPTER THIRTY

**A HELEN MURDOCK** from CSU in Fort Collins called the next morning to say that the meat I'd sent was definitely equine. I asked her to email a written report to Sheriff Plackmon and to the BLM headquarters in Washington DC. She promised to do that immediately.

Next, I called the BLM in Washington DC to explain about the CSU email and provide Sheriff Plackmon's contact info. The first guy I spoke to put me on hold, then passed me along to a series of lengthy holds. The BLM's repetitious message "Your call is important to us, thank you for your patience," was increasingly irritating, but I used the time to send an email about Gannon's equine meat to the sheriff. Finally, a woman with an authoritative tone and an impressive title came on the line and listened to everything I had to say, starting with my suspicions about both Joe Gannon and also Juan Gomez. The latter wasn't under her direct control, of course, but United Energy Federation companies were drilling on BLM land. I briefly explained about the mustangs' dis-appearances, the large quantities of equine meat in Joe Gannon's freezer, the expansion of his saving account, and the possibility that Luke Barnes might've been killed because of something he knew or something he saw at the Cliffs. She asked a number of questions, first asking what my connection to the mustangs. When I explained that I was a horse trainer and also interested in establishing a mustang rescue, she seemed shocked that Joe Gannon hadn't approved my rescue and said she'd see to it that it'd happen, and soon. Then she asked me to send videos showing Soda Creek Cliffs mustangs and the illegal capture pens and finished by saying she'd contact Sheriff Plackmon and her office would "take it from there" and that she'd contact me again soon about my plans.

As soon as the call ended, I let out a whoop! "It's happening, my rescue, my rescue!"

Roy came running, picked me up and whirled me around and around, both of us laughing.

Even I wasn't ready to accuse Gannon of murdering Roy. As for Juan Gomez, he'd be even harder to implicate in any illegal scheme, but if Joe was involved, Gomez and the drilling companies might be snagged by association.

Roy and I invited Jessica and Frank along with their entire crew to the ranch later that afternoon for a picnic, and the talk centered about Jake Campbell and all that'd happened. I pulled Evelyn aside and asked her if she knew anything about what'd happened to Jake. She immediately began crying and then said she'd paid Jake to pretend he was Jessica's stalker, that it was all just an act for more publicity.

"Did Jessica know?"

"No way. No one besides Jake and I knew. He was such a sweet kid," she said through more tears. "I didn't mean for him to get hurt, to die!"

I wasn't sure what to say. I had no idea how Jake ended up in my round pen with Big Red. It didn't seem Evelyn would want him harmed. But who did? Who killed him, and why?

Frank was still talking when Evelyn joined the others. He thanked the crew for sticking together during a difficult time and assured everyone that they'd move on to better times. As far as pep talks go, it was successful, although it was easy to tell that the crew was still shocked about all that had happened.

"On a happier note," Frank continued, "I have marvelous news. I just returned from a flight over Soda Creek Cliffs."

Everyone began talking at once.

"You did?" Jessica asked.

"Wow, cool," Damian said.

"A flight?" I said.

Frank held up his hands for silence. "It was a helicopter, actually. The idea occurred to me for two reasons. I had heard so much about the area that I felt compelled to see it for myself. It is quite amazing, much more rugged than I'd imagined. And I have decided—"

Zap, Fetch and Louie all barked at once and ran down the driveway to escort Sheriff Plackmon's truck to the house. He exited the truck, bent to pat first one dog and then the other, dipped his head and touched an index finger to the brim of his hat. "Afternoon," he said, stepping onto the porch. "Thought you'd want to hear this first hand, Mr. and Mrs. Parker."

Jessica's smile was uncertain. Frank grasped her hand.

"We verified that Jake Campbell and Michael Turner were one and the same. Had one good set of prints from that last letter he sent. Perfect match with the body."

"That's such a relief," Frank said.

Bianca stepped forward. "Did a horse really kill Jake?"

"No Ma'am," the Sheriff replied, and then he looked at me. "The facial wound was an almost perfect hoof shape, and there were traces of blood on one of your gelding's rear horseshoes, so maybe the horse kicked him." He paused before adding "however, the coroner determined that Jake Campbell died of other head injuries as well as a broken neck."

"Meaning what?" I asked.

"Meaning the horse's kick wasn't fatal. Either Campbell fell and hit a fence post hard enough to kill himself or someone came and killed him. Also, there was a high level of methamphetamine in the deceased's blood."

"Drugs?" Evelyn said, swaying. "No way. Jake didn't use that stuff. None of us does."

"Blood tests don't lie," Frank said. "Such a shame."

"So what exactly would a high level of that do to a person?" Jessica asked.

"Hype him up, for one thing, make him act crazy," the sheriff replied.

"Meaning he may have stumbled into Big Red's round pen, gotten the horse all frenzied," I said.

Sheriff Plackmon rubbed his chin, then frowned. "I need to speak with you in private, Margo. You too, Roy."

We followed him to his truck.

"I received a call from a BLM head honcho in Washington DC just a short while ago," he said, "and she directed me to confiscate all Joe Gannon's rifles, his computer, and oddly, his freezer and all the contents. A deputy and I did that before I came here. The two of you are behind this, right?" He gave us a stern look. "False accusations are a serious matter."

"It was me, not Roy," I said, "and I didn't accuse Joe Gannon of anything. I just told the BLM what I'd found out."

"But you didn't consider telling me?"

"I'm sorry, sheriff, I really am. This all happened so fast. I did send you a detailed email explaining what I know so far."

"Uh-huh. I don't see emails right away. Calling is better."

"Again, I'm sorry."

He shook his head. "I might as well make you a deputy so you can sniff around legally."

"Thanks, but no," I said.

Roy laughed, then asked, "any results on Luke's rifles?"

"Yes, matter of fact. The ballistics on his rifles are entirely different from the rifle found by his horse."

I nodded. "Not surprised. Does this mean you can confiscate some or all of Nick Dickson's rifles for comparisons?"

"Yes, I'll be doing that after I leave here."

"Okay, so back to Jake Campbell. His mother called and mentioned a large amount of money in Jake's bank account. Also, Evelyn handles publicity for Jessica's group, and she admitted to me that she talked Jake into acting as a 'fake stalker' because it could generate lots of news."

"Maybe drugs made him escalate," Roy said, "so he started stalking Jessica for real."

The sheriff rubbed his chin. "Possible."

"Which could account for his swollen bank account," Roy said.

"Seems he made bad decisions, paid the ultimate price. I'll talk to the mother, then to Evelyn."

We talked some more, and then he tipped his hat and left.

Back on the porch, Frank drew Jessica close and kissed her. "I was about to announce a most wonderful plan," Frank said. "Now that poor Jake is gone and this unfortunate stalking business is over and done with, we can turn our attention to promoting 'Running Wild, Running Free.' The very best way to do that is for you ladies to have one more ride at Soda Creek Cliffs."

"Great idea, Frank," Jessica said, squeezing his arm.

He kissed her again, then continued. "We did see an injured horse out there."

"You did? What was wrong?" I said. "And where was it?"

"I am no expert, of course, but it was limping about, not keeping up with the others. The pilot said it was in a place called Box Canyon. I thought perhaps you could ride out there and check on it or some such."

"Maybe," I said, but Roy was frowning.

The BLM was officially responsible for caring for the mustangs, but injured horses were left on their own. Either they healed, or nature claimed them. Survival of the fittest.

"Did you see other mustangs with it?" I asked.

"Quite a few, maybe a dozen, as I recall," he said. "I have to leave early tomorrow to finalize things in Oklahoma, but you ladies and the crew have one final day in Colorado."

"Oh, I didn't realize everyone is leaving so soon," I said. "I'll check my schedule, see if I can clear tomorrow. I should check on that lame mustang anyway." I was getting used to having Jessica around, and one more ride with her sounded good.

I turned to Roy. "How about you? Can you ride tomorrow?"

He shook his head. "I have a zoom meeting with the Salt Lake City people. At least I don't have to travel."

After a while, the crew headed back to town, but Jessica, Bianca and Evelyn stayed with us since we planned an early morning ride.

We'd just gotten inside the house when Ruth Dunn called.

"Doris just stopped by my place, crying so hard I could barely understand her," Ruth Dunn said. "Did you have anything to do with getting Joe in trouble?"

"What do you mean?" I asked, thinking she was referring to the fact that Sheriff Plackmon had confiscated his rifles.

"He just boarded a plane for Washington DC, told Doris some woman from the BLM called and placed him on administrative leave, arranged for him to come immediately to headquarters. Doris also said she'd heard that the FBI took Juan Gomez into custody for questioning."

"You don't say."

"Don't be coy with me, Margo."

"Ok, Ruth. Doris isn't the one in trouble, but Joe Gannon has a freezer full of equine meat."

"What!"

"I was shocked too, and there are likely more things waiting to unfold, but it's up to the BLM and whoever else needs to be involved. For what it's worth, I feel sorry for Doris."

"Right. But I considered Joe a good Christian man. You just never know, though. I'll pray for them both."

"That's good of you, Ruth."

The evening passed quietly with an early bedtime. When Roy and I were alone, he told me to be careful on tomorrow's ride, reminding me to take the satellite phone, a rifle, a pistol and to keep a watch out for whatever might come along.

As I drifted off to sleep, I thought about Luke Barnes and Jake Campbell, both dead under strange circumstances. Nick Dickson. the sharpshooter, seemed the likeliest killer of Luke and Spirit.

Jake Campbell's death seemed different. Even if Evelyn did think up things like the knife, the box of bullets and the all-too-real-threatening letters, maybe Jake morphed from a pretend stalker into a very real threat. And what if he'd finally given in to using meth. That still didn't explain who'd killed him. Or why.

Everyone seemed fond of Jake. The only one who didn't seem upset by his death was Frank. But then Frank cared more about himself than others. I was glad to know he'd be leaving early tomorrow.

# CHAPTER THIRTY ONE

THE MORNING SUN was comfortably warm, the breeze mild, the horses calm. We'd ridden for an hour, and the day promised to be memorable. I was always happy to ride Phantom anytime, anywhere.

"I'm sneaking back one dark night to steal Hawk," Jessica was saying. "I love this little pinto."

"You look good on him," I told her, "but if you make off with him, I'll hunt you down and give you a good thrashing."

"You wouldn't," she said, laughing.

Bianca giggled.

"Try me," I said.

Bianca was happy to be back on Wizard, and the mustang's steady gaits were a bonus when she lifted the video camera to record stretches of scenery that caught her eye.

Evelyn brought up the rear on Flash and seemed content too.

We hadn't seen any mustangs yet, but they moved around so much that it wasn't unusual. Still, this was a good day for a ride, with one exception. That one thing was the thought of Spirit's body, of his flesh beginning to rot away. Eventually the skin and bones would melt into the earth, leaving only memories. I hoped Luke hadn't seen his horse fall dead. I hoped Nick Dickson would spend the rest of his miserable life behind bars.

"Are we going on the same trails, Margo?" Bianca wanted to know.

"Yeah," Evelyn said. "Do we have to see…"

We'd already traveled the length of Coyote Bluff Trail, and were now on Rock Creek. "It's okay," I said, "We won't be riding where Spirit is. I couldn't face that."

Bianca sighed. "Phew, us either. I mean, I'll never forget him there, but…"

"I know," I said. "I understand. So today we could stop at Cougar Spring again for lunch, but then we'll head into Box Canyon."

"Sounds good," Bianca said.

"That's where Frank said the lame mustang is," I said.

"What can we do for the poor thing?" Jessica asked.

I shrugged. "Depends on what's wrong. Unlikely that we can catch it unless the injury is slowing it down a lot, but I might tranquilize it if we get close enough."

"You can do that?" Jessica asked, wide-eyed.

"I brought a dart gun," I said, "keep it for occasions just like this."

"Wouldn't that hurt it?" Bianca asked.

"No, just put the animal to sleep for a few minutes. I have first aid supplies that might help. I can splint the leg, or just wrap it, depending on how things look."

"Wow," Bianca said, "that's great."

"We'll see," I said. "Hopefully the injury is such that nothing at all needs to be done. If it's really bad, the options aren't good."

"Oh, don't tell me that you'd put it out of – " Jessica said, making a face.

"No," I said, understanding her drift. "For one thing, that would be illegal, even if it is seriously injured. I'd hate to have to put a mustang down, but I'd have to get permission from the BLM first." I knew they didn't want to hear that mountain lions culled the lame and the weak before humans intervened.

"Do you think Luke would ever have shot a horse because it was lame?" Bianca asked.

"No. No way," I said. "What I do think is that we need to change the subject."

The talk turned to scenery, possibilities of seeing more horses. At the mention of mustangs, though, Evelyn frowned. "I just don't think they're all that great."

"How can you say that?" Bianca asked.

"You love horses," Jessica said.

Evelyn shrugged. "Like I said before, they're scrawny, just... well, it's like the difference between purebred dogs and run of the mill mutts."

Jessica shook her head and looked at me.

I rode on in silence, the comradery of the morning had fractured. By the time Cougar Spring came into view, we attempted to rekindle ease by adopting food for a main topic. We dismounted, tied the horses so they could graze, and settled down to eat. Bianca had spent a secretive two hours in my kitchen last evening helping Roy put together today's lunch consisting of chicken and mango salads, rolls, a jug of iced tea. For dessert she produced chocolate chip oatmeal cookies, which disappeared in a flurry of grabbing.

"Let me guess," I asked Bianca. "Your Granny's recipe?"

She giggled and nodded.

"Is she, uh, sort of fat?" Jessica wanted to know.

"No way," Bianca said, giggling some more. "But my Grandpa is a bit round."

"I can imagine," I said. "It's hard enough eating Roy's cooking and trying not to make a pig of myself."

"Bianca always spoils us," Jessica said. "Cookies are her specialty."

"How about Damian?" I asked. "You haven't fattened him up yet."

"I'm trying," Bianca replied. "We figure on getting married one of these days, making a few babies to keep us company on the road." She smiled and started humming. "Hey, Girls, how 'bout let's sing."

Evelyn looked down at her hands. She'd stayed silent during lunch.

Bianca reached over to pat Evelyn's hand. "Hey now, it's okay. Everyone is entitled to their opinion. Right Margo?"

"Absolutely."

Evelyn turned to me. "I'm sorry. Shouldn't have dissed the mustangs. It's not that I hate them."

"Never mind," I said. She was doing me a favor of sorts, reminding me that many people thought mustangs had no place in the wild. When my own mustang refuge was up and running, I'd open it to the public, encourage people to come see the animals for themselves.

"Now, though, I like Bianca's idea about you three singing."

Jessica grinned. "Why not. What would you like to hear, Margo?"

"What else?" I asked. "Out here, it's got to be 'Running Wild, Running Free'."

So they sang, a cappella. Sounded beautiful, even better than at the concert. Bianca handed over the video before they began, and I recorded them, zooming in on their faces, then panning the surrounding scenery.

Afterwards, Jessica hugged me. "I'm glad we got back together," she said. "I'll never forget this time."

"Today has been perfect," Bianca said, her eyes moist.

Evelyn smiled too.

"As for you, Bianca," I said, "if you ever get tired of traipsing around with the band, just come and help with the ranch."

"You got it!"

Jessica was beaming, looking beautiful and content. I couldn't imagine her giving up performing. Maybe all she needed was a vacation, a few weeks to relax.

"Your fans will love the videos of these Cliffs," I said.

"When will your mustang rescue open?"

"Just as soon as I can hang out a sign. But really, with the BLM behind my plan at last, it'll happen fast."

"And we're all coming back to see it," Jessica said.

"Great," I said. "Now we need to get going, check and see if the lame horse is still in Box Canyon."

The canyon had only one narrow entrance leading to a good-sized meadow enclosed by steep cliffs. A natural enclosure which might serve as a corral if the entrance were closed off. Mustang bands were lured in by grasses which grew taller due to the sheltered nature of the place, and by the cool water from a meandering stream. They seldom lingered because wide open territory made detecting predators easier. If that lame horse or any others remained very long inside the canyon, it would be more from necessity than desire. Not every part of the interior meadow was visible from the entrance due to rock outcroppings and scattered cottonwoods.

Phantom and I led the way through the bottleneck opening into the canyon. The first thing I noticed was one long black tail, then another, swishing back and forth on the muscled butts of two mustangs. They were a ways from us, grazing in about the middle of the canyon, but their heads shot up when they heard us. One of them snorted, both turned and trotted away toward the back of the canyon to join additional horses, about two dozen of them, which meant that for some reason several herds had gathered here.

I'd never seen that many in the canyon at one time, and it made me vaguely nervous.

Jessica and the other two followed me.

"This is gorgeous," Bianca said.

I was about to reply, shush her a bit so we wouldn't spook the mustangs more than we already had. Most of them hadn't reacted to our presence yet. We were just inside the canyon, and I needed to approach the horses, see if one was still lame. But then there was a loud sound, sort of a popping that reverberated off the cliff walls. Maybe a rock tumbling down from above.

My nerves kicked into high gear.

# CHAPTER THIRTY-TWO

I **LOOKED UP**, searching.

Nothing seemed out of place, and yet something was wrong.

Another sound followed, this time from the entrance. I swung around, saw the shadow of a something that looked like a gate, closing us and the mustangs in.

"What's going on?" Jessica asked, her eyes wide.

"Shhhh," I said, holding a finger to my lips. "I dunno," I whispered.

I motioned for Evelyn and Bianca to bring their horses closer. The narrow mouth of the canyon opening that we'd just passed through was partly obscured by high twisting cliffs. Someone lurked out there, hiding until we'd passed by.

We were trapped.

The first person I thought of was Joe Gannon, but he was over in Denver. It wasn't even remotely possible that he'd returned to the Western slope late last evening. The woman at the BLM would still be questioning him today, was maybe in the process of doing so at this very moment. Sheriff Plackmon was questioning Nick Dickson, maybe had even arrested him. But maybe Nick had escaped, had come out here. I hadn't seen Juan Gomez for days, hadn't spoken to him since the town meeting several weeks ago. I had no idea why he would want us trapped in this canyon. As far as I knew, he didn't even know Jessica and the others, had no reason to harm them.

Frank was the one who'd told us about the lame mustang in Box Canyon. He'd known we were coming here. So the question was who had he told, who would want us trapped and why. Maybe Frank thought this would be a good publicity stunt.

Evelyn served as publicist for the band. She'd admitted concocting the stalking, paying Jason to play a part that led to his death. I glanced at her. If she were involved in whatever was going on now, she was in as much danger as the rest of us. And she looked every bit as scared as Jessica and Bianca.

Ruth Dunn said she'd seen Frank at least once with Joe Gannon. Maybe Frank had told Joe about today's ride, and then even though Joe himself wasn't around, he could have arranged for someone to get revenge because I'd ruined his money grubbing plans and his career. If Gannon was involved with Luke's death, he might be behind this too.

Another loud pop echoed above us, followed in rapid succession by several more. Had to be a gun, but the cliff walls distorted the sound so that I couldn't be certain of the shooter's location.

At the far end of the canyon, the mustangs milled from one cliff wall to the other, a pack of explosive horsepower with nowhere to go.

Someone cried out. I swung around, saw red oozing through Bianca's white blouse. "Oh, I – oh" she said, slumping forward.

Evelyn screamed. "No, Bianca no!"

"Oh my God, Bianca!" Jessica shouted.

I jumped off Phantom, threw the reins over to Jessica and hurried to Bianca, calling over my shoulder for the others to dismount, squat down low to the ground. Seemed doubtful that the horses were the intended targets. "Hang onto the horses," I told them, "grab the reins." Our fastest way out of here would be on horseback.

The mustangs dashed a ways toward us, heading for the entrance, but soon whirled and galloped back to far end of the canyon, huddling together, agitation mounting.

"Lean over toward me," I told Bianca.

She pulled herself up straighter on Wizard, blinked at me, said, "I've been shot."

I was grateful that Wizard hadn't panicked and run, although his head was up, eyes wide. The term bullet proof was being put to the test. I reached up for Bianca, pulling her toward me, easing her down from the saddle. Wizard stood still for that much, but had his limits. He snorted and took off running toward the back of the canyon and the mustangs.

Evelyn stood frozen, staring at the red on Bianca's blouse.

Bianca herself looked a little pale, but her breathing seemed okay. I sat her down on the ground, bent over her and opened her blouse. There wasn't as much blood as I'd feared. She'd been hit high on the shoulder. I withdrew a handful of tissues from my pocket, pressed them into the oozing wound.

"Why?" Bianca began.

I shook my head. "No idea." Nor did I know when or if more bullets would come.

"Hurts, but not bad," she said.

"You'll be okay," I told her, hoping I was right.

"What can I do?" Evelyn said.

"Tell me if you know anything about what's going on," I said.

She shook her head. "No... honest, no."

I had my doubts about that. Lots of suspects, no time to differentiate. "Press here," I told Evelyn, "on Bianca's shoulder."

She sank down by Bianca, murmuring to her friend.

I stood up, scanned the cliff in one direction and then another. The rock walls were jagged, pocked with ledges and hiding places. Movement, just slight, about twenty feet above us but deeper inside the canyon. So far, Jessica had managed to keep hold of both horses. I reached over to Phantom, crouching low, slipped my hand inside the saddle bag, withdrew the handgun and the dart gun. No way to hide the rifle, but I slid the dart gun and the handgun inside my back waistband, under my shirt. I was glad Roy made me take a rifle. I had never shot anyone or anything except paper targets. But I'd never been faced with an ambush, a sniper.

My heart thumped, my breath became shallow. But this was no time for panic. I made myself take deeper breaths, assessed our situation. The shooter was behind that movement I'd just seen, I'd bet on that. And whoever it was must be toying with us, scaring the hell out of us to begin with.

We were sitting ducks in this canyon. At least two people involved; the shooter and the one who'd barred the entrance. They wanted to keep us in here. But if killing us outright was the objective, the shooter could've done that right off. Scaring the hell out of us had been accomplished. Adrenaline overflowed, tempting me to run or scream or both. The others looked like they were about to faint. If we turned around, we'd run into the blocked entrance and whoever waited there. If we moved forward, we'd be even closer to the sniper. No good options.

Fear bubbled over into anger. How dare someone ensnare us, turn us into helpless targets. No way was I about to just stand here and let someone hidden behind a rock outcropping pick us off one by one.

"Who are you and what the hell do you want?" I shouted.

Silence.

There was no more movement that I could see.

Seconds and then what seemed like hours passed without a sound.

Finally, a man stepped out of the shadows to the front of a ledge at the very spot where I'd first noticed movement. He looked in our direction, pointing a rifle right at us.

Jessica was the first to speak. "Frank? You?"

"Yes indeed, my Darling."

The anger in his tone made me gasp. I could only stare, dumbfounded.

"Drop your rifle on the ground, Margo. Do it now!"

I dropped the rifle.

"And now your other gun, the handgun I am sure you have."

I removed the gun from my back waist, lifted it to show him, dropped it.

"You shot Bianca!" Jessica was saying.

"Yes, but I was aiming at you, my Darling," Frank's voice dripped with sarcasm.

Jessica said, her jaw dropping as she too saw the rifle. "Oh God, Frank, what…"

"I pulled the trigger, my Darling, but you must assume the blame."

"What are you talking about?"

"Let us not play games. You know," he said, enunciating each word slowly, increasingly loud until he was yelling, "quite well what I'm talking about."

Jessica shook her head, stunned.

"I loved you," he continued, "gave you everything. I made you as much of a star as I could. But you," he paused, shaking his head. "You chose him."

So Frank knew about Eric, had probably known for a while, let his anger simmer until it boiled over.

"I still love you, Frank," Jessica was saying. "I really do." She closed her eyes. "I didn't want to hurt you."

"You are a beautiful woman, Jessica," Frank said, softly, and then he sneered. "And a whore. You are shameful, a liar, a God damn liar!"

"No, Frank, I'm not lying."

"Do not argue with me. Do not dare argue. Too late, anyhow. Everyone has a day of atonement. Today is your time."

"You're going to kill me, aren't you?"

"You have always been smart, my Darling."

"Then let the others go," she said. "They've done nothing to you. This is between us."

"And to think I just said you were smart. Perhaps not. Evelyn and Bianca, they both knew about you and Eric. They are guilty. Although it is unfortunate that you were shot, Bianca. You must pardon me, it was not my intent to shoot you."

Evelyn began whimpering and Bianca stared at him, wide-eyed.

He shrugged at them, turned toward me. "And you, Margo the best friend, you let Eric come into your home and share my wife's bed. Guilty."

"The bodyguards spy for you," I said.

"Naturally," he said. "And Eric is not the first man Jessica has slept with."

"You've done so much for me," Jessica said, beginning to cry.

"You are so right," he said. "I built you up, made you a star."

"And I've always been grateful," she said, crying more.

"Now, now, my Darling," he said, sneering, "tears will only mar your beauty, ruin your makeup. It is far too late for regret."

"I'm sorry, Frank," she said. "I really am."

"How very touching," he said, repositioning the rifle.

"Oh God, oh God, I don't want to die," Bianca whispered.

Evelyn began sobbing.

But he was no longer aiming the rifle at us. He'd turned toward the back of the canyon, toward two of my horses and the wild mustangs. I felt a wave of increased panic, wondering if he intended to kill the horses first. He'd just said he wasn't planning to shoot us. I had to keep him talking until I could maneuver closer to him, use the dart gun.

"Why here, Frank? Why now?" I asked.

He looked at me without lowering the rifle.

One of the women whimpered.

"It is too late to bargain," he said.

"I am not bargaining," I said, trying not to let my voice shake. "But don't we deserve to know how we're about to die?"

The rifle lowered. "But of course," he said. "This began some time ago, soon after I verified the truth. My plan is quite brilliant, guaranteed to keep all of you in the news and at the same time ensure continued cash flow for the Parker Company long after you are crushed to death in an unfortunate but spectacular stampede of wild horses. Imagine the headline: Bodies found by bereaved spouse of once famous singer."

I glanced from him to the mustang band. So that was it. He'd shoot at the mustangs to get them riled, make them run toward the canyon entrance. And us. There'd be nowhere to go, no way to avoid all those thundering hooves.

"Tell me about this plan," I said, looking up at him, sliding one step closer. Anything to keep him talking.

"The first phase was one bullet, one horse."

My jaw dropped. "You killed the mustang?"

"No, no, of course not. I have, shall we say, others to handle such matters. That was necessary to enhance the sentimental aspect of the new song as well as for added publicity."

Jessica closed her eyes, shook her head. "A hit man? You really did?"

"Yes, Darling, I really did. Money can buy almost anything, except love."

"What about Luke Barnes and his horse?" I asked. "Did you have them killed too?"

"Unintentional, but unavoidable. He was in the wrong place at an inopportune time."

I shook my head. "Joe Gannon, was he involved?"

"The BLM man? Hardly. He answered some questions for me, but I employed only a reliable man for these matters."

"So you hired Nick Dickson." I'd never thought of him as a hit man, but then again, he was the type.

"Matter of fact, he was available. Quite taken with guns, too. Seemed anxious to go after the horse, might have even done it for free, but no, I paid him and hired the helicopter ride that took him out there."

I clinched my fists. "You bastard."

"Why, Margo Richards, how unkind. But no matter. At any rate, as we have recently seen, horses are powerful. Hooves are so very dangerous, killing machines, really, striking the body with incredible force."

"You..." I said, "you killed Jake Campbell too."

"Score another one for the horse trainer," he said, nodding at me.

The only thing I'd scored was a wave of nausea, a taste of bile at the back of my throat.

"Did you hire Nick for that?"

"Inconsequential, at this point."

"So you killed Jake yourself, then."

"Jake was useful, for a time. Such an exuberant young man. Quite taken with you, too, Darling. Did not require much enhancement to turn him into a proper stalker, right, Evelyn?"

"Turn him into?" Evelyn said. "What do you mean?"

"Evelyn, you handled that so capably. I am grateful. If you had been honest with me about my wife and Eric, I might spare you now. I considered letting Jake take the blame for today, for your deaths. Could have happened that way. But he became a liability."

"So you made it look like he'd been kicked in the face," I said. And suddenly I knew just how Jake had died. "You nailed a horseshoe to a block of wood, used that to bash Jake's face after you injected him with meth."

"Margo, you are truly intelligent," Frank was saying. "My compliments on your powers of deduction. I shall make certain you are amply mentioned in the headlines. 'Jessica Parker and Best Friend Die Under Thundering Hooves of Wild Horses.' People so love tragedy. Sales of 'Running Wild, Running Free' will soar."

It'd been easy to get us out here this time. There was no lame mustang, of course, just several dozen wild horses that someone he'd hired had lured into this canyon, kept here.

He turned to Evelyn and Bianca. "Nor will you two be forgotten, at least not right away," he said, smirking.

They both sucked in air audibly.

"Now now, Ladies. You both had ample opportunity to come to me, tell me about my Darling and Eric, did you not?"

Evelyn began sobbing again.

Bianca turned pale. "Please, Mr. Parker."

"Sorry, my Dears, far too late to grovel. So, now you all know the story, how your end shall come. Jessica, Darling, this is it, then." He paused, shook his head. "I loved you, trusted you. A mistake I regret. Oh, and as for Eric Jakowski. I considered having him killed, but decided to let your lover boy drown in sorrow."

Jessica stared at him, her mouth open. "I don't love him the way I love you, Frank. It was just…"

"I know, Darling. It was just sex. Same with Sidney and I."

Jessica's eyes widened. "Sidney? You mean that blonde you met in Kentucky."

"And why not? She threw herself at me. I may just make her a star. Someone will need to take your place, of course."

"We could start over, Frank."

"I hardly think so." Frank raised the rifle again. "I could have entrusted this final task to the, ah, hired man, but doing this myself will bring a better sense of closure. Now let go of those two horses."

Phantom and Hawk stood still for a short time before trotting off toward the back of the canyon.

"Yes, marvelous," Frank said. "Now you four step back, into the narrows."

No one moved.

"Now!" Frank said. "Move there now!"

Jessica closed her eyes, and Evelyn began swaying.

"And don't bother trying to escape , because the man posted at the canyon entrance will shoot to kill."

I motioned for the others to move back first, and I looked up at the steep canyon walls, trying to find a place we might scramble up out of the way of thundering hooves. There didn't appear to be any such places. As soon as Frank shot at the mustangs, they'd stampede directly toward us, knock us down. Trample us to death.

My guns were gone, but I still had the dart gun. If the thing could tranquilize a mustang, it'd surely take down Frank. He turned away from us, raised his rifle toward the mustangs, and I grasped the dart gun, held my breath, aimed at him, fired.

The dart hit in the middle of his back.

A startled look crossed his face, his mouth opened. He wobbled back and forth, fired the rifle into the air as he crumpled down off the cliff, ended up on the ground not far from the narrows.

The mustangs thundered toward us.

Evelyn screamed.

Bianca fainted.

I ran to the women, lifted Bianca, tried to push everyone out of the narrows toward a wider place, but there was no time. The mustangs were upon us. Jessica held onto Bianca, and I pressed the women back against the cliff wall, waving my arms like a wild woman to keep the frenzied animals as far from us as I could. Even inches would help.

They came in single file to begin with.

The worst danger would come after they got to the canyon entrance and couldn't escape. They'd turn and pile up in the narrows, crushing each other and us in their panic.

The mustangs filled the narrow space, their hooves mere inches from us. They veered away from my flapping arms, but my nostrils filled with the musky scent of them. Our four horses ran amongst them, equally frenzied. Any moment now, their attempt to gain freedom would be rebuffed, their panic would increase.

But that never happened. Either they'd knocked down the entrance gate or it'd been opened for them.

Within moments, the pounding of hooves faded into the distance, then ceased.

The mustangs and our horses were gone.

Then came silence. And questions. I motioned for the women to remain still while I dashed back inside the canyon to grab the rifle and the hand gun Frank made me drop.

And there was Frank himself, sprawled face down on the ground, the back of his head bloodied, his white shirt reddened as blood flowed, his legs at impossible angles. He'd fallen into the mustang's path. I knelt beside him, felt for a carotid pulse. Nothing. The women gathered. I stood, shook my head.

Jessica ran up, hands over her mouth. "He, oh God, oh Frank." She sank to the ground, sobbing.

Evelyn and Bianca began sobbing too.

But Frank was not the only person in this. Someone appeared out of the shadows, a big someone coming through the narrows.

I suspected Nick Dickson.

But no, was one of the bodyguards.

"Stop!" I yelled. "I'll shoot."

"No," he yelled, hands in the air, still coming.

I kept my rifle pointed at the guy. "I said stop."

He stopped, hands still in the air. "He forced me to help," the guy said, staring at Frank's mangled body.

"Forced you?" I asked, frowning.

"I'm on parole. Served my time, but he threatened to fix it so I'd go back to the joint if I didn't do what he said."

"So you were going to kill us," I said.

"Kill? No way. I was nailed for robbery, never killed nobody. He had the helicopter round up these horses yesterday, herd them into this canyon. Some kinda' prank on Jessica, he said." He shrugged. "He said it was in fun, nobody hurt. I thought he was crazy."

Crazy indeed.

"He made me stay here all damn night, said not to let the horses out no matter what, then hide myself and the gate when you women came. I figured it was time now though, with all the commotion inside, so I threw the gate a ways off."

I looked at the big guy, kept my rifle trained on him. "Who are you?"

"It's Rodney," Jessica said. "He's one of the bodyguards."

"Yeah, I'm Rodney. Uh, Bishop. Rodney Bishop. Ain't got no middle name."

Still keeping my rifle on this big guy, I told him to take off his shirt, throw it to the side, same with his belt, his pants. I asked Evelyn to empty all his pockets, make sure he had no gun, no pocket knife. Last, I had him remove his shoes and socks. Evelyn checked those, too. Then I let him get dressed again.

"How're you doing, Bianca?" I asked.

"Okay. Barely bleeding. Jessica is helping me."

"Good. Evelyn, you know how to shoot a rifle?"

She nodded.

"Ok, take my rifle, keep it aimed at Rodney while I go to call our horses."

"Will they come?" Bianca asked.

"Phantom will, if she's in hearing range, and the other three should follow."

But before I even called, Phantom showed up, trotting through the narrows, coming right up to me. I leaned against her, wrapped my arms around her neck. And let the tears come.

My black mustang mare stood quietly, soothing me the way only she could.

Accuse me of anthropomorphizing Phantom, accuse me of whatever. I know my mare, and she knows me.

The others weren't far away, and Hawk soon appeared, followed by Wizard and Flash.

Phantom's reins were intact, and so were Hawk's, but Wizard and Flash needed some of the spares I kept in my saddlebag.

I called Roy on the satellite phone, told him it was done. All over.

I mostly just needed to hear his voice. He understood, knew there'd be plenty of time for explanations, coming to terms.

Next, I called Sheriff Plackmon. He listened, said the helicopter would be out with him and paramedics.

I took one last look at Frank, felt sick to my stomach. He'd seemed so charming, at first.

When the sheriff saw Frank Stanza's body, he shook his head, took photos, asked questions. He took control of Rodney Bishop, ushered the big guy into the chopper, which had landed a ways outside Box Canyon. Bianca wanted to ride back with us, but the paramedics strongly advised against that, so she let them bandage her up and she hopped in the chopper, said she'd wave to us from the air. The paramedics helped the sheriff place Frank's body in a black bag.

Before he left, Sheriff Plackmon came over and hugged me, then smiled and said, "Drop by my office. I might as well give you a badge, make you official."

I smiled too. I really should start calling him Ben.

He asked me if there was any way I could dial down the drama in future.

I said I'd consider it.

Evelyn and Jessica shook their heads no when I said they could take the chopper back if they wanted to. After the chopper left, the three of us sat down, drank some lemonade and ate a handful of nuts and raisins to fuel us for the ride back. Phantom wandered over, so I fished in my saddle bag for some horse cookies. Maybe the reason she loves me is that I feed her lots of treats.

It might look that way, but I don't think so.

The thing I love most about Jessica is that we came together again. To friendship. Always.

The thing I love most about Roy is that he understands. Always.

The thing I love most about Phantom is that she understands too. Always.

# EPILOGUE

THE DAYS AHEAD brought a blur of funerals, first for Luke Barnes, the next a thousand miles away for Frank. I bought a black dress, wore it to both. I read Jake's obituary, didn't attend the service, but I sent a long note to his mom. After the black dresses came off, there was a flurry of good byes. And more of the same as what remained of the Parker Company fragmented in separate directions.

A fog of sadness and regret lingered. Jessica stayed with us for a week or so, ignoring the media circus snapping photos and shoving microphones toward her. She and I hugged, wept, tried to make sense of it all with little more success than we'd had back when we were thirteen, crying together over my parent's fatal plane crash.

I threw the black dress in the trash, pulled on breeches and boots. All the horses, as always, were my solace, my escape. They regarded me with solemn brown eyes, peered into my soul and understood almost as much as Phantom and Roy always did.

He came home grinning one day and handed me a package wrapped in fancy paper topped off with a gigantic bow. I took it with a grin of my own, found it was on the heavy side. Shook it, but nothing rattled. Finally, I ripped it open, and laughed out loud. This was the best present ever, something I'd wanted for years. Inside all that fussy paper was a big wooden sign with artistic lettering: Mustang Rescue Ranch – Welcome! I hugged Roy so hard he said I was about to squeeze all his stuffings out.

Either he's kidding or I'm stronger than I look.

Thanks to a new friend of sorts at BLM headquarters in Washington, D.C., Roy and I are expecting seventy-five mustangs fresh off the Soda Creek Cliffs range to be shipped directly to the reinforced fencing pasture at Bow's ranch next door. Arrival due in ten days. More expected in due time.

One Sunday before the mustangs came, Roy and I arose earlier than usual, hurried through chores, then loaded Phantom and Mutt in our trailer and drove to Soda Creek Cliff. The summer sky was a cloudless blue, an altogether perfect day. We saddled our horses and headed out on familiar trails, halting to watch the magnificent bay stallion and his herd race into view. This was the moment we came for. I reached into my saddle bag, withdrew the chunk of Spirit's mane that I'd removed from his still body not long ago. I gave some to Roy and together we made an offering to the sky. The strands glistened in the sun before settling slowly down while the mustangs disappeared into the distance. Roy and I held hands, imagining Luke and Spirit together forever in another realm.

## Acknowledgements

First of all, thanks to everyone who reads my books. A special thanks to proofreaders: Colleen Greenan, Sue Catterall, Jan Turner, Elizabeth Taylor and Don Schrecengost. And a shoutout to Damonza for a great job with cover creation and interior design.

You might love horses, and it's no doubt clear that I'm writing the Everything Equine Mystery Series because I'm a total horse fanatic. If you are one too, welcome to the club. What is it about horses? I think the magic is that they communicate without the need for words, they manage to teach us about life and help us connect to nature. If you have never owned a horse but always wanted to, consider sharing board on a horse or volunteer at a horse rescue to spend time around these amazing animals.

Some of us just need barn time, preferably often. Any barn will do as long as horses are present. Donkeys are a bonus. One fabulous place guaranteed to scratch this particular itch is Rocky Mountain Horse Rescue in Arvada, Colorado. Bini Abbott is the heart and soul of the place and Kris Nixon, her daughter, is the hardworking manager and also judges horseshows as far away as Wellington, Florida. The rescue horses range from large all the way down to "What's that? A mini, you say?" The mini horses and donkeys are impossibly cute, mostly sweet, and never shy about begging for carrots. With the help of JoJo, an opinionated black and white mini horse who has lots of hilarious stuff to 'say,' Kris and her husband, Rob, compose an annual multipage newsletter full of RMHR happenings. Check out the web site for heartwarming and sometimes heartbreaking stories. Donations are always put to good use. https:www.rockymountainhorserescue.org

When I was a kid, all I ever wanted to do was ride a horse. During vacation car trips, I watched for horses, then rolled down my window and whinnied at them. Friends of my parents owned a farm where I got to ride a big white mare named Lady. She probably seemed big because I was little then. Anyhow, she carried me bareback at a slow walk under shady cottonwoods, and I adored her. When I was about eleven or so, I babysat to save enough for an occasional hour's ride at a nearby stable. I was twenty-six and mom of a toddler when I got my first horse. A couple years later, we moved to a home with a few acres and a barn. That's where I kept Babe, my 'one in a million mare,' a fabulous dark chestnut half-Arab with four white socks, a blaze face, and a perfect disposition. She came to us at age three and taught me and my daughters about riding and a lot about life during the thirty-seven years we were privileged to share with her. She and I took dressage and jumping lessons, but we excelled at competitive long-distance trail rides and accumulated over a thousand miles total in sixty-mile increments. Other horses lived with us too, and when my 'toddler' grew to be a teenager, she and I traveled to Britain for a week of riding lessons on the forty school horses at Yorkshire Riding Centre. Both of my daughters not only grew up around horses but joined me in a lifelong love of 'Everything Equine.'

www.ingramcontent.com/pod-product-compliance
Lightning Source LLC
Chambersburg PA
CBHW031216260626
47169CB00007B/2083